MURDER AT
DEVIATION
JUNCTION

The suit coat was open, and beneath it was a yellowish stuff like pasteboard – the flesh of the man himself. There was no head, but then I saw the skull, resting by the waist. One of the blokes picked it up, set it down on the blanket at the top of the suit coat, and then stepped back to look, as if he'd just finished a jigsaw. The skull seemed too small: just a topknot, a tiny, dinted stone – something to be going on with until a more impressive object was found . . .

Presently, one of the blokes said, 'Seen better days, that lad has.'

Further praise for Andrew Martin

The Necropolis Railway
'Guaranteed to make the flesh creep and the skin crawl; a masterful novel about a mad, clanking, fog-bound world.' Simon Winchester

The Blackpool Highflyer
'Genuinely gripping . . . The sort of thing D. H. Lawrence might have written had he been less verbose or been blessed with a sense of humour.' Peter Parker, *Evening Standard* (Books of the Year)

The Lost Luggage Porter
'Unerringly sharp and pioneeringly original, it locks the reader in from start to finish.' Andrew Barrow, *Spectator*

Murder at Deviation Junction

A Novel of Murder, Mystery and Steam

ANDREW MARTIN

faber and faber

First published in 2007
by Faber and Faber Limited
3 Queen Square London WC1N 3AU

Typeset by Faber and Faber Limited
Printed in England by Mackays of Chatham, plc

A CIP record for this book
is available from the British Library

ISBN 978-0-571-22965-9

ISBN 0-571-22965-4

2 4 6 8 10 9 7 5 3 1

For J. B. Martin, forty years a railwayman

Acknowledgements

I would like to thank Charles Morris of the Cleveland Industrial Society; His Honour, Judge David Lynch; David Secombe (for his heroic attempts to explain Edwardian photography to me); Mike Ellison of the North Eastern Railway Society; the Whitby Literary and Philosophical Society; Roy Burrows of the Roy F. Burrows Midland Collection Trust; Kevin Gordon; the Highland Railway Society; the Tom Leonard Mining Museum, and the staff of Wick Library.

All departures from historical or technical fact are my own.

Author's Note

This story is not intended as a depiction of anyone who might actually have lived in the North of England in 1909.

PART ONE

The Mentor Reflex

Chapter One

'Cut you in half, it will!' shouted the bloke.

He was talking about the wind coming in from the river.

He called to me again: 'Step over here, lad,' and I walked into the lee of the five great blast furnaces. They were as big as railway tunnels set on end, and joined by gantries at the top along which ironstone tubs ran. In between stood banks of coke, which made the sound of the wind different on this side, but just as loud. Men worked at the hearths set into the bottom of the furnaces – on this freezing day, men without shirts.

'I'm looking for a bloke!' I shouted to the bloke. He grinned and looked up; there came a fast upwards roaring, and the sky above the furnaces turned red. The redness held – like a man-made sunset – and when I looked down again, the bloke was closer to me.

'Name?' he shouted.

I couldn't bring to mind the name of my quarry, although it was set down on the arrest warrant in my pocket, and I carried a photograph of the bloke there too. I knew him as 'Number Nine'; and I knew his place of work.

'Hudson Ironworks!' I bawled at the bloke, and he pointed with his right hand, an action that came easily to him, for he had only one finger attached there. He began to smile, letting me see he had no teeth either. Eighty feet above our heads, I could feel the heat descending, and the wind rising again. I looked at that lonely finger, and the bloke shook it, as if to unfasten my gaze, and get it fixed where it ought to have been: upon the roaring Ironopolis of Middlesbrough.

I began crossing the railway lines half-buried in hot cinders, making towards the centre of this city of blast furnaces. Strange trains criss-crossed in front of me, like black curtains being drawn and redrawn, all towed by short tank engines that looked as though they'd been run hard into a wall and made taller than they were long by the smash.

Some of the lines were operated by the company that employed me – the North Eastern Railway Company, I mean – and some were not. Over towards the black River Tees, I watched a line of small hopper wagons move forward, and then it was taken *up*, a little mineral train rising through the sky towards the top of a line of furnaces, brought by the turning of the endless iron rope. The inclined line was mounted on steel struts, and they were shaking in the wind, but the little train kept on. The tops of the blast furnaces were fifty feet high, and the track was – what? one in fifteen for five hundred yards? Men waited for it on the high gantry.

And then I saw giant Hs painted on a row of three. That would have to be Hudson's furnaces. I moved across the ashfield with my coat wrapped round me blanket-wise. I had entered the iron district directly from the Whitby train, without having fastened the buttons, and now my hands were too cold to do them up. I was in want of a decent pair of leather gloves.

As I made towards the Hs, I opened my coat to reach in for my pocket book, and the wind came at me. That's pneumonia right there in that single stab, I thought. I fished out the arrest warrant, and my warrant card. The arrest warrant was inside an envelope, and my hands wouldn't work to open it. I thought again of the bloke's name, but no, it wouldn't come.

I was supposed to lay my hands on Number Nine – orders from Detective Sergeant Shillito, the bastard who breathed beer fumes at me all day long across the floor of the Railway Police office in the station at York. Number Nine was evidently inclined to rowdiness, and Shillito had promised there'd be a Middlesbrough constable to help with the arrest. But no man could be spared, as Shillito had told me with satisfaction just before I'd set off.

Number Nine was a centre forward; turned out for Middlesbrough Vulcan Athletic (Vulcan being the name of the

4

road that skirted the west side of the iron district). At a game played at York on Saturday last he'd crowned Shillito in a football rush. As well as being my governor, Shillito was captain of Holgate United. But I wasn't being sent after Number Nine on account of that first assault. No, I was to arrest him because he'd then laid out the Holgate United goalie during an argument over a penalty kick. The goalie was called Crowder, and his skull had been split. He was at death's door in the York Infirmary, if Shillito was to be believed.

I walked on with head down, thinking again that the affair was not, rightly speaking, a railway police matter at all. Yes, Holgate was the railway ground, but neither of the teams had been Company teams. It was Shillito's personal war that I'd been sent to fight.

I was now directly before the Hudson furnaces. Red molten iron was flowing away from their bases, just as if they were bleeding. Men wearing undershirts or no shirts at all attended the streams with long steel poles as they flowed away into a great building near by.

I began trying to work my hands. I took the warrant from its envelope. Clegg – *that* was the footballer's name: Donald Clegg. Nickname 'Cruncher'. I felt in my pocket for the photograph Shillito had given me. Middlesbrough Vulcan Athletic played in a strip that made them look like a pack of playing cards: shirts dark coloured on one side, light on the other, and a crest over the heart. Clegg, the biggest of the lot, stood in the centre of the back row.

'You there!' one of the blokes was calling to me from the bank.

I looked up.

'Step away!' he shouted.

'I'm looking for Clegg!' I called up, but he didn't hear. I held up the photograph and my warrants.

The bloke was striding down the bank now, stepping over the flowing iron channels as he came crosswise towards me.

'Put your boot in one of these and you'll know about it,' he said when he was level with me. He wore a coat over his bare chest, as if he couldn't decide whether it was hot or cold: and the queer thing was that, this close to the furnaces, it was *both*.

'I'm looking for Clegg,' I said, showing him the photograph.

5

'Works here; turns out for this lot Saturday afternoons. There's been a complaint of assault made against him . . .'

'Clegg's a bloody good player; marvellous at dribbling.'

'What?' I said.

'Dribbling. He's brilliant at it.'

I just looked at the bloke; I did not follow football.

'I know Clegg,' the bloke continued. 'He's a good lad.'

'Well, there's a man lying half-dead in the York Infirmary.'

'Shamming, I expect,' said the bloke.

'Twenty bloody stitches,' I said, 'and you call that shamming.'

'An artist, is young Clegg,' said the bloke. 'An artist and a *poet*.'

'"Cruncher" Clegg, I believe they call him,' I said.

The bloke kept silence.

'Where does he work, mate?' I asked, and the bloke craned his head up towards the over-world at the top of the furnaces, where tiny men moved silently along gantries amid the snow. What was put into blast furnaces to make iron? I tried to think. Ironstone, coke and . . . something else. Limestone.

I joined the bloke in looking again at the high gantries. Had this been Shillito's programme all along? To get me sent up there? But the bloke tipped his head down again, his gaze now roving between the roaring sheds behind us.

'You'll find him over yonder,' he said.

I nodded thanks and turned on my heel.

In the heart of the shed, four men were pacing about in front of a strange and mighty vessel. It looked like a forty-foot-high brick head that pivoted on its own ears, these being formed of two mighty steel wheels held in place by giant iron stays. As I approached, the head tipped upwards, as if to say, 'Who is this come to visit?' And the men stepped back from it.

A bloke came at me from the darkness. 'Look out, mister,' he said, indicating behind. I turned around and a huge ladle of molten iron was rattling towards me, suspended from a moving crane. I tore my eyes away directly, for the sight burnt them. I stood aside as the ladle passed. It was like a piece of the sun put into a bucket, and it was approaching the great swivelling head, which was turning again, ready to receive its drink of hot iron. This was steelmaking.

The roof had been cut away above the thing's head, and some snowflakes that fell through the gap escaped melting, and swirled towards the watching blokes. I fixed my eye on a particular one of the four: the tallest. His right hand was bandaged. He was Clegg, I was sure of it, but the only light I had to go on was that from the iron in the ladle, which had now stopped short of the blokes. It swung in the cold wind that came through the open roof, making weird shadows.

I turned to the bloke who'd warned me of its coming.

'Is that fellow Clegg?' I said, pointing to the one I'd been eyeing.

The man's glance travelled from my warrant card to the four blokes. He said nothing, but I could tell I'd hit the mark. I stepped over towards the blokes and the head somersaulted so rapidly that I thought it might leave its moorings. At that moment, the one behind called:

'Look out, Don – he's a copper!'

I turned about to see the man sprinting to the mouth of the shed. I started after him, running hard over the hot cinders. At the shed mouth, the bloke turned left. I did the same, and one of the red iron streams was right before me. I leapt it and, in the middle of the air, saw another just where I was about to land. I tried to make my leap into a dive, and cleared the second stream with inches to spare. I rolled away from it and lay still for a moment, feeling its warmth all along my left side. I stood up and looked across the territory of Ironopolis. The men who worked in it were made tiny by the size of the blast furnaces; and Clegg could have been any one of the hundreds of tiny blokes in view. I stood up, and tried to brush the red dust off me. One false move in this bloody place, and you were done for. I had no chance of running in an ironworker in the ironmen's own stronghold. If Shillito wanted the job done, he could bloody well ride the train north and do it himself.

I walked back towards the bloke who'd warned Clegg.

'What's your game?' I asked him.

'You could have been anyone, walking to him. He'd have

7

jumped out of his skin if he'd turned round to see you – and that's not safe in a spot like this.'

He looked me up and down

' . . . big fellow like you.'

I was half his size, and getting on for a quarter of his thickness.

'It's obstructing a police officer, that's what.'

'I don't think so.'

'Look, I'm *telling* you. Don't make an argument of it or I'll run you in as well.'

'As well as what?' he said, and a slow grin spread across his blackened face.

Mastering myself for the cold, I headed back towards the mouth of the mill, where snowflakes were swooping about in confusion. I picked my way back through the towers and smoking ore rivers of the iron district, presently hitting Vulcan Road where once again things were human-sized: snow floating down on motor cars, carts and traps; people pushing on grimly, heads down. This was the town that iron had made. I saw a woman at some factory gates over opposite. She was all folded in on herself, quite motionless under accumulating snow. She looked like Lot's wife, and I thought: this party is frozen solid, I must *do* something – but as I approached, she lifted up her head and smiled, as though it was quite a lark to be snow-coated.

Chapter Two

In the middle of town, Queen's Square was a white ploughed field, the ruts made by the cartwheels stretching away towards the railway station, where I saw the wife waiting in her woollen cape and best winter hat. She held her basket with one hand, and young Harry's hand with the other. She'd come up to Middlesbrough with me, and she'd told me she would be at the station for the mid-afternoon York train, should I be able to finish my business with Clegg earlier than expected. (The plan had been for me to take him into the Middlesbrough Railway Police office, for questioning and possible charge.)

'It's snowing, our dad!' young Harry bawled out, as soon as he saw me.

Lydia stooped down and said something to the boy – 'our dad' being a vulgar expression he was forever being told not to use. I looked again at the wife's hat, and I was glad to see that it was the same one as she'd been wearing that morning. She'd come up to Middlesbrough because she'd fancied a look at the new millinery department in the town Co-operative Store, and I'd been fretting that she might have gone on a bit of a spree.

'You've got a bit frozen, Jim,' she said, when I walked up.

Harry asked, 'Where's tha bin, dad?' and Lydia corrected the boy: 'Where have you been, *father*?' She was a kind of echo to Harry, who generally paid her no mind at all.

'I've been to see a man about a dog,' I said.

It was something when your business was unmentionable to your own son.

'We had spice cake,' Harry said.

'As if your father couldn't guess,' said the wife, leaning down to brush a scattering of crumbs off Harry's coat.

'And was it nice?'

'It was *expensive*,' he said.

The wife laughed, looking for my reaction as she did so. The topic of money had been a delicate one between us of late.

'And what else did your mother tell you?'

'Eh?'

'To keep your muffler up to your chin.'

I tried to make from his muffler and coat a seal against the snow. Then we turned and made towards the station, which was a curious mix-up: made of about four churches by the looks of it, with one great hump in the middle. Steam and smoke leaked out from the seams and rose upwards.

'You didn't lay hands on the man then?' said the wife.

'He scarpered.'

She sighed.

'He's a footballer, isn't he?'

'Aye,' I said, 'amateur.'

'And you know which team he plays for?'

'We do.'

'It's pretty easy to track down football teams, you know. They're generally to be found on football *pitches*.'

'His lot dodge about a fair bit.'

'Give over. It's all league and cup, league and cup.'

'There's friendlies as well,' I said. 'That's where he split the goalie's skull – in a friendly.'

'It's a queer town, is this,' said the wife as we walked on towards the station. 'There's red dust everywhere . . . especially on you.'

She lifted her hand up towards my bowler hat.

'It's iron,' I said. 'The air's full of iron. Puts most of the populace into an early grave.'

'I *like* it!' said Harry from behind.

'Get *in*!' Lydia called, stamping her boot, and holding open the booking office door. But Harry had stopped in the snow for a good cough.

'Connection's gone,' Lydia said, shaking her head. That was her expression for when Harry was off into his own world, which was a good deal of the time. She walked out into the snow again, and fairly dragged him in through the station door, where the air was a little warmer from the unseen engines waiting. He was a funny, forward little lad, our Harry, but a very good speaker, considering he was just two months short of his fourth birthday.

Lydia took from her basket the cough cure and spoon she'd carried with her to Middlesbrough, and fed it to the boy amid the swirl and bustle of the ticket hall – for now the evening rush was starting.

We found the Whitby train waiting on the main 'up' platform, and then . . . well, Harry would have to have a look at the engine. He never missed. I led him along to the front, and there stood an M1 Class 4-4-0. 'Outside steam chest – good runner,' I said to Harry, although of course that went over his head. 'It's eeeee-normous,' he said, which is what he almost always said. He then removed his mitten, threw it down on to the snowy platform, and there in his palm was a tiny tin engine.

'I got this today,' he said. 'I keep it in my hand.'

'Where did you get it from?'

'Monster lucky tub,' he said.

'Which shop?'

'Don't know.'

'It's a bobby-dazzler, that is,' I said.

I was glad he'd fished a locomotive out of the bran tub, even if he ought not to be getting presents so close to Christmas. I fancied Harry might make an engineman one day – succeed where I'd failed. But the wife wanted him educated to the hilt, make an intellect of him. Even at a little under four years old, she swore he had all the makings.

Harry was coughing again, so I whisked him back along the platform to where the wife waited, and we climbed up. The steam heat was working in the carriage, but Harry still coughed. He was on the mend from his latest bad go, but he had a weak chest: at age two he'd had pneumonia. Three months in the York Infirmary, pulse at a fever rate for days on end. Our sick club didn't cover the cost, and most of our savings were gone.

We settled ourselves in an empty compartment, and I took out from my pocket the *Middlesbrough Gazette* for Monday 13 December 1909. A succession of polar lows were moving south in an Arctic airstream. There had been much freezing of water taps and gas mains, and now widespread snow was forecast for the district.

The train was being quickly boarded: it was the main service of the evening down the coast to Whitby. You could go by the country way, but I wanted to see the sea. People clattered along the corridor, carrying snow on their shoulders, shouting about the weather: 'Bad weather for thin boots, this is!'

Harry settled eventually, and the wife took out her library book – something on the women's movement, probably with a dash of religion. She always had something like that on the go.

The whistle blew and we were fast away. A moment later, a man and a woman walked into the compartment, and Harry immediately fell to staring at them, which I couldn't stop without drawing attention to the fact that he was doing it.

They were both small. The woman carried a big basket stuffed with parcels. As she pulled the white fur mantle off her shoulders, I caught sight of Lydia's flashing eye. It meant this was the fashionable kind of mantle, worthy of notice. The woman sat down quickly, but took a long time settling herself. The man wore wire-rimmed spectacles, a flat, snow-topped sporting cap, black suit and a green topcoat of decent quality. The cap didn't belong, for he did not look the sporting type.

He carried a valise and a canvas case about a foot and a half square. He looked twice at the notice on the string rack over the seats: 'Light articles only'. He took off his specs and blew on them, as though thinking about that sign. Then he stowed the case on the rack anyway. He put his topcoat up there, and whipped off the cap; he was bald, except for a line of hair that ran round the perimeter of his scalp. It was just a memory of hair, marking the boundary of where the stuff had been. His nose was queer as well. It was an arrow, coming out sharply and going in again quite as fast. It was just right for supporting his specs, though.

Sitting down, he gave me a quick nod, which made his red face turn redder still.

As we rocked away from Middlesbrough station he took some papers from the valise and began leafing through them at a great rate, while occasionally making jottings in a notebook. I looked out of the window. The iron district was to my left, the mighty furnaces burning under the snow. The woman was reading a picture paper – *Household Words* or some such. I caught sight of the question: 'A lemon cake for Christmas?'

The man lifted his feet and rested them on the seat over opposite, at which Harry's mouth opened wide. I knew what was coming, but could see no way of stopping it.

'It's not allowed!' said Harry, pointing at the boots.

Lydia shook her head, though she was almost laughing at the same time. The man coloured up and – continuing with his note-making – took his feet off the seat.

'Don't bother on our account,' I said to this clerk-on-the-move, who acknowledged me once again with a nod.

Harry was now looking out of the window.

'The boy's quite right though, isn't he?' the woman was saying. 'Where would we be if everyone put their boots on the seats?'

She looked at the man.

'Where would we be, Stephen?'

'I'm sure I don't know, Violet,' he said, hardly looking up from his scribbling.

(She did not look like a Violet – too pale.)

'I think it comes from his being a policeman's son,' said Lydia, at which the clerk looked up over his glasses at me.

'The man two doors down from us in Wimbledon is on the force,' said the woman. 'He's quite high up – an inspector, I think.'

She was pretty but, like her husband, small in scale – like a child playing at being an adult. Whenever she spoke, she caused a commotion, or so she seemed to think, for she rearranged herself afterwards, refolding the gloves that rested on top of her basket and patting down her skirts.

'He's only been in the street for a year,' she went on. 'Well, we all have. But the milkman for the area, who was known to give short measure . . . he doesn't try it in Lumley Road.'

She looked at us all.

' . . . that's because of the Inspector.'

'James is on the North Eastern Railway force,' said the wife, after a moment. 'Detective grade. He's going for his promotion on Christmas Eve.'

And because we were in company, she left off the words: 'He'd better get it as well.'

Lydia had spent the past two years fretting about our futures – mine and hers both. Would she end up at the kitchen sink? That was her leading anxiety. She was a New Woman, forward thinking. There was to be a sex revolution, and you knew it was coming by the speed at which Lydia went at her typewriting. Whenever Harry slept, or was at school, she would be at the machine in the parlour by which she got her living, writing letters for the Co-operative Movement or the women's cause in general or the Co-operative Women's movement, which was a frightening combination of the two. She got a little money by this, and now she'd been offered a position in the Northern Division of the Co-operative Movement: half-time secretary to Mrs Somebody-or-other. Three days a week, ten bob a day. Very fair wages, all considered. Lydia was to give her answer by the first week of the New Year, and she would only be able to say yes if I achieved promotion to detective sergeant. That would be a big leap, for it would all but double my pay, letting us take on a girl who could do the weekly wash and mind Harry for the three days.

My interview was to be with the chief of the force himself, Captain Fairclough, and it was fixed for twelve noon in the spot we were now leaving behind: Middlesbrough, to which the head-quarters of the North Eastern Railway Police had lately removed, having been first at Newcastle.

We rolled through Redcar station, for we were semi-fast to Whitby, where we would change for York. I caught a glimpse of the beach as we rocked through Redcar station. It was snow-covered. A torn white flag planted in the sand flew the word 'TEAS'.

The ladies in the compartment were developing a conversation.

'Do you wash at home?'

'*Some*,' the wife said, very cautiously. 'Only handkerchiefs and the like.'

That was a fib (we washed everything at home), and I flashed the wife a sideways glance, which she avoided.

The woman started in with another question: 'Do you wash the – ?' But she broke off at the sight of three rough-looking blokes whisking along the corridor, shouting at each other as they went. Iron-getters most likely, I thought, and half-canned at the end of a turn. Harry was kicking his feet, looking out of the window at more furnaces – set high on a hill in the weird light.

'Everything's on fire, dad,' said Harry, and it was evidently fine by him, for he spoke the words calmly.

'Wimbledon's home to us,' the woman was saying. 'Lumley Road.'

She would keep on mentioning it.

'It's well away from the railway,' she said.

Was that good or bad? She found the railway noisy, I supposed. But there'd be no Wimbledon without it. I remembered the place from my days on the London and South Western company – a medium class of houses, and seemingly more of them every week you rode by them.

I looked again through the window. A little light left in the day; lonely cottages here and there; snow landing slantwise on the sea beyond.

'Do you know London?' the woman was saying.

'I'm from there myself,' said the wife.

'Oh, where?'

She was cornered now.

'Waterloo,' she said, and that was the end of the conversation for the moment. You could not say the lodging house the wife had kept there had been well away from the station; it had been almost *in* it. Lydia frowned at the gas lamp over Harry's seat. He suddenly smiled and waved at her with the full length of his arm, as though she sat half a mile away, but she did not respond. She was fighting for the sisterhood, but that didn't mean she had to like all individual women, or even very many of them, and it was ridiculous of me to think so, as I had often been told upon raising the point.

Harry was keeping rhythm with the train, repeating over and over, 'Rattly ride, rattly ride, rattly ride,' until Lydia, ever so gently, kicked him on the knee, after which he fell to *whispering* the words.

I turned to the boy, saying, 'Those hills are full of miners, Harry – getting the ironstone from which the iron and steel is made. There's a whole world underground: miles of tunnels, workshops, storerooms, even horses and stables.'

'Have you been doing your marketing in Middlesbrough?' Lydia asked the woman.

'I did a little *shopping*,' said the woman. She was not the sort for marketing.

The village of Marske was to our left – a big house on a hill stood guard over it, but snow fell on village and mansion alike.

'We had tea at Hinton's,' the woman was saying. 'The main dining room, you know.'

We crashed over some points and there was a winding gear suddenly hard by us, all lit up.

'We had lovely macaroons,' the woman was saying, 'and then Stephen smoked a cigar in what they call the *More-ish* Room. It's rather select.'

At this, the man was finally provoked into speaking.

'The *Moorish* room,' he said. 'After the Moors, who come from North Africa or wherever it might be . . .'

'Or the *Yorkshire* Moors,' said the wife, grinning, and the Wimbledon pair both laughed at this: the man quite briefly, the woman for longer. It surprised me that she should have laughed, and made me better disposed towards her.

I turned to Harry. 'Have you seen that we've been passing wagons full of the stuff? They're taking it to Middlesbrough, but must wait for the passenger trains to go by.'

'Why?' said Harry.

'Because,' I said, 'people come before lumps of stone.'

'You *reckon*,' he said, and Lydia touched his knee with her elastic-sided boot again. This was another of his regular expressions she considered coarse. I looked at the wife, and she grinned. I liked those boots of hers. I wanted to see what she looked like standing in them with nothing else on, but had not quite had the brass neck to ask. I would do, though – I would do it come Christmas Eve if everything had gone all right in Middlesbrough, and we had more money in view.

We were now winding our way towards the new seaside town of Saltburn. The black sea was to our left; a slag breakwater stretched out like the black hand of a clock. More shouts came from along the corridor, and the Wimbledon man had stopped work to listen. Harry was coughing again.

We began rolling past tall houses. The cornerstones of some did duty as telegraph poles, and the wires between were thick with snow. Too heavy a coating and they'd come down. Was the blackness I could make out beyond them the sea or the sky? We stopped against the station name: 'Saltburn'. It hung on chains, restless in the sea wind, and I imagined the sea as vertical beyond the houses, like a great wall.

'Want a turn along the platform, son?' I said to Harry.

'Don't be daft,' said the wife. 'He'll catch his death.'

So I went out alone.

As I stepped down, a gang of big, raggedy, snow-covered blokes climbed up. They carried long articles in sacks, and they were not Saltburn types at all. It was rum. There were more like them already aboard.

Saltburn was a terminus – you left by the same direction you arrived. Beyond the buffer bars towered the Zetland Hotel, facing out to sea, which meant views in summer and a terrible battering from the wind come winter. I looked up. A bit of the fancy wooden edging of the platform canopy was coming away in the wind. I stared as it rocked back and forth, thinking: this might come down on the carriage roof at any moment.

I heard the bell before I expected, and was back up in an instant. As I returned to the compartment, Stephen the clerk-on-the-move was coming the other way along the corridor. There was something in his hand, which he put behind his back somewhat as I looked on.

He stepped into the compartment after me, and whatever had been in his hand was now gone. We rumbled backwards, then forwards again; more shouting from along the corridor. Skelton came; Brotton; Huntcliffe – a tiny spot, with no station, but we stopped there anyway. I looked to the left and saw only blackness. But I knew it to be the sea.

Harry was asleep, and the ladies were nodding off too.

The train went on its slow, jerky way for another minute, then came to rest again. At once the gleaming whiteness of snow began to build up against the window frames to the left. There was a sound far off like a war, but it was only the rumbling and booming of the sea. And still the shouts came from along the corridor.

'Irregular, is it?' the man said after a space. 'To come to a stand here?'

'Just a little,' I said, and I couldn't resist adding in an underbreath, 'We're not more than six foot off the cliff edge.'

The clerk moved his boots in a way that made me think he didn't like that idea, so I added, 'Should be away shortly.'

I ought to have introduced myself to the fellow, but something told me he didn't want that. The sharp scream of the train whistle came, and we rolled slowly on. Stephen the clerk said, 'There's some strange working on this line, I'll say that much.'

The train motion sent the ladies' heads rocking, and *Household Words* slipped to the floor between them, but we hadn't made more than another half-mile before we stopped again. The banks of a cutting enclosed us on either side, and I was ready for the jerk of the applied brake, for something was certainly amiss. We creaked on past a lineside cottage that looked tumbledown, and with a badly smoking fire. Then came a high signal box followed by brighter lights rising to meet us, and we were into a station. There came more shouts, the sound of running boots along the platform.

The Wimbledon woman was awake.

'Where is this?' she said, just as we came to rest with the station sign conveniently filling our compartment window: Stone Farm.

The snow was flying at the words as Harry said, 'It's like Christmas here.'

He always woke up just as though he'd never been asleep.

'Are we booked to stop here?' asked Lydia.

'No,' I said, 'and not much ever is.'

I'd suddenly had enough of the compartment, and all the uncertainty brought on by the weather.

'I'm off for a scout about,' I said. 'See what's going on.'

The rough-looking blokes were moving along the corridor.

'We mustn't be stuck here for all hours,' said the wife. 'Harry wants his bed.'

'Do not,' he said, but he said it quietly, which proved he *did*. The mysterious Stephen watched me go as I pulled the door closed behind me. The fellow hadn't put pen to paper since Saltburn.

Chapter Three

I stepped down on to the platform into a blizzard – no other word for it. The rough blokes were streaming away along the platform towards the 'up' end – the direction of Whitby – and their sacks held shovels and lanterns. Snow gang, that's what they were. I saw the train guard come running towards me. He was heading the opposite way to the blokes.

'Bad blockage is it?' I shouted to him.

He was making for the signal box – he would telegraph from there.

'Reckon not,' he said, still running. 'If it is, we'll work back to Saltburn.'

In that case, the Company would have to put us up – perhaps at the Zetland Hotel. Lydia would like that.

I turned to face the engine again, which was harder to do, since the snow blew from that direction. The engine driver and his fireman were holding a low conversation on the platform while a few feet beyond them stood a bloke in a waterproof cape. He would be the stationmaster. He was directing the snow gang to the site of the blockage, and they looked like a foreign army, trooping off in their long coats and no-shape hats. But I now saw that they were just ordinary railway blokes: men from every corner of the sheds at Middlesbrough and Saltburn who'd fancied a bit of overtime. I looked again towards the stationmaster. The cape threw me off a little, but there was something familiar about the man's brown bowler, snow-covered as it was.

'Fighting King Snow,' said a voice at my ear. It was Stephen from the compartment. He stood there in his topcoat, blinking in the snow and holding out a travel flask. The canvas case dangled from his shoulder, and I knew it now for a camera case.

I took a belt of the stuff in the flask.

'Much obliged,' I said, handing it back.

He poked his glasses to the top of his beak of a nose, and took another go on the flask. His hot little head looked stranger still when tipped back. I gave him my hand.

'Stringer,' I said. 'Jim Stringer.'

'Stephen Bowman,' he said. 'Call me Steve.'

He was holding out a business card; I read it by the train light.

'S. J. Bowman. Correspondent, *The Railway Rover*. Also author: *Railways Queer and Quaint*; *Notes by Rocket: A Compendium*; *Holidays in the Homeland*; &c.' The address given was not Wimbledon but 'Bouverie Street, Fleet Street, E.C.', which I took to be the address of the magazine.

'We're running a special feature on the North Eastern company,' he said.

I could think of no real answer, so I said, 'Why?'

'We started one last year but it had to be called off.'

It was no answer, of course.

'I'm a detective on the Company force,' I said.

We were making for a little open-fronted shelter that lay just beyond the 'down' end of the platform.

'Your wife said you were a policeman,' he said, as we stepped under the wooden roof. 'How's the line, by the way?'

'Be cleared soon, by all accounts.'

The snow was finding its way through my boot soles, and I kept moving my toes, trying to recall them to life. Bowman was at his flask again. With head tipped back, he resembled a spectacle-wearing bird. Having despatched the snow gang, the stationmaster was staring along the platform at me.

'I know this fellow,' I said to Bowman, nodding in the direction of the man. 'His name's Crystal.'

'Know him from where?' said Bowman.

'Grosmont.'

'Never heard of it.'

'You wouldn't do, living in Wimbledon. It's not ten miles from here – a little way inland from Whitby.'

'"Twixt Moor and Sea",' Bowman said, prodding his glasses up his nose.

Crystal was approaching through the blizzard. The brim of his bowler was loaded with snow.

'Had my railway start as a lad porter there,' I said. 'This chap was my governor.'

As Crystal walked up, I felt sorry for him. He'd had hopes of becoming an assistant stationmaster at Newcastle, only to fetch up in a place that was a comedown even from Grosmont. Here was his allowance in life: the single line, the one small station, half a slice of moon and the black sea rolling away three fields off. The only point of interest was the passing loop that ran around behind the station building. Twelve mineral wagons waited there, loaded with ironstone and snow. They were illuminated by four lamp standards.

'Interesting fellow, is he?' said Bowman, now with notebook in hand. 'Think there's a paragraph in him?'

'A short one, maybe,' I said.

'I might write him up,' said Bowman. 'Life of a stationmaster at Sleepy Hollow – you know the sort of thing.'

'I wouldn't say that to him,' I said.

'Give me a line on the fellow,' said Bowman, as Crystal continued to approach. 'Sum him up in a sentence.'

'You could say he was a stickler for duty and detail,' I said, 'with working timetable and appendixes always to hand.'

'Append*ices*,' said Bowman.

'Or you could say he was a complete bloody pill,' I added in an under-breath.

Crystal was now standing directly before us.

'You do know you're on trespass here, don't you?' he said.

His head was smaller than before. Or was it just that his moustache was bigger? Anyone could grow a bigger moustache.

'How do, Mr Crystal,' I said, and then he clicked.

'Stringer,' he said. 'What the blinking heck are you doing here?'

I recalled that Crystal was a regular at chapel – never gave a proper curse.

'Spot of business took me up to Middlesbrough,' I said. That I had *failed* in my business up there would have come as no surprise to him. Crystal had been down on me from the moment we'd met.

'I thought you'd gone south to learn footplate work.'

'I had a few adventures in that line, aye.'

'But you were found not up to standard, let me guess.'

The snow fell slantwise between us.

'I'm with the North Eastern Railway Police just now,' I said. 'Detective grade. This is Mr Bowman,' I added. 'Journalist with *The Railway Rover*.'

Crystal turned to Bowman. 'You're a journalist and he's a detective, but what I want here is another twenty snow gangers.'

'How's the line?' Bowman asked, and he nodded towards the snowy shadows of the 'up' end, into which the gangers had marched.

'Blocked right to Loftus,' said Crystal. 'Has been this past two hours.'

It was worse than the guard said, then. Or was this just Crystal being his miserable self?

'Important to have a good man in place here,' said Bowman, looking all about the station. He was trying to butter Crystal up for some reason.

Crystal nodded back at him, saying, 'The marshalling yard gives a deal of trouble – or would do to a chap lacking experience,' and he waved his hand over towards the abandoned mineral train.

Marshalling yard! It was nothing but a passing loop with siding attached. Over Crystal's shoulder, beyond the 'up' end of the platform, I could see the white bank that led up to the black edge of the woods overlooking that end of the station. It was lit up by the danger lamp of the signal standing at the foot of it. As I looked on, two of the gangers seemed to be fired out of those woods and began scrambling down the bank.

'Takes the worst of the weather, does this place,' Crystal was saying.

Under the red display, the two gangers tumbled fast down the incline, creating an explosion of snow.

'Quick judgment,' Crystal was saying. 'That's the leading requirement of a man in my place . . .'

The first two had gained the 'up' end of the platform now, and here they started to run. Behind and above them, four more men came out of the woods, though at a slower pace than the first four; and these four slow men were carrying a cricket bag between them (that was my first thought, at any event) which they kept level as they came down the bank, boots first, in a controlled slide.

Crystal was saying, 'And of course, the rule book only gets you so far . . .'

The first of the running blokes was level with us now.

'Mr Crystal,' he panted, 'you've to send . . . You've to get . . . You've to get a wire . . .'

The bloke was out of puff, couldn't get the words out. Crystal, about ready to blow up at this impertinence, was turning slowly towards him. The cricket bag was no cricket bag, but a horse blanket, and it was coming up fast behind Crystal like a dark wave.

The four men spread it before the stationmaster's boots, under the rushing snow: cricket stumps threaded through black broadcloth. That's what the body looked like. The suit coat was open, and beneath it was a yellowish stuff like pasteboard – the flesh of the man himself. There was no head, but then I saw the skull, resting by the waist. One of the blokes picked it up, set it down on the blanket at the top of the suit coat, and then stepped back to look, as if he'd just finished a jigsaw. The skull seemed too small: just a topknot, a tiny, dinted stone – something to be going on with until a more impressive object was found.

We all kept silence.

Mr Crystal's arms were tightly folded. I could not recall him standing like that before, but I knew what he was thinking: *paperwork*. He stared down at the body as the snow fell.

Paperwork by the armful.

Presently, one of the blokes said, 'Seen better days, that lad has.'

Crystal turned towards the nearest bloke:

'Why d'you bring it to me?'

'You're the governor, en't you?' said another of the blokes.

'Was it discovered inside station bounds?'

One of the four who'd carried the blanket jerked his thumb in the direction of 'up':

'Wayside cabin over yonder. Stowed under a load of stuff, he was.'

'What stuff?'

'Fire irons, coal, sacking – general railway articles.'

Crystal flashed into rage.

'That cabin's disused. It's for the old line that was taken up. What were you doing in there?'

'Tommy Granger –' said the spokesman, pointing to one of his fellows. 'He was hunting up a shovel.'

'Why did he not have his own shovel?'

'That doesn't matter,' I put in.

'Every man was specifically instructed to fetch his own shovel,' Crystal was saying, as I held up my warrant card in the view of everyone.

'Very likely a felony's been committed,' I said. 'I'll take charge.'

'A felony?' said Crystal. Then: 'You'll bloody not take charge' – and he'd cursed. He coloured up immediately, but carried on speaking. 'As stationmaster it falls to me to investigate all the circumstances, and make up a report for the line superintendent.'

I thought: I'm going to have to arrest the bugger. He'll lose his position.

'This falls under the head of "accident occurring on railway premises",' Crystal was saying, as I spied another man advancing through the snow at the platform end. He carried some object I couldn't make out.

I watched him for a while and then bent over the body, pulling the flap of the man's topcoat and making a search of his pockets. They were all quite empty. The last of the snow gangers was level with us now and, looking up, I saw that he held two objects. The first was a length of rope.

'Cut it down from the roof beam just above him,' he said. 'Bloke hanged himself,' he ran on, and he was looking at all of us as he spoke, making a kind of appeal.

The second object he held was a camera case of similar design to the one slung about the neck of Stephen Bowman. No – although weathered, it was the very *spit*.

'Found this half-frozen into the stream,' he said. 'Just on the edge, like. It was only a little way below the cabin –'

The man was shaking with cold. Everybody was eyeing him, and he didn't like it.

'I was making to step on it . . . use it as a stepping stone for crossing the brook . . . Then I thought it might be his –'

He pointed at the bones.

'What is this?' said Crystal, looking from the dead man's camera case to the one hung about Stephen Bowman's neck. 'A flaming camera club?'

Taking the case from the man, I turned about to look at Bowman, and the silver flask was in his gloved hand. I opened the carrying case and took out the camera, which was a black cube in fair condition, given where it had been. There were round switches more or less at the corners, so that it looked as though it was meant to move on wheels – a miniature wagon. Attached to the back of the thing were rusted clips that ought to have held another part of it. I moved a catch and a rubber pyramid rose up. You looked through that to take a picture.

I had my eyes on Bowman as I held the camera.

His words came slowly through the snow.

'The changing box is missing – the box that holds the slides.'

'That holds the . . . exposures?' I said.

The colour was all gone from Bowman's face.

Crystal stood stock still, his moustache collecting snowflakes at a great rate. Most of the snow gang had had enough, and were moving away towards the station house. It was that or become like the man in the blanket. This was not bad weather but something more – this stuff falling from the sky was out to bury us. I looked back at Bowman, and he was all wrong, could not hold my eye. I made a lurch towards the station buildings. I then heard a sound which was not snow falling, but a coloured spray flying from the mouth of Bowman. His hand wiped at his mouth as though he'd just eaten rather than done the opposite, and looking down at the pinkish stuff now lying on the whitened platform, I realised how beautiful the snow had been until that moment.

Chapter Four

Nine hours after the discovery, I looked out of the window of the station building, and the night air was suddenly clear, like a stopped clock. The train was long gone. The engine had detached from it, and taken a run at the drift that lay around the bend. It had just gone bang at the snow and had cut through it directly. The train had then carried on towards Whitby, taking the wife and Harry with it. They were in for a weary drag, but Lydia had made Harry a pillow with her wrap, and they would be in time to connect with the last York train. Duty required me to stay at Stone Farm, and Lydia had quite understood:

'No sense in shirking with your interview coming up.'

She was pushing the pace all right.

I'd then waded through the snow on the bank with two of the blokes from the snow gang, and they'd showed me the cabin where the main discovery had been made. It had been used as a shelter by the platelayers when the direction of the line had been slightly altered years before. The line now went the seaward side of the bank rather than the landward side. A short stretch of the old line remained as part of stationmaster Crystal's empire: Deviation Junction.

The cabin was soundly built, and there were three roof beams at a good height for hanging. Toppled over on the floor of the shelter was an old wooden chair. Had the man stepped on to it while fixing the rope, and then kicked it away? There was a mix-up of rusted tools, railway line catches and clips and baulks of timber on the floor. The body had lain amid this stuff, having fallen away from the noose when the rot set in. It was a queer kind of comfort to know that a man could not remain hanged for ever.

On my return to the station, a loco had run up light engine from Saltburn to take away the snow gang. Every man had stood on the footplate, most with beer bottles in hand.

It was now three-thirty a.m. I closed the doors that gave on to the platform, and poked the fire in the little room that made shift as the Stone Farm booking hall. Through the ticket window, I could see Crystal counting coppers in the ticket office, attending to the business he'd been kept from by the arrival of our train. The body was in there with him, stretched on a table top, and muffled in the blanket. Those bones were Crystal's property, and he growled like a dog if anyone came near. This didn't bother me overmuch: I'd sent two telegrams from the signal box – one to the Middlesbrough office of the railway police, one to the local force, whose nearest office was at Loftus, five miles down the line. And I'd kept my hands on the length of rope and the camera. Nothing would happen until morning, and I had no desire to be at close quarters with Paul Peters in the meantime.

That was the fellow's name. I'd had it from Steve Bowman, who'd also decided to stay at Stone Farm. After seeing the body, and chucking up on the platform, he'd seemed in a great state of nervous tension, wandering about in a daze. He'd said it was the shock of realising that he'd known the dead man; and it was certainly a strange turn-up – far too strange to be explained by coincidence, in my view.

Bowman had got sensible at about midnight, though – which was about when he'd been able to lay his hands on some strong waters. He'd then found his tongue, and told his story to Crystal and myself.

Peters was a photographer. He'd been sent north with Bowman this time last year to tour interesting spots on the North Eastern Railway and get articles from it. They'd put up at the Zetland Hotel in Saltburn for a week in order to look at the easterly parts of the Company's territory. It had been snowing heavily then as now. Peters had kept going off on his own, taking the train at all hours over the Middlesbrough–Whitby stretch. Night photography, weird railway scenes in the half-light or strange weather – it was the coming thing, and he was a demon at it. Peters was a young lad, barely seventeen, and Bowman had known he ought to accompany him. It had troubled his conscience at the time, and was doing so with compound interest just now.

'There'll be an investigation of some sort, I take it?' Bowman said, from the booking-hall bench. He would keep asking that.

'It'll go to the coroner,' I said, for the umpteenth time. 'But what I want to know is: why wasn't more of a fuss made when he went missing?'

Bowman kept silence, taking another go on a beer bottle. He'd been doing excellent justice to a crate of John Smith's – a consignment without a label – that Crystal had given over in exchange for the pair of us staying out of his way. I could see Crystal now through the ticket window. Having got the gist of Bowman's story – which seemed to have fairly bored him – he'd retreated to his desk and begun counting coppers.

'It wouldn't do for the magazine to give the impression it didn't know where its own men were,' Bowman said at length. 'Not that he was on the staff. He had an arrangement with the editor, that's all.'

Silence for a space.

'Peters was a free agent,' Bowman continued. 'Not married – parents dead, if I remember rightly.'

His camera was in its box at his feet. He stared at a poster of Whitby and sighed. Everything he said seemed to come with a sigh.

'Was he the sort likely to make away with himself?'

Bowman nudged his spectacles again.

'Well, he wasn't very amiable,' he said. 'Not much conversation. Taking photographs was everything to him.'

'But was he the sort to kill himself? The nervous sort, I mean?'

Bowman looked down at the floor, looked back up again.

'He didn't like it if you said, "Take a pot – go on, take a pot of that engine." That would annoy him.'

'But you wouldn't say he was at breaking strain?'

Bowman took a long go on his beer bottle.

'The boy took postcard views for Boots – that was how he really got his living. He'd go to any town and make it look interesting: cathedral or castle if the town ran to one, or failing that, a fine view of the bloody fish market. He was only a kid but he did pretty well by it.'

Bowman raised the bottle to his lips again. He was queer-looking all right: thin legs, little pot of a belly, head too small, nose too big. He might have been built from bits of several other men.

I said, 'You take your own pictures now, I see.'

He tipped his little head up towards me, pushed at his specs.

'The editor was minded to make economies, as he is in every matter except those touching on his own salary and expenses. He said, "You go roving about so much – it costs fortunes to have you always accompanied. Take your own pictures."'

He leant forward towards the fire, staring into it as he warmed his hands.

'Not to boast, Jim, but I *am The Railway Rover*. Apart from anything else, I'm the only one who ever leaves the bloody office. As regards the pictures, I do just take a pot, you know, and it seems to work.'

He was reaching into the valise he'd carried off the Whitby train.

'I've a mind to stop writing altogether, and go all out on photography. It's a good deal quicker – at least, it is the way I do it. There's one of mine here, if you'll just hold on a second.'

He took out a journal, and I had my first sight of *The Railway Rover*. Bowman leafed through it for a while, before handing it over kept open at a certain page.

'What's your opinion?'

The article was entitled 'Some Drivers and Their Engines', words and pictures by S. J. Bowman. The photograph in question showed a smart o-8-o at some station or other.

'It seems a first-rate picture to me,' I said, 'but –'

'Be straight now,' said Bowman, giving a twisted little grin.

'Well – that telegraph pole does appear to come straight up out of the locomotive chimney.'

Bowman sighed, sitting back again.

'But that's down to the driver stopping directly in *front* of the telegraph pole.'

31

'He's stopped there for a signal, or for whatever reason,' I said. 'Aesthetics don't come into it.'

'Well, I was damned if I was going to ask him to move the engine,' said Bowman. 'Peters would do that, you know. He'd go up to the driver, and he'd say, "Could you just reverse out of this shadow that you're presently standing in?" and the chap'd say, "Reverse out of this *what*?" Couldn't believe it.'

He shook his head and looked away as I said, 'But if *you'd* moved . . .'

He was back at his bottle; back to gazing at vacancy.

I dragged my own bench closer to the fireplace, leafing through *The Railway Rover* as I did so. 'Notes by Rocket' came at the back. They were light items: 'In a trade supplement recently appearing in *The Times* newspaper, an article on "New Railway Locomotives of the Midland Railway" gives prominence to a picture of a 2-6-0 engine of the GWR. As any schoolboy knows, this is not an Atlantic, is not new and does not belong to the Midland. Otherwise, we can have no complaints whatever as to the accuracy of the representation.'

It was well-turned, I supposed; a little fancier than the common run of railway writing.

I went through the pages again, heading backwards this time.

'What time's this milk train due?' Bowman asked, after a while.

'Twenty to five,' I said.

We were to go on to Whitby by the first train of the day. It was the morning milk, but one passenger carriage was carried along behind the vans.

'Can't think why we've hung on here after all,' said Bowman.

Why *had* he stayed? He could've told me what he knew about Peters in good time to re-board the Whitby train. But I reserved that particular question – along with about a hundred others.

'Will you be investigating the matter yourself?' Bowman asked.

'Shouldn't think so,' I said, and I lifted my eyes from *The Railway Rover* to think of Detective Sergeant Shillito. That bastard would put the kybosh on any independent action on my part. Besides, this was a matter for the Northern Division of the railway force, whereas we in York belonged to the Southern Division.

Crystal was eyeing me once again through the ticket pigeonhole.

'What are you reading?' asked Bowman.

'An item called "The Railways in Spain".'

'They fall mainly on the plain,' said Bowman, leaning back on his bench. He kept silence for a minute, before muttering 'Fawcett' and shaking his head. The article was, I saw, by B. R. M. Fawcett.

I took it up again. The clock ticked.

'I'm surprised at your sticking with that, quite honestly,' said Bowman. 'I mean to say, do you not find the style rather antiquated?'

I read on, while Bowman watched me.

'"We must advert to –",' he said, after a space. 'That's Fawcett all over. I will not "advert".'

'He knows his stuff on the railways of Spain,' I said.

'Yes,' said Bowman. 'Well, he's better up on train matters than I am.'

'How do you mean?' I said, looking at him. 'That's the whole subject of the journal.'

Bowman shrugged.

'You have no interest in railways?' I asked him.

'I started penny-a-lining around Fleet Street after school – got afloat on railways, that's all. Railway topics were the easiest ones to get rid of.'

'Did you not play trains as a boy?'

'Must've done, I suppose. I really can't recall.'

He took another pull on the beer bottle.

'I'm done, I don't mind telling you,' he said. 'I was up all hours last night as well.'

'Up at Gateshead, weren't you?'

This had come out earlier on.

Bowman nodded.

'Function at the Railwaymen's Institute there,' he said, yawning. 'Presentation of a cabinet gramophone to a fellow who'd done fifty years of service. I thought it might make an item in "Queer and Quaint".'

'And will it?'

'If I'm desperate come press day,' he went on, walking over to the window that gave on to the station yard. 'When a function bores the daylights out of me I'll generally put "Several interesting speeches were made", and leave it at that.'

Bowman had spotted something through the window, for he fell away from his speech and craned closer to the glass. I joined him at the window. In the light of dawn there was a bike half-buried in a drift, and a young lad picking himself off the road. It was me six years ago: Crystal's lad porter, arriving for his day's work.

He lifted the bicycle and started pushing it through the snow, kicking the stuff up as he went.

He walked through the station door, the left side of his uniform covered with snow. I nodded at him, and he shot me a funny look – 'Morning, mister' – before blundering through into the ticket office and closing the door behind him.

I heard his cry of 'What the bloody hell's that, Mr Crystal?' and then Crystal came down on him like a ton of coal, vociferating away for a good half-minute, as Bowman finished off his beer bottle.

'Rather wearing, the company of a chap like that,' he said, leaning forward on his perch, and pushing his spectacles up his nose.

When he'd finished bawling at the kid, Crystal furnished some sort of explanation, and although I couldn't make out the whole scene through the ticket window, the lad must have been permitted a look under the blanket, for he exclaimed, in a voice loud enough to be clearly heard beyond the ticket office, 'Hold on, I know that bloke!'

This checked Bowman, who was setting about another beer bottle. He froze with the opener in his hand, all ears. I was on my feet straightaway, and into the ticket office. 'You don't ruddy know him,' Crystal was saying, as he put on his topcoat. (Having worked all night, he was about to be relieved by a spare man from Loftus up the way). He eyeballed me for a moment, then relented.

'Best talk to him if that's your fixed idea,' Crystal said to the lad, nodding in my direction.

I took out my notebook and indelible pencil, and asked the lad to say what he knew about Paul Peters.

'Bloke came through here about this time last year; stepped down off the one-thirty stopping train to Whitby. Only a young fellow, and he'd a camera slung over his shoulder – camera on legs, it was. No, wait, he had *two*, now that I think on – just like this here.'

The kid looked at the camera I wore; looked at me.

'I'd just finished me dinner,' he went on, 'and I was scraping snow and laying down sand as per instructions from Mr Crystal. Bloke came up to me. He said, "Would you mind putting some of the snow back down on the platform?" I said, "Come again, mister?" Bloke said, "Could you put some of it back, as it makes for a better picture?" I said, "It might be pretty, but it en't safe." He looked a bit put out, so I said, "Can you not take a picture of summat else?" "Such as what?" he said, and I said, "We have a passing loop here, you know."'

'Marshalling yard,' rapped Crystal.

Bowman was at the doorway, listening hard.

'Well, bloke re-slung his camera, and went off to have a look. About ten minutes after, he came back and said, "I think I'd better be off up to Middlesbrough. When's next train?" I said –'

'Hold on a moment,' I cut in. 'Had he taken a picture of the loop or marshalling yard or whatever it's known as?'

'I can't say,' said the lad porter, 'but I reckon he might well have. I mean he was loony. Any road, like I was saying –'

But he'd forgotten what he was saying.

'You said the bloke was after going to Middlesbrough,' I prompted him.

'That's it. I said, "If it's views you're after, you'd be better off in Whitby." He said he didn't want "views" but railway interest, anything out of the common for a magazine, so I said, "If you take the next Middlesbrough service you'll get there in time to see summat a bit that way." And he said, "What?" and I said, "Why, the Club Train."'

'Club Train?' I said, and there came a fearful crashing from the station yard.

'Milk cart's here,' said Crystal. 'You,' he continued, pointing to the kid, 'stop yarning and get to work. I'm off home.'

And he pushed his way past Bowman, at which point the lad porter seemed to take in the journalist for the first time.

'You all right, mister?' he said. 'You don't half look seedy.'

Chapter Five

Behind the lad porter, I spied the steam jets of the day's first train.

'Bloke boarded the train for Middlesbrough,' continued the kid. 'I closed the door behind him myself. He was after photographing the Club Train.'

He and the bloke in the milk cart had the churns lined up on the platform ready for loading. As the engine came past the snow-crowned signal box, the kid was leaning on a churn, going over his tale as I made notes in my book with my indelible pencil. The lad held a long ladle in his hand. He'd lately dipped it into the churn, and he kept looking down at it rather than drinking from it.

'But as soon as you'd done so, you realised you'd made a bloomer over the time?'

'Aye,' he said. (He seemed very happy to admit the fact.) 'I worked out that he wouldn't get there in time to see the Club Train. It would have left Middlesbrough before he arrived.'

'Can you recall the date?'

He shrugged. 'Run-up to Christmas time.'

'Why was he so dead set on seeing the Club Train?'

'It's a swanky thing, en't it? Luxury carriage set aside for the toffs. All modern conveniences carried. Newspapers, hot drinks, ice refrigerator – that's for the champagne, you know.'

The train was beside us now, adding its steam to the whiteness of the air, but the lad didn't stir himself.

'Why don't you drink that milk?' I said.

'I like to watch it,' he said, still gazing down at the bowl of the ladle. 'I like to see the cream rising to the top.'

He pitched the milk on top of the platform, and made ready to load the train.

'That's what's going to happen to me,' he said, as the train guard jumped down from the brake van, ready to give a hand. 'I'll rise to the top.'

'I started under Crystal myself,' I said. 'I was his lad porter for a while at Grosmont.'

The milk train was in now. Thirty tons of engine stood along-side the kid – a B16 class 4-6-0, very nice motor, and he paid it no mind. Instead, he was thinking over my remark.

'And what are you now?' he asked, giving me a level look.

'Detective,' I said. 'Detective . . . sergeant,' and of course it was a lie. 'You'll be hearing from me again,' I said, re-pocketing my notebook.

I had in that moment determined to investigate the matter of Paul Peters, and not leave it to others. I was bored in my work and in need of distraction. I found myself thinking: if this is suicide, there will be nothing to plunge into, and I will be straight back to hunting up ticket frauds and petty hooligans. But as my thoughts ran on, I found that I was trying to picture whoever had done for the boy and made it *look* like suicide.

Why would a man come all the way to Stone Farm to make away with himself? Peters was a young fellow doing work that he enjoyed and with everything before him. He had not committed suicide. He had been killed – I was on the instant certain of it – and Stephen Bowman was mixed up in it somehow, or knew more than he let on. He was standing by the milk train now, having stepped across from the station building, camera once again over his shoul-der. Why had he come to this station on this day? But no – he had-n't made the choice to come. We had all been turfed off the train against expectations. And as for the reason for his being on the *line* . . . well, he *was* staying at Whitby. But there was more to it than that.

Crystal, ready to depart for his bed, stood in the booking office doorway. I would show him what I was made of – him and Shillito both. I would search for the truth about Peters, and if I made enough headway before Christmas Eve, I might be DS by New Year.

I climbed into the one passenger carriage with Bowman. We were railway rovers, him and me both. Any man who wanted to make his way in the modern world had to be. We stowed our cameras on the luggage racks. Bowman, not looking at me, said, 'Your wife said you were detective grade. But you gave out to the boy that you were detective sergeant.'

I coloured up while removing my topcoat. He didn't miss much, for all the booze he put away. He must have a head like cast iron.

'I have the grade "detective sergeant" on the brain,' I said, 'what with forever thinking about this interview I have coming up.'

Bowman gave a short nod.

'Christmas Eve's the big day,' I said, 'at the headquarters in Middlesbrough.'

Bowman, taking his seat, said, 'I can hardly think for tiredness just now, but when I get back to London I'll fish out last year's diary. It's in the office somewhere, and I have a note in there of Peters's wanderings. Come down, and I'll stand you dinner. Make a day of it.'

'Up,' I said.

'What's that?'

'It's "up" to London as far as the railways are concerned.'

I wondered at his not knowing, being a railway journalist.

He nodded wearily, saying, 'But what if you're going across country: Stafford to Birmingham, for instance? What's that? It's neither up nor down.'

'The kid says that Peters carried two cameras. That right?'

Bowman nodded and yawned at the same time.

'He would generally take two on a job, yes.'

'Why?'

'In case one broke – even though the model he used, the Mentor Reflex, is about the sturdiest portable available. He was over-keen, you see.'

Bowman made do with one Mentor Reflex. The job did not justify the precaution of taking two – was not important enough. He had arranged his topcoat over his legs, making a blanket of it. As we pulled away from Stone Farm, he looked through the window at the snow-covered fields. It was all like so much spilt milk.

'Beautiful railway ride!' he said, in his sarcastic way.

A moment later, he was asleep, and the stop at the small town of Loftus – where more milk was taken up – didn't interrupt his slumbers. As we rolled on parallel with the high street, the sea came into view once more, and I looked down to the left, towards the ironstone mine that stood on the low cliff there. This was Flat Scar mine, one of the biggest, and it squatted at the seaward end of a great valley that had been cut by a tiny beck.

The wheelhouse of the mine was at the centre of a web of wires. Iron buckets were being sent out along these, running to and from the mine's own railway station. The mine was its own little black town, with its own gasworks and its own black beach behind the main building, on which rusty lumps of machinery and slag were dumped as required. A wooden jetty stuck out to sea, but this was disused now. No stone went north by boat.

From the mine station, ironstone was taken up a zigzag railway towards the furnaces at Rectory Works. I looked up to the right, and saw the Rectory (as the works was generally known) with its line of fiery towers – only they were not blast furnaces but kilns, and they did not make iron but burned the lumps of ironstone down so that there was more iron and less stone. It was then cheaper to carry to the blast furnaces of Ironopolis.

The iron cloud over the kilns was slowly changing from one shape to another, moving like a person in agony.

As we rumbled on towards the Kilton Viaduct, which would carry us across the valley, I looked down at the mine, and up at the kilns. Here was a pretty situation: a train was setting off from the mine station. It was making ready to climb the zigzag. I stood up in the compartment to watch the exchange. The zigzag line, running east to west, would take the iron train between the hundred-and-fifty-foot-high brick legs of the Kilton Viaduct while we crossed over the top, heading from north to south.

A wind gauge fluttered beyond the compartment window – a

strange-looking contraption. It was like a small windmill, and it operated a 'stop' signal in high winds. It was not safe for a train to be on the viaduct in those conditions, but we were rolling across it now, going at the precautionary slow speed over the great ravine. The walls on either side of the single track were low, and I looked over the one on the left to see the iron train still climbing. At any moment, it would be passing underneath. The falling snow, the rising iron cloud, the crisscrossing of the trains, the rise and fall of the tide and the slow approach of Christmas – all were part of the larger machine. The transition I'd taken a fancy to happened out of sight, with black smoke rising from below. The little ironstone engine had been on the left; now, having passed underneath the viaduct, it was rising to the right, taking its dozen wagons to the waiting kilns of the Rectory Works, where more fun lay in store – for the wagons would be picked up bodily by a mighty winch, and carried to the top of the kilns, there to be upended. I had seen that business carried on, and it was like watching a hungry giant feed itself. An account of it might have been interesting for readers of Bowman's magazine, and what could match it for photographic opportunities?

But he slept on.

He had no enthusiasm for his work. He was like me: fixed in a rut. I gazed at his fiery little face, which was suddenly blotted out as we shot into the Grinkle Tunnel. Three quarters of a mile of blackness . . . and we came out into the beginnings of day. Bowman had rolled forwards somewhat. He was the same sleeping man as before, only now shaking with the train.

He was not shamming.

He had wanted to know my line of questioning – that was why he'd stayed on at Stone Farm. But I must lose him in Whitby, for I intended to make straight for the siding where, the lad porter had told me, the Club Train had been kept; and was kept still. It no longer ran, and nor did Peters, who had been closely interested in it, and I thought those facts might very well be connected.

We were now gliding across the viaduct over Staithes. That village was packed tight in the mighty ravine below. During the short stop at the station, I watched fishermen walking between boats on the snowy beach, wondering whether to put out. 'All weather is a warning.' Where had I heard that? A man led a pony with a sack slung on either side across a white field. Kettleness station came next; then the viaduct of Sandsend, which was like the legs of a giant iron man walking, and the houses below looked as though they'd been pitched off the cliff by that same giant.

I was not tired, despite having been up all night, and I knew the reason: in the months and even years beforehand, I'd done too little. I had been biding my time in the York Railway Police office, avoiding the chilly stares of Shillito, listening enviously to the sounds of the engines and enginemen coming and going in the station beyond. An office in a station was a ridiculous thing: a ship forever docked.

We were now rolling across the snow-covered cliff-tops – and our train was the only moving thing on those tops as we made for the terminus, Whitby West Cliff. As we came in, I woke Bowman with a touch on the shoulder.

'Copy's come up short,' he said, quite distinctly, at the moment of waking, and then he looked at me for a moment as though he didn't know me. But he quickly apologised, and collected up his things.

Whitby West Cliff station was a little way out of the town, which was silenced by snow. Bowman walked beside me through the drifting whiteness, the camera slung over his shoulder. We stopped outside a bakery that was responsible for all the activity in one particular narrow street just above the harbour.

'Which is your hotel, old man?' I said.

'Oh,' he said. 'The Metropole.'

'I know it,' I said, and I pointed seawards. 'The alley past the chapel will see you directly to the door.'

'Right-o,' he said, but he made no move.

A low tugboat was rocking across the water from the west to the east harbour wall – nothing more to look at than a floating chimney. A church clock counted sadly to five.

'To think that it's twelve hours until I can take a drink,' said

42

Bowman. 'That's if I stick to my fixed rule . . . which I never do.'

'Well, I'm for the town station, and home,' I said.

He nodded and we shook hands.

'You'll keep me posted as to your investigation?'

I nodded. 'I'll be in touch,' I said.

But he still didn't move off, and it struck me that he'd been clinging to me like a barnacle right from the start. He now muttered something while looking down at the snowy pavement.

'What's that?' I said.

'Peters,' he said, looking up. 'It comes to me now . . . He'd had one of his two cameras stolen.'

'Where?'

'Middlesbrough – in the vicinity of the station, I think.'

'Did he report it?'

'Not sure.'

'When did this happen?'

'Couple of days before I saw him for the last time. I must look at my diary, as I say.'

And he nodded again and moved off in the direction of the sea.

Chapter Six

Down to the sea, up again a little way, and I came to the other Whitby station: the Town Station. It overlooked the harbour. Two trains were in steam, but there were no takers for them. A line of footprints in the snow ran along the platform, and I followed them to a porter who was sitting on a barrow reading the *Whitby Morning Post* instead of scraping up the snow. I held up my warrant card to him, saying, 'How do? I'm cutting through to Bog Hall, all right?'

I wasn't really asking but telling him.

I stepped down off the platform and walked into a wide railway territory across which snow flew right to left, seawards. Here was the main line to York, running away through a mass of sidings and marshalling yards. Beyond lay the estuary of the river, where signals gave way to the masts of schooners. I was making for a mass of carriages by the river's edge when a tiny pilot engine moving under a great tower of steam checked my progress. The driver kept his face set forwards but the fireman turned and smiled down at me.

'Now then!' he called down.

'You wouldn't know the whereabouts of the yardmaster?' I said.

Just then a man stepped around the smokebox end of the engine, which straightaway began a fast retreat, the fireman grinning at me all the while.

'Who wants me?' asked the man. I explained what I was about and showed him my warrant card, and he gave his name as Mackenzie. He was a big bloke, and seemed to fairly roll over the rails and barrow-boards on our way to the farthest corner of the siding, where the railway land met the half-frozen river.

'Mothballed,' said Mackenzie, coming to rest, with his fingers in his waistcoat pockets, before a train of oddments. We were looking directly up at a dirty but good-class bogie carriage. It was in Company colours, but 'CTC' was written in gold on the side.

'Cleveland Travelling Club,' said Mr Mackenzie. 'Ran from Whitby to Middlesbrough and back every day for nigh on twenty years.'

'When was it decommissioned?'

'One year since,' he said. 'Fancy a look up? Pride of the line, this was,' said Mackenzie, hauling himself up towards one of the high doors. He was proud of it himself too, as it seemed to me.

He got the door open after a bit of struggle that cost him his perch on the footboard, pitching him on to the mucky snow beneath. He clambered up again, motioning me to follow.

The carriage smelt of past cooking, and it contained coldness: a special damp kind.

'Subscribing Club members only in here,' said Mackenzie. 'That was always the rule. No guests allowed – not even if they paid treble. You after taking pictures?'

He was pointing at the Mentor Reflex.

I shook my head. I was looking at a great boiler in a cubby-hole all of its own.

'Tea-making machine,' said Mackenzie, as he squeezed his way forwards.

'Galley's next,' he said, sliding back a door that gave on to a little dusty kitchen. Half a dozen dusty wine glasses in a basket; two cups rested on a short draining board. I picked one up.

'Gold trim,' I said.

I knew the design. Best Company china. I'd first come across it at the Station Hotel, York.

'Where's the rest of the service?' I asked Mackenzie, and his cheeks rolled upwards and outwards as he smiled. 'Tom Coleman's back parlour, shouldn't wonder.'

'Who's he?'

'Whitby Town stationmaster as was. Took superannuation nine months since. Took himself off to Cornwall 'n all.'

'That's handy,' I said. 'Who else would know about this show?'

'You might try the traffic department,' said Mackenzie. 'They supplied the Club tickets.'

'They'd be seasons, I suppose?'

'Aye,' said Mackenzie. 'Whitby–Middlesbrough annual returns. *Specials*, like.'

We were moving along the corridor again.

Mackenzie said, 'The Club never had a full complement of members, you know.'

'The club cars *I've* heard of,' I said, 'on the Lancashire and Yorkshire and the Midland and suchlike – there'd be twenty-five members or so. That amount was needed before the Company would lay out money for the carriage.'

'Well, this club was different,' said Mackenzie.

You'd have thought he was the Hon Sec or some such.

'*Richer*,' he added, after a space. 'Membership never over-topped five.'

We were moving along the corridor again, passing two compartments. Inside they were like a rare sort of First Class accommodation: wood panelling with walnut trimmings, fancy electroliers bunched up into railway chandeliers. Photographic views were mounted in glass frames above each of the dozen seats – all the photographs showed country houses instead of the usual water-falls or whatnot. One of the window panes was cracked, and there was a single bootprint on one of the seats.

Mackenzie was shaking his head as we pushed along the corridor. 'It was fitted on to the morning Whitby–Middlesbrough train,' he said. 'Came back with the evening Middlesbrough–Whitby.'

The corridor now brought us into a saloon: a railway sitting room with two settees facing each other under another brace of chandeliers. The seats had their backs to the windows. At either end were more chairs: two rockers facing a third sofa, and this one with a drop-head, for lying back.

'You'd have your glass of wine on your way home from business,' said Mackenzie, 'and you'd drink it stretched out flat! Bit of all right, wouldn't you say?'

'But only one of them could do that,' I said.

'All right if you were that *one*, then –'

'I just can't picture the sort of men who might have rode up here waiting on the platform at Whitby Town every morning,' I said.

'The train ran from Whitby,' he said. '*They* didn't. Nobody who rode up here boarded at Whitby as far as I know. They lived at different spots further along the line.'

'Where?'

'Wherever a good house was to be found. Places around Saltburn.'

Stone Farm was near Saltburn. Was this a Club of murderers?

'They lived closer to Middlesbrough than to Whitby, then?'

He nodded.

'It's an hour and a half all the way from Whitby to Middlesbrough. You wouldn't want to do that every day.'

'They all rode every day?'

He nodded.

They were not gentry, then; not county people but businessmen. They could run to the smaller sorts of country houses. They'd have carriages and half a dozen servants apiece, but were still obliged to turn up daily at their place of business.

'Who put the Club together?'

'Search me. One of the members?'

'How come you know so much about the club yet can't put a name to any of the members?'

He let this go by, saying, 'The one who put the Club together would be the same bloke who put in for this carriage.'

'Did you ever set eyes on any of the Club people?'

'Don't reckon so. The carriage was always empty when it left here, remember.'

'What about Tom . . . whatsisname?'

'Coleman.'

'That's it – Whitby SM as was. Might it be worth writing to him in Cornwall?'

'You'd be writing to a dead man,' he said.

'When did he die?'

'This summer.'

'Of what?'

Mackenzie shrugged.

'Heart.'

He was enjoying this: the back and forth, like a game of tennis.

'Why did the Club have the two compartments *and* the saloon?'

He shrugged again, saying, 'Why do some folk have sitting rooms and parlours? Comes down to brass.'

The wind was getting up, and the carriage shivered for a moment like one of the boats in the harbour, but Mackenzie held his footing.

'Where are all the members of this Club?'

'All gone,' he said, grinning.

'Gone where?'

He was shaking his head vigorously now, as though trying to shake off the smile.

'That,' he said, 'is not known to any of the blokes along the line.'

PART TWO

The Gateshead Infant

Chapter Seven

The great tower of the cathedral, seen from the train, seemed to pin York to the ground. The city had been about for ever, and would go on in the same way. It was as cold as the coast but felt safer.

It was *too* safe, and the station police office seemed like a sort of prison – one building trapped inside another. It stood between Platform Four (the main down) and Platform Thirteen – a small bay platform used by trains from Hull and nowhere else. The Chief was in the office on my return from Bog Hall, along with two of the ten constables, Wright the chief clerk (who was also the only clerk) and Langbourne the charge sergeant. Detective Sergeant Shillito had not been present, which suited me, for it meant I could report direct to the Chief, who took one look at me and ordered me home for a day's sleep, this even though I had started in on the story of the dead body. Dead bodies were nothing to the Chief. He had killed men, and not just in war.

I did not go home directly, but sent a telegram and wrote a letter. I then biked home to Thorpe-on-Ouse, where I discovered that Harry had a low fever. There were so many medicine bottles by his bed that he would play soldiers with them – cod-liver oil, menthol, camphor – but none seemed to answer. Removal to a temperate climate was recommended for chronic bronchitis by the *Home Doctor*. Meanwhile in York, snow threatened, and I biked through an icy wind without gloves in order to book on at the office for Tuesday 14 December.

Present in the cold office at seven-thirty were Wright the chief clerk and two constables: Crawford, who was at Langbourne's desk, and Baker, who was by the fire. The constables didn't have desks, and the fact that I did was one of the few privileges that I, as a detective constable, had over them.

Wright, who was pushing seventy, was eating an orange prior to distributing the mail on to the desks. The orange was the only colourful item in the office, which was cold and smoky – dirty green in colour. No Christmas cards stood on the mantelpiece, nor were any likely to. A Hull train was simmering just beyond the door. Wright ate a few pieces of the orange very noisily. Everyone watched. After half a minute, he broke off, saying, 'I've got four of these oranges.'

It was like a threat.

'Four for a penny, they were,' he said.

'One for each of us, is it then?' enquired Baker.

'Eh?' said Wright, ripping at the fruit with his teeth.

'I can't stand oranges of any description,' said Crawford.

'What do you mean, "oranges of any description"?' asked Baker. 'All oranges are the same.'

'I hear you struck a dead body on your travels?' said Wright, who might have been old but was also very curious.

'I did,' I said.

'Reckon it was one of your murders?' he said.

The first case I'd taken on in the force had been a murder, and it seemed no one in the office had been able to get over the fact.

'I'm sure of it,' I said, and as I spoke the words, I wondered about them: yes, the connection of the death of Peters with the Travelling Club that had disappeared made the matter a certainty.

'All oranges are the same,' Baker said again.

'What about tangerines?' Crawford was saying.

'Tangerines are not oranges,' said Baker.

'They fucking well are,' said Crawford.

Wright, wiping his mouth with his mucky handkerchief, pointed to the swear box that sat on his desk, which was a shortcake tin with a hole stabbed through. *Necessary* swearing was permitted – swearing in the line of duty, so to speak – but Crawford's remark hardly counted.

Crawford ignored Wright, who looked at me again.

'Reckon you'll be permitted to investigate?' he said.

'It's up to the Chief,' I said.

Wright shook his ghostly old head, which was about two inches above the level of his desktop as he gnawed at the fruit. 'No,' he said. 'It's up to Shillito. He's your governor.'

'Tangerines are oranges,' said Crawford. 'That's what they're called: tangerine-oranges.'

'Answer me this then,' said Baker. 'What colour are tangerines?'

'Orange,' said Crawford.

'No,' said Baker, 'they're *tangerine*-coloured.'

'Leave off, lads, will you?' said Wright, who turned to me again, saying, 'It'll be a matter for the Northern Division, any road.'

'Tangerines are a sub-species of oranges,' Crawford said. 'Take this office now: we're all policemen, but some of us –'

'– have got more pips than others,' said Wright.

Everybody looked at him.

'That's funny, is that,' he said, but he was as surprised as anyone; and if anybody meant to laugh, they hadn't got round to it by the time Detective Sergeant Shillito stepped into the room.

'Morning all,' he said, removing his topcoat and bowler and taking his seat at his desk, which was directly opposite mine. 'Your book please, Detective Stringer.'

I stood up, and passed him my notebook. He was supposed to initial it at the end of every turn, though he always made a great palaver out of doing so. Everybody watched him as he read. They all knew I was going to be rated by him – it was just a matter of when. Beyond the window, a train was leaving Platform Four, and I wished I could do the same.

I looked at Shillito's wide, sloping face. I sometimes fancied that he looked like a big Chinaman, though he was from Grimsby originally, and not at all yellow but bluish about the jaw and otherwise red, for he was a keen tippler. Why was he down on me? There'd been the matter of that murder case three years before, the biggest piece of business ever seen in the York office, and only me and the Chief in on it. And then there was the fact that I was aiming to be made up to his rank, even though a good deal younger than him (twenty-seven to his thirty-four). I also knew very well that he saw me as a dreamer, a schoolboy train-watcher, whereas he was on the railway force only by default.

Engines and the pages of a Bradshaw held no fascination for Shillito, but if there was anything coming off in the way of sport, he had to be involved: football, cricket, rugby, billiards – and especially football. He'd play most weekends, but sometimes had to be content with running the line, or shouting on his mates, for he was forever under suspension for violent tactics, and he was forever moaning about it. He'd sit in the office composing letters to the *Yorkshire Evening Press* complaining about referees, signing himself only 'an interested spectator' or 'one who is concerned about standards' or such, and never letting on that the referee in question had sent him off the previous weekend for loosening some poor bloke's teeth. Shillito ought to have *been* a sportsman. He'd been on Northern League forms for some professional lot or other – before he'd blown up with the gallons of beer he put away. Instead, he'd joined the police, and missed his mark in so doing. His perpetual fear was that all the business of investigation, diary-keeping and report-filing would spin out of control if he once relented in the regime of drudgery that he imposed on himself and others.

He fell to reading the notebook, frowning at the pages as was his way. He himself wrote in a tiny backward-sloping hand, and anything in a slightly freer style he took against. Turning from the third to the fourth page of my account, he sighed and said, 'And the ink flows on, Detective Stringer.'

Up your arse, I thought.

He continued reading.

'Must you always set down the type of engine that has pulled your train?' he enquired, after a further minute of reading.

I kept silence.

'Answer me, man,' he said, not looking up.

'Can't help it, sir,' I said.

'What do you mean by that?'

'I'm coached up in observation.'

Did this amount to insubordination or not? It seemed that

Shillito could not quite decide, which is what I had intended. I wished I had the courage to show him my mind: to let him know that I considered him failing in his duty by never providing any encouragement. The wife had told me to speak out, not understanding that my position would be at risk if I did so.

He looked up again.

'And what's all this about the weather: "the snowfall was now severe . . . the snowfall, continuing severe . . ."?'

'It had a bearing on events,' I said.

'What events, Detective Stringer? You were sent north to bring in Clegg. Why did you not give chase when he ran out of the steel mill?'

'That's not the place for a sprint, sir,' I said.

Again he digested the remark. Ought he to flash into rage? I could see him weighing the question. He rarely did so in his place of work, and that was where he differed from my first evil governor, Stationmaster Crystal.

'Now this business of the body –' said Shillito. 'It's a simple enough matter: you are right to make mention of the discovery and of the fact that you stumbled on an acquaintance of the dead man. But then we have page after page about this journalist, and yet more about this Travelling Club and their special carriage.'

'The dead man was interested in it.'

'Well, I'm not.'

Why would he not sign the bloody book and have done?

'If this becomes a murder investigation,' he said, 'the Travelling Club *may* become of account. But it seems to me a clear case of suicide.'

'It warrants investigation,' I said.

He shook his head.

'Do you intend asking my permission to pursue the matter?'

'Yes,' I said, and he looked at me until I put in the word 'sir'.

'I thought so. And yet you won't keep abreast of the baggage claims.'

This was the only reasonable grounds for complaint that he had. I found the interception of fare-avoiders dull work, but I stuck at it nonetheless. Baggage claims were a different matter. Whenever luggage was reported stolen, and compensation put in for, I was required to write a report – a 'flash report' as it was called for some mysterious reason. If I found any suspicion of fraud, the Company would fight the claim, but I never did find any. It was all old ladies who'd lost cats, folk thrown into despair by the loss of some article quite useless to the general run of humanity – and very *boring*.

'And what about the cardsharpers on the Leeds train?' asked Shillito.

There had been reports of gaming on York–Leeds evening trains.

'You are also to see Davitt arrested and charged.'

Davitt was a York citizen and notorious fare-avoider. He travelled all over the shop, always without a ticket, and it seemed to me that not paying the fare was the whole *purpose* of his travel.

The constables were now quitting the office for fear that Shillito would begin asking about their own neglected duties.

'Above all, you are also to go after friend Clegg again,' Shillito continued, '– and this time you are to gain your object, Detective Stringer. These are your priorities. As for starting up murder investigations in the territory controlled by other divisions of the force – how do you think that will go down with the Middlesbrough fellows?'

Now this was the meat of the question, and I could see Shillito weighing it in the balance just as I had – only where my aim was my own advancement, his was to check me.

Captain Fairclough, who was to interview me on Christmas Eve, had particular responsibility for the Northern Division as well running the entire North Eastern force. By interesting myself in the Paul Peters business . . . well, he might not take kindly, nor might his men. Set against that was the fact that here was a chance to make an impression. I might throw light on the Peters mystery before the interview, then make free with my findings.

There *again*, whatever I discovered, Shillito would discover also, through his reading of my notebook. If I turned up anything of interest, he would claim the discovery as his own, and so get points with the Middlesbrough men for himself.

I had been going over this most of the night before, while attending to Harry at hourly intervals, and it seemed I had no choice. As my senior officer, Shillito would write a report for consideration by Captain Fairclough. It would not damn me on all counts. Shillito would try to seem mild, and outside the field of play he was not up to any really bold stroke. But it would not be favourable, no matter how many flash reports I filed between now and Christmas. My best hope of promotion was to bring off something sensational that would outweigh all of Shillito's carping.

'You are to go north again tomorrow,' he said. 'You are to lay hands on the suspect, and this time no excuses will serve. I will make arrangements once again for you to take Clegg to the Middlesbrough station police office.'

He knew I would use the opportunity to bring up the matter of Paul Peters, to ask after any crime reports touching on it. Shillito had decided to give me enough rope to hang myself.

'Do you not have a home address for Clegg?' I said, not fancying another visit to the iron-making hell, horribly fascinating though it was.

'No,' said Shillito, 'but I do know that they change shifts on Wednesdays. Tomorrow is Wednesday, and they'll be stopping work at two o'clock, when Clegg and his pals always go off to the same public house.'

I kept silence as he eyed me; this low pub of his would be another lion's den. He was turning the pages in his own orderly little notebook.

'It's called the Cape of Good Hope,' he said presently, 'and it's on Randall Street.'

'Where's that when it's at home – sir?'

Now this *was* pure sauce on my part, and Shillito tilted his head back and looked at me over the top of his wide, flat nose. It was the danger signal, as I knew. For all his methodical ways, Shillito was not above clouting any man. I counted my heart-throbs as he contemplated me, but the situation cracked when Wright spoke up:

'That game of yours, Ernest – how did the score stand when the scrap broke out?'

'There was no scrap, Mr Wright,' said Shillito, making great play of the 'Mister'. 'There was simply an aggravated assault, committed by a man who unaccountably remains at large.'

Silence in the police office – for he had not answered the question.

'As to the score – do you mean the score as adjudged by the referee?'

'Well . . . yes,' said Wright.

'According to the official it was nil-nil,' said Shillito, 'he himself having disallowed two perfectly good goals scored by our own team.'

Somebody would be getting a letter about that. He was still in fits about it: you could tell by the redness rising in his face as he at long last initialled my notebook, returned it to me and swept out of the office with carefully folded topcoat under his arm.

When he'd gone, I set about some flash reports.

My backlog included twelve reported losses, of which only two had come in from York addresses, which was fine because regarding these I was required to pay a visit to the complainant. Otherwise, a letter asking for more particulars was required. Many of these went unanswered, and the more the better as far as the Company was concerned, because then the matter could be dropped.

When Shillito had gone, Wright stepped over and placed a letter on my desk. He smelt of oranges, which somehow didn't sit right with his ancient white face. He sat back and looked on as I picked up the envelope.

It was addressed in a shocking hand, and the nib of the pen had flooded between the words 'Stringer' and 'York Station Police Office.' The postmark was Whitby. I looked back at Wright, who had now set about another bloody orange, the clicking of his ancient jaw in rhythm with the ticking of the clock, and the two together making the sound of a rocking chair. He watched me with eyes fairly bulging.

The letter was one sheet of paper, and it came out backwards, so that I saw the signature first, which was a long word, running across half the page. I turned the leaf over: the address was set down as 'Shunters Cabin, Bog Hall Siding'. It was Company paper, though of an old style. 'Dear Stringer of the Rly Police York', the letter began. 'Mr Mackenzie, Yard Master (Nights) told me what you were about, and I have set my mind to it, and there is one from the Club you were asking after that I have heard of. That was Mr Moody. He was an old man but I heard he went under a train somewear north in summer, and is dead. His son I know is still living. He is in Pickering. He is a gentleman like his farther and deals in chimbeny sweaping eqpt like his farther did to.'

It was signed: 'E. Handley'.

It was good of the fellow to go to the labour of writing.

I wouldn't need a gazetteer to find a man called Moody in a small place like Pickering, but when would I get the chance to go there? It didn't matter. I would go. Meanwhile, I had a telegram to get off: to Mr S. Bowman of *The Railway Rover*, Bouverie Street, London E.

Chapter Eight

Once again, I sat on a train shaking across the cliffs with Whitby behind me, heading for Ironopolis. It was all Middlesbrough today, for I also had in my pocket two written communications from the iron town. I had collected these from the office before crossing the footbridge and boarding my train from Platform Fourteen. I had read them as I crossed, with all the thunder of the morning peak going on below: the first was from a Detective Sergeant Williams of the Middlesbrough Railway Police, and it was in response to a telegram sent on my behalf by Shillito: 'Confirm suspect Clegg can be brought here for questioning or charge. Holding cell at your disposal.' That second sentence was by way of a joke, perhaps. At any rate, this was Shillito arranging a second bout between me and Clegg.

The other letter was more curious, and no less anxious-making. It was from the secretary to the passenger traffic manager, Middlesbrough District. A search had been made for the file requested: that concerning the subscribers to the Cleveland Travelling Club, and 'It is very regrettable to have to relate that the documents in question appear to be missing. It is possible that the Club subscribers were, or are, registered with us as ordinary First Class Season holders, but we have so many of these listed that we would need the names of the parties in order to be able to provide confirmation.'

My telegram to Stephen Bowman of *The Railway Rover*, Bouverie Street, London E., had so far gone unanswered.

Sandsend came and went, then Staithes, the train crossing over the mighty cliff-gaps by means of the towering viaducts. To the folk below, our engine driver must seem more like an aviator. After the long darkness of the Grinkle Tunnel, the mine workings began to appear once more. We slowed on to the Kilton Viaduct, passing the whirling gauge that was meant to warn of high winds. I looked down towards the Flat Scar mine: the sea beyond was grey, the sky white. Two men were on the jetty of the little harbour, standing thoughtful-like. But there were no ships. In the fields and on the grey slag piles around the mine, the snow remained, though worn away by footsteps, hooves and machinery here and there. It was as though it had overstayed its welcome, the novelty having worn off, and I thought of the pub in York that had started out as the Bay Horse and had gradually become the *Grey* Horse owing to the quantity of smuts on the sign.

There was no train ascending the zigzag line this time. Instead, one man toiled up the bank towards the viaduct. A dog walked alongside him, and he seemed to have an extra, bright white arm, but it was the neck of a shot goose, carried on his shoulder. I looked to my left and saw the Rectory smoking.

We came into Middlesbrough station dead on time at midday. I hung about on the platform watching some of the gentry climb down from First; all the porters in Middlesbrough were attending those select carriages, offering to carry even the smallest of black leather valises or just holding open doors. One fellow in a silk topper climbed down with a cigar in his hand, and I could have sworn he was about to give it to a porter to hold as he put on his gloves; or perhaps he would content himself with putting it out on the little bloke's cap. But what became of the cigar I never saw because, looking to my right at that moment, I saw the word 'Police' painted in white on a green door.

The Middlesbrough police office was much homelier than the York one. It was long and narrow like the railway carriages that were forever pulling up alongside. The crackling of a good fire mingled pleasantly with the ticking of a good clock, and the men worked at desks behind wooden screens – a very snug-looking arrangement. Even the constables had desks, for two of the men working wore that uniform. There were two others in plain dress, and one of these came towards me with hand extended.

'Detective Sergeant Williams?' I said.

'Ralph,' he said, nodding, 'Ralph Williams.'

He was a pleasant, restful-looking sort of man, with sleepy eyes and sleepy moustache.

'Where's that hardened villain Clegg, then?' he enquired, grinning. 'We have a very comfortable cell waiting for him.' And he pointed towards a stout door at the end of the room, indicating at the same time an old fellow surrounded not by a wooden screen but by a barricade of filing cabinets. I knew him straightaway for the Middlesbrough equivalent of Wright, the chief clerk.

'Clegg's known to this office, is he?' I said, removing my cap.

Ralph Williams smiled slowly. 'Well, I can't say he is.'

'I'm expecting to run into him come opening time at the Cape of Good Hope,' I said.

'The Cape?' he said, thoughtfully. 'An ironman, is he?'

'Aye,' I said. 'Works at Hudson's.'

'You'll be wanting a constable to go with you,' he said, which was exactly what I'd been hoping he wouldn't say. 'I think we have a man spare, if you'll hold on a moment.'

But before he could turn around and call to one of the uniformed men, I heard myself say, 'No bother. I'm sure I'll manage.'

'You'll have your whistle about you, I suppose?'

Once more that slow smile – which made it very difficult for me to gauge the true level of any danger waiting in the Cape of Good Hope.

Having spared the Middlesbrough office the inconvenience of lending me a constable, I felt entitled to ask a favour.

'I'm curious to know whether a photographer reported a camera stolen about this time last year. It might have happened somewhere on the railway territory.'

'And this is touching on –?'

Williams was making circles with his right hand, as though winding up his memory.

'– Paul Peters,' I said.

'Yes, the body turned up at Stone Farm,' he said, nodding.

62

'He was a photographer,' I said. 'He generally carried two cameras, but suddenly he had one, and I think he'd been in Middlesbrough in the meantime. I'm told somebody had one of his cameras away while he was up here, just before he copped it in the woods.'

Williams kept silence for a second, before saying:

'They're all luck, some blokes, aren't they? Billy's the man for that,' he added, pointing towards the clerk at the far end. 'We'll ask him to hunt up the crime reports for last year.'

But old Billy was listening with ears cocked, and by the time I'd walked down to his end of the office, he was already at it. He was the Middlesbrough equivalent of Wright, but he smoked pipes instead of eating oranges. There were two on his desk and one in his mouth as he fished the right file out of a drawer. It was labelled 'Crime Reports, December 1908'.

I looked through 'Stolen Albert', 'Stolen pony', 'Assault', another 'Assault', 'Damaged fencing', 'Trespass' and then about ten 'Drunk' or 'Drunk and Riotous', all threaded together with green string. 'Stolen Camera and Assault' came right after, as I'd somehow known it would, in this most obliging office. Complainant: Paul Peters, professional photographer.

In the afternoon of Thursday 3 December, Peters had been set upon by two men at Spring Street, which was evidently close to Middlesbrough station. He had not been badly hurt – that would come later – but one of two cameras he carried had been stolen. It was noted that Peters had been unable to provide a useful description of his assailants except that they wore dirty working men's clothes. The report had been made out by a Constable Robinson. I pointed to the name, and asked Billy if the man was about. He shook his head.

'Patrolling the line just presently,' he said.

Well, at least he wasn't dead, as everybody else connected to the Peters business seemed to be. I thanked Billy and signalled thanks to DS Williams, who was now working the office telephone; I then quit the station bounds for Middlesbrough town centre.

The streets were all at right angles, as though built quickly to the

63

simplest plan, and all carried very honest and straightforward names: Council Street, Corporation Road, New Street. All was new-looking and spruce in the bright winter light, for the sun had emerged at last, but a price had been paid for the forcing of this town, and I saw it in the shape of the giant, red-smoking blast furnaces to the east. It was heaven and hell, with the station and the high-level lines leading in and out the barrier between the two.

As I headed away from the station and its viaducts, the sound of a very majestic arrival made me turn back around.

It crossed the viaduct like bloody royalty: the Gateshead Infant, so called because of its incredible, titanic size. There'd been twenty of the beauties built – V Class Atlantics. You never saw them south of Darlington. For ten seconds in imagination, I was up there on the footplate, closing the regulator for the cruise into the station. I tried to recall from my firing days the braking procedure for an engine of that size, and realised in panic that I could not.

I turned about to face the river wind, the Cape of Good Hope and the man Clegg.

Chapter Nine

The Cape of Good Hope was a corner house looking over a wide road. On the other side, high metal gates opened on to an empty stretch of scrub that made a clear channel between two congested parts of the ironworks. The scrub led to the docks and the sea, where stood another infant of the north: a mighty, gleaming steamship, backwards-sloping chimneys giving a great impression of sleekness and speed even though it stood stationary.

I pushed through the door of the Cape, which was not at all the smokehole I'd expected but a wide, peaceful place, church-like with a window of red and green painted glass on three sides.

I was closely watched, as I crossed the threshold, by half a dozen blokes who all had their backs to the bar. Three sat on high stools, three stood. They were arranged somewhat like a football team posing for a photograph, and I reckoned this was half of Middlesbrough Vulcan Athletic standing before me. But they looked just as much like hospital patients as footballers: coats worn askew, shirts buttoned up anyhow or not buttoned . . . and the giant in the centre with the bandaged hand was Clegg.

'Here's trouble,' one of the men said, as I stepped over to the bar.

None moved as I fished in my pockets for gold, and for my warrant card. As I held up the card, one of the blokes cut away from the bar, and he was off – out through the front door. I watched him go. Well, I was a sneak and a spy, the enemy of working men.

I asked for a pint, and the barman broke from the gang to serve me. He was friendly enough, but my ale came in a glass where all the other blokes had pewters.

'Donald Clegg,' I said to the centre forward, removing my

bowler and holding up my warrant card. 'There's a complaint of aggravated assault laid against you.'

'Aggravated now, is it?' He stood, and walked over to give me his right hand, which was the one bandaged.

'Go easy,' he said, as I gave him my own.

It was not normal to shake hands with a man you were about to arrest.

'How did you come by that, Mr Clegg?' I asked him, and he was unwinding the none-too-clean linen as I spoke. He showed me the wound, as the other blokes drank on thoughtfully behind. The back of Clegg's wide hand was a black mass.

'Boot studs,' he said. '*Football*-boot studs. The knuckles are cracked n'all. I was nearly bloody well stood down from work over it.'

'Whose boots, mate?' I enquired, but of course I knew the answer before he spoke.

'Shillito's fucking boots.'

'Turns out he's a copper,' said one of the blokes from the bar – he wore a beard, whereas all the others had moustaches. You didn't reckon to see footballers with beards.

'If it was Shillito came at you,' I said, 'why did you crown his mate?'

Clegg lifted his shirt: more blackness.

'That was courtesy of their number six. So I belted him with my left. If I'd used my right, he'd have known about it.'

'You've put him in hospital any road,' I said.

'Hospital? Is he buggery!'

'His head had to be sewn.'

'Don't believe it.'

'We'll swear to what happened,' said the bearded player, 'every one of us.'

'It'll come to court,' said another, 'and it'll be the fixture all over again, only with swearing in place of ball skills.'

'That's just about what it was before,' said beard, who gave me a grin as I took out my notebook.

'Shillito's a cunt,' said one of the blokes.

66

I looked up, but couldn't make out which one had spoken. It wasn't Clegg.

I said, 'That's –'

'That's what?' put in beard.

'– That's as maybe.'

A sort of shimmer went through the football team. One of the blokes said, 'Stand you another pint, mister?'

I nodded.

'Won't say no,' I said, and one of the tall stools was pushed my way.

As the pint was poured, I asked, 'Who was the bloke that just bolted?'

It was Clegg who answered.

'Alf Wood.'

'Where's he gone?'

'Don't know, mate,' said Clegg.

I nodded thanks as the second pint was passed over.

'He went just as soon as I held up my warrant card.'

'Happen he doesn't like warrant cards,' said the long-haired bloke.

Clegg was grinning. 'Never mind him,' he said. 'What about the business in hand?'

I had made up my mind not to take Clegg in. The situation did not call for immediate arrest, and Shillito could go hang.

'I'll take statements,' I said, 'starting with you, Mr Clegg.'

With pint and notebook in hand, I removed to a table under the window and Clegg followed me over. He sat down, and told me of the fight. He was about of an age with me, and I liked him, and I believed his account. After Clegg, I took statements from three other blokes, who wandered over one by one. Each man, when speaking to me, was out of earshot of his confederates, and each said the same, or as near as made no difference. As the third man spoke, I reasoned that Shillito might want to make an end to this investigation, for it was becoming obvious that he ought to be the one charged. I was just stowing away my indelible pencil when the pub door opened, bringing a freezing wind, and sight of the bloke who'd scarpered a minute earlier.

'Hi!' I shouted. 'I'd like a word, mate.'

He stood his ground this time, and one of the team said, 'You're all right, Alf. He's white as they come, this lad.'

Alf Wood stepped into the Cape of Good Hope. Judging by the speed with which he'd made off, he was certainly a vagabond – which might prove useful.

'You'll take a pint?' I asked him.

He nodded, and I called for the drink with a flash of anxiety at the amount I was spending. If I made no arrest, Shillito would not permit me expenses. The football group stood in a somewhat looser arrangement now, but they all watched as one man as I turned towards Wood, saying, 'Would you mind answering a couple of questions?'

'Why me?'

'I think you know this town.'

'I bloody don't.'

'But you've lived in it all your life?'

Long silence on this point.

Presently, Wood said, 'Two questions only?'

'Aye.'

'I'm saying nowt about the business at Langton's place, mind.'

'What's Langton's place?' I said.

Wood looked at me for a space.

'I'm saying nowt about it.'

'You've one question left,' one of the football blokes called out to me.

'Mr Wood,' I said, 'have you heard of any operator in this town – any man who might at some time last year have had away a good-quality camera?'

'Camera? What for?'

'How do you mean, "What for?" The camera was taken from a professional photographer in a street robbery this time last year. It happened in Spring Street near the railway station.'

'Camera?' Wood said, making a question of the word again. 'Never heard of any such article being taken.'

'Then do you have any idea where a good camera might fetch up having *been* taken?'

I was nearer the mark with this, for one of the footballers said, 'You give him the tip, Woody, and he'll do all right by us over the little bit of bother we had in York.'

He didn't have this *quite* right, but I kept silence.

'Let's be right,' Wood said to me. 'I'll take you to a likely spot, but the bloke there – he doesn't want any bother from you lot.'

'I'm after the camera,' I said, 'and that's all.'

Wood nodded, and fixed his cap back on his head.

'We'll take a walk then.'

I picked up my hat and notebook. Turning to Clegg and his mates, I said, 'I'll show these statements to Detective Sergeant Shillito, but I'm going to recommend the matter goes no further.'

Clegg nodded at me.

'Obliged to you, mate,' he said. I then turned and followed the little bloke, Woody, into the street.

Woody pushed on ahead, red-faced from anger or shame at helping out a copper; or just from the bitter cold. It was washday in Middlesbrough, and we moved under great glowing white banners of towelling and sheets suspended across the streets. Turning a corner in the half-light, I fancied that I saw two great snowflakes swooping down towards us, but they were seagulls. We were on the edge of the town centre, and rows of shops began to appear amid the red houses, but the place that Woody found was something *between* a shop and a house. The door was ajar; there were words painted on it that I did not have time to read, because Woody pushed it open directly and then, saying something in an underbreath, he was off down the street like greased bloody lightning.

A man in a dusty topcoat stood by a small fire looking thoughtfully at a great mix-up of goods, as though he'd lately bought it as a job lot and was wondering whether it had been a good investment. There were bits of bicycles, gramophones, sticks of furniture, a tangle of overmantels, with the ornamental items that might once have stood on them – and that might, but probably wouldn't, do so again – tumbled into wooden boxes hard by. There were a lot of clocks, some of which turned out to be barometers, and a whole corner was given over to musical instruments, including half a dozen fiddles, one of these being labelled 'violin' as though it was a cut above the others. I nodded at the man, holding up my warrant card.

'Detective Stringer,' I said. 'Railway force.'

The man stood up straight.

'You wouldn't have taken delivery of a camera, I suppose, some time over the past year?'

The man looked at his boots for a while, then up.

'Hold on,' he said, and turned on his heel. He disappeared into a back room, and after a couple of minutes of scuffling and cursing, came back carrying a camera.

'That was quick,' I said.

'Don't hang about when you lads come calling,' he said.

He wanted me off his premises, just like most of the folks I met in the course of my work.

He handed it over to me. It was the same as the one that had dangled from Bowman's shoulder, and the one that had been found in the brook near Peters's body: the Mentor Reflex. But this time the changing box that held the exposures – or might do – was fixed in place at the side. If the doings was all inside there . . . that could only mean that this camera had not been stolen by people interested in what Peters had photographed. It must, in that case, have been taken by the common run of street thief, a man interested only in the value of the camera. Why else would the camera have been brought to the man standing before me?

If the exposures proved to be in place, the villains concerned in the Middlesbrough theft must have been a different lot from the ones who did for Peters at Stone Farm – that was my first thought, at any rate.

'Have you had this off, mate?' I asked the man, pointing to the changing box.

He shook his head.

'And I don't believe the bloke who brought it in had done either.'

'Why not?'

'He didn't look my idea of a whatsname – photographic artist.'

'Who was he?'

'Reckon I'd let on if I knew?'

'Er, no,' I said.

'That's just where you're wrong,' he said. 'I'm not bent, though you might think it from the looks of this place. A bloke came in, sold me a stack of stuff for a tanner. I took it sight unseen, granted. But that en't a crime now, is it?'

'Would you recognise the bloke again?'

'Big cap . . . thick muffler . . .' said the shopkeeper.

'That's narrowed it down to about thirty million.'

'I can't help that, mister,' he said.

I believed him, just as I'd believed Clegg and the men of Vulcan Athletic. They seemed to be part of an honest network – or had they been guying me from start to finish?

'Mind if I take it?' I said. 'It's evidence.'

'You're the boss,' he said.

Anything to get shot of me.

I carried the Mentor Reflex into the middle of town. The wide, new streets were all in straight lines, and the trick was to avoid the ones along which the sea wind raced. The streets were prettily lit, for all the cold, and the shops crowded with Christmas tomfoolery. There was a clear-cut line between the sexes: the men were moving fast, thinking of business, the women moving slow, thinking of Christmas. I was turning a corner in the locality of the railway station when I was checked by the sight of a small fir tree from which dangled little medicine bottles of coloured glass. 'Milner,' read the sign above the window. 'Druggist.' The important notice was in the corner of the window: 'Photographs Developed'.

I pushed open the door, entering a sort of warm, chemical Christmas. Approaching the counter, I removed my gloves and loosened the catch that held the plates on to the camera. A man waited at the counter: white-coated and clean – struck me as a doctor who'd missed his mark, like all druggists.

'Can you do these for me express?'

'Two hours,' he said, and whether that was express or no, I couldn't have said from his tone.

'How many exposures in here?' asked the man, taking the tin from me.

'Well, there'd be two at most, wouldn't there?' I replied. 'Or there might not be any.'

He looked at me narrowly, saying, 'If there aren't *any*, it won't take two hours.'

I requested the largest print size, and then went off for a bite and a warm, eventually walking into Hintons, although not the select parts used by Steve Bowman and his wife, but a smoke-filled, pub-like part of it, where I ate fried eggs and drank a cup of cocoa.

It was five o'clock when I returned to Milner, the druggist.

'Anything doing?' I asked, and by way of reply he handed over an envelope, saying, 'Two and fourpence.'

Chapter Ten

I paid the money over without a thought for the cost, and pulled first from the envelope the two negatives. Five men stood on a platform before a special carriage. It was the one I'd viewed at Bog Hall Sidings, Whitby. Above it was visible a part of the platform canopy, and I knew that right away for the broken one at Saltburn. The men's eyes seemed to be burning, and all about their boots was a mass of rough blackness – snow in reverse.

I then pulled out the prints. Going from left to right, the first man was clean-shaven and wore a silk hat (which he held in his left hand, along with his gloves) and a topcoat buttoned right up; there would be a smart black morning coat underneath, no doubt. He was handsome, and his hair went backwards in waves. His dashing looks put me in mind of fine copperplate handwriting.

He looked slightly sidelong at the photographer, as if to say, 'Photograph *me*, would you?' and his left arm somehow did not belong about the shoulder of the next man, number two, but that's where it was. Number two was perhaps half the age of number one. He had a friendly face and smiled straight at the photographer. He carried a folded copy of a newspaper, the name of which I could make out: it was the *Whitby Morning Post*, which served the whole of the coast of North Yorkshire. He wore a derby hat, and had a fine winter flower in his buttonhole, as did the next man, who was about of an age with the first; his rough, grey hair and beard were all of a piece with his tweed suit. He might have been an explorer, freshly returned from the Arctic Circle. The fourth had a round face (he was bareheaded and bald) and round glasses. He gave a cautious smile. The flower in his buttonhole did not suit him. It was too *flowery*. Number five was older than the rest. He wore a stovepipe hat, and had blind-looking eyes; he looked dirty and confused, but also *rich*. He might be Moody – the man who'd gone under a train, father of another Moody now living in Pickering. I looked them over again, thinking of them in turn as handsome fellow, young fellow, wild-looking fellow, bald fellow and old fellow.

The second print was more or less the same, save for the fact that the young man was looking down, and I saw immediately that this was the difference between a photograph that could be used in a picture paper, and one that could not. The prints themselves made an impression not very different from that of the negatives – and this, I believed, was on account of the strangeness of the snow light; I could not tell whether the picture had been taken in the morning or afternoon.

What had become of these men?

I had already been told that one was dead, and I knew this much: that there was only one way your fortunes could go once you'd attained the distinction of your own railway carriage, and that was down the hill. I found myself turning one of the prints over, half expecting the druggist to have written their names on the reverse. I looked at the man, now serving a cold cure to another customer. Smart shopkeeper like himself – he might know one of the Club gents; he might know all six. So might any man in Middlesbrough, come to that . . .

I had meant to take my trophy straight to Detective Sergeant Williams, but a new notion came to me as I exited the druggist's, and I struck out for the largest building in my line of sight: the Middlesbrough Exchange. I crossed a wide square that was filled with trams come to the rescue of the freezing citizens. In the cold darkness, the iron-making smell had descended on the middle of the town: the strange, out-of-the-way smell of burning sand.

One of the mighty double doors of the Exchange was being swung to as I approached, and the place was evidently closing up. A fossil in a gold-braided uniform watched me go in, as if to say, 'I won't trouble to ask your business; you'll be ejected before long in any case.' In the great hall of the Exchange, the remaining groups of buyers and sellers talked under clouds of cigar smoke. Wooden stands were placed at intervals, each one an island under its own electric light. Notices were pinned to the stands: the day's prices of coal, ironstone, iron, steel and ships, as I supposed – all the goods that had raised Middlesbrough from nothing to a city of a hundred thousand souls in less than a lifetime.

Some clerks remained at the counters that were set into the walls beneath a great gallery, but most were already shuttered. I walked towards one group of businessmen with my warrant card and the photograph held aloft. 'Detective Stringer of the railway police,' I said, and they turned to me as one. It cost them quite an effort to look civil, but the warrant card made them do it. What did they see? A thin, youngish bloke with a camera over his shoulder; topcoat a little out at the elbows. It was my work coat. A new one, in a better grade of cloth, would be served out to me if I gained my promotion. As they eyed me, I felt very strongly the want of that word 'Sergeant' – 'Detective Sergeant' would have testified to at least one promotion successfully secured. One of the men took the photograph and passed it among his fellows. The second one to clap eyes on it spoke immediately.

'It's Falconer,' he said, and he pointed to the rather wild-looking one, the explorer type.

The next man to take the photograph nodded, and he too said, 'Falconer.'

'How would I find the man?' I asked.

'How would you *find* him?' asked one of the men, in a wondering tone. 'Well, that's the *question*, isn't it?'

Another of the group was speaking:

'And that one's – why, that's Lee.'

'Which one?' I said, craning to see, and I was aware of not appearing to be a fellow of quite the right sort.

'This one,' said one of the men, indicating the bald-headed and spectacle-wearing gent, while another at the same time asked, 'Is some connection discovered between the two?' But in fact they were all speaking at once now, and their black-gloved hands were all over the photograph as they each sought a better look.

'It's a travelling club,' I said, but the remark was lost in the scramble.

One of the men was asking, 'You're on the Middlesbrough force and you've not heard of poor George Lee?' The first one to have spoken gave me a narrow look, saying, 'You seem to stand in need of some enlightenment.'

'I'm from the railway force,' I said, 'stationed at York.'

'You're operating independently of the Middlesbrough constabulary?' one of the men asked. He seemed to quite credit that I might be, and that this might be a rather clever notion. He looked a little more amiable than the rest, but the situation was too humiliating for words. I must break away.

'Does this represent some new line in the investigation?' asked one of the men as I reclaimed the picture.

'Yes,' I said.

'But isn't it a little late for that?'

Christ knew whether it was or no, but Detective Sergeant Ralph Williams would be the man to tell me. Reclaiming the photograph, I fairly sprinted towards the double doors but one of the group – the amiable chap – was keeping pace, and as we crossed the exchange floor, he held his gloved hand out before him as though grasping an imaginary cricket ball.

'George Lee,' he said, waving his cane enthusiastically. 'If I had in my hand a quantity of ironstone, he could tell me the percentage of iron in a trice. Not just a rough indication of quality. I mean, he'd shoot a verdict straight at you. "Thirty-five per cent," he'd say, which is a good deal, and in which case, of course, you were on velvet. Twenty-five per cent? Oh Lord, *then* you had a headache – do you sink your shaft or no for that grade of stone?'

He'd stopped in the lobby or vestibule of the Exchange before the great double doors, and he was pressing the question on me:

'For twenty-five per cent stone?'

'If you could mine the stuff cheaply . . .' I said, groping in the darkness, and the amiable man gave me a sort of wink at that. We were pushing on towards the tram-packed square, the man's cane ticking like a clock on the new-laid pavement.

'What were George Lee's origins?' I asked, reasoning that no disgrace ought to attach to ignorance on that point.

But the amiable man had his arm out, and was saying, 'This is me.'

A hansom had stopped for him, and it had whisked him away as I looked on.

Not three minutes later, I was in the warm police office, where Ralph Williams – who was also amiable, but steady and quietly spoken with it – was inviting me to sit down at his desk chair. He himself perched on the desk.

'Now you have some further questions as regards the dead photographer?' he said, once I'd explained the absence of my quarry Clegg.

'I've discovered his camera,' I said, indicating the Mentor Reflex, 'and I've found the pictures in it. Now it all comes down to the identity of these fellows –'

I took the photograph from its pasteboard sleeve. 'They're the Whitby–Middlesbrough Travelling Club – went every day from country stops along the line into this station.'

Williams seemed a good fellow, but I'd been hoping to stifle that grin of his, and in this I had succeeded.

'The shot was taken at Saltburn,' I said, 'by Paul Peters.'

'Well, this *is* a turn-up,' said Williams, eyeing the photograph.

I told him how I'd come by it.

'Now this man,' I said, pointing to the bald, spectacle-wearing one, 'is George Lee, mining engineer. Some blokes at the Exchange just told me.'

Williams nodded.

'I believe it is.'

'What's become of him?'

'Lee?' said Williams, still looking at the photograph. 'Why, murdered.'

'Like Peters,' I said, 'and this picture makes a connection between them.'

Williams might have frowned at that, but his pleasant face didn't suit frowning. I asked him, 'Was it known that Lee was in this Club?'

'The connection was certainly not made in court,' said Williams. 'I do not believe that the matter of this . . . Travelling Club . . . I do not believe it was brought in.'

Williams called to the old clerk at the far end of the room. 'Prosecution register please, Billy – the Lee case.'

Williams put the photograph on the desk between us.

'The case was prosecuted?' I asked him.

Williams nodded.

'Somebody swing?'

Another nod, and Williams slowly pronounced a name: 'Gilbert Sanderson.'

'And this one,' I said, pointing to the wild-looking explorer type. 'This is Falconer?'

'I was coming to him,' said Williams.

'Was he murdered as well?'

'Maybe,' said Williams, and for the first time there was shortness in his tone. 'Theodore Falconer was reported disappeared about this time last year; picture widely circulated at the time. You'll find his woodcut in the *Police Gazette* most weeks. Billy has papers on him.'

Billy was on hand, giving me a file marked 'Crown vs –' somebody – I couldn't make out the name. There was another piece of paper being passed over. 'Telephone message,' said Billy. 'Call came through ten past three.'

He was a marvel of organisation, this Billy. Thanking him, I read the note: 'Detective Stringer to telephone Mr Bowman. Urgent.' The number given was 2196 London EC.

Detective Sergeant Williams was putting his coat on. I'd rattled him with my discoveries, no question. Billy moved away, and returned with a second file, this marked simply 'Theodore Falconer'.

'How about the other three in the picture?' I asked Williams, and he shook his head.

'This one,' he said, pointing to the clean-shaven, handsome man in black. 'The face seems –'

But he shook his head again. He'd seemed to have the name on his tongue, as had the blokes in the Exchange. Williams, smiling again, said, 'You're at liberty to take those papers away for a little while. I'm booking off just now – I have the job of collecting the family Christmas tree on the way home. Do you have children yourself, Detective Stringer?'

'One boy,' I said.

'I've three girls.'

Well, a fellow could run to three on a detective sergeant's wages.

'They're each after a doll's house,' he said, reaching for his bowler, 'so we'll land up with a whole street in miniature.'

'My boy wants a toy aeroplane,' I said. 'One that really flies.'

And it seemed to be quite typical of Williams that he should have responded:

'Now I know just where you can get one of those. Brown's,' said Detective Sergeant Williams, backing through the door. 'On Corporation Road here, but there's a York branch, I believe.'

'But how does it fly?'

'Why, *elastic*,' he said, with a parting nod.

Billy wound the magneto for me at his end of the office, and handed me the instrument. Half the telephone talkers in London seemed to come and go in echoing waves, and then I was put in connection with a very sad-sounding man who might have sighed very loudly when I asked, 'Am I through to *The Railway Rover*?' or that might just have been the noise of the line. Anyhow, it *was* *The Railway Rover*, and Stephen Bowman had evidently just left the office in a tearing hurry.

Chapter Eleven

I nodded thanks to Billy, who said, 'Would you care to read those papers here? It's cold out.'

'Much obliged,' I said.

I sat down and he brought me a cup of tea, which I never touched because on turning to the prosecution file marked 'Crown vs Sanderson', it straightaway came to me that here was the business that had been known to York newspaper readers as 'The Lame Horse Murders'. The case had been tried in Durham nine months previously; I had forgotten that the defendant was called Sanderson, and the two victims were called Lee.

George Lee's wife was of superior rank to him. Lee himself had had no schooling to speak of and had started work in the iron mines at fifteen. He was a joiner at various places, rising swiftly to foreman joiner. He was good at his job; couldn't be beaten for energy and push. Aged thirty-one he was injured in a cage accident at New Mine, which was somewhere on the cliffs near Saltburn, for which he was handsomely compensated. He'd used the money to undertake a degree in mining engineering at Leeds University, obtaining a first-class certificate.

He then worked at a certain Marine Mine, and here he invented a whole new contraption for the mines: the Lee Picking Belt, which had put him in funds for life. His next move was to become a consulting engineer, employed at umpteen mines, and he'd also become an investor: shareholder here, seat on the board there.

In 1904, Lee had bought The Grange: a tidy-sized place a mile or so inland of Staithes, and so about a dozen miles south of Saltburn. Here, he'd set up as a country gentleman in a small way.

It was mentioned in the report that he 'travelled every working day to the office he kept in Middlesbrough', but it seemed to be nowhere stated that he had done so as a member of a travelling club. That had been my own discovery, and all of a sudden it didn't seem of much account.

I looked up just then to see the door of the police office opening.

A constable came in holding another man by the elbow. This second fellow was smartly turned out. He held a well-brushed bowler lightly decorated with snow, and had a pleasant lemony smell to him: good-class hair oil. He was being led off to the holding cell nonetheless. A couple of minutes later, the constable came by my desk again. Introducing myself, I asked whether he might be Robinson, the man who'd interviewed Peters about the theft of the camera, but he was not. At this, I wanted to get back to 'Crown vs Sanderson', but the constable, nodding towards the holding cell, said, 'Notorious fare-avoider, that bloke.'

'Caught him at it, have you?'

The constable nodded. He was holding a cup of tea, provided by Billy.

'Making for Scotland on a doctored ticket, he was.'

'Looks like he came along pretty quietly.'

'Like a lamb,' the constable said, draining his tea. 'He's wanted by the town police here on a number of other points besides.'

He just *would* be, I thought, as the constable returned his teacup to Billy, gave me good evening and quitted the room.

In that perfect police office, I turned back to the file.

Gilbert Sanderson, George Lee's murderer, had followed evil courses from an early age, and had practically grown up in the reformatory at Durham. It was believed he'd got his living mainly by burglary from then on, although he'd held some subordinate positions in some of the Cleveland iron mines, and had described himself on his marriage certificate of 1897 as a 'tinker'. Sanderson kept quarters at Loftus, in the heart of the iron-mining district, but he was of a roaming disposition, and travelled throughout the North Riding buying and selling, which is where the horse had come in. It was a white mare, an ex-Middlesbrough cab horse that had suffered a collision with a motor in Middlesbrough city centre and been ripped open along the flank. But the mare – name of Juliette – had been stitched and survived.

A year ago, the paths of Sanderson and Lee had crossed.

Sanderson broke into The Grange on 11 December 1908, and was stowing candlesticks in a haversack when the owner came upon him. Lee was stabbed through the heart. The wife came next into the room, and got the same treatment. Both died instantly; the manservant was blinded in one eye, and he was lucky at that, for the knife point had stopped just short of causing injury to the brain. The boy, who was seven years old at the time, survived the attack and now lodged with the late Mrs Lee's sister in London, with all the property held in trust for him.

It was the manservant's description that had done for Sanderson; that and the discovery of the horse in the garden. It had been found lame, with a crack in the right foreleg, and this was taken to be the reason for Sanderson having made his escape on foot. He was well known to the local police (having twice before got hard labour for burglary), and he was arrested the next day at his lodgings in Loftus.

Sanderson was hanged at Durham Gaol on 4 March 1909, and a newspaper account of the hanging was contained in the file. At the head of it was a woodcut of Gilbert Sanderson: he was a big, pug-looking man with a bald head and long side whiskers.

I bundled up the papers, together with the camera and the photographs. I walked out on to the platform. It was crowded, although the Whitby train that everyone was after wasn't due for a quarter of an hour. A lad walked the platform shouting, 'Papers, cigarettes, chocolates,' and I wondered which of the three offered the best defence against cold. I let the lad go by, even though the *Middlesbrough Gazette* was offering its seasonal 'Complimentary Calendar'. I ducked into the refreshment room, where there were even more black-suited businessmen than on the platform. A fire blazed at each end of the room, and the bar was in the middle, under a gas ring that was kept rocking by the opening and closing of the door, to the annoyance of the steward, who kept reaching up to steady it. All the Complimentary Calendars had been chucked anyhow across the floor, and were being trodden to bits beneath the boots of the drinkers.

Hot milk and rum was on the go, so I bought a glass (in spite of the long cost) and turned to the second set of papers: the 'missing' file on Falconer.

Theodore Falconer was the son of a well-to-do Whitby ship's master. At sixteen, he'd gone to sea himself in a small coaster, against his father's wishes, returning four years later with a pronounced stutter, which he never cured. He never spoke of this adventure, or gave out where he'd been except to say 'Northern waters'.

He had been welcomed back like the Prodigal nonetheless, and after attending Oxford University he in due course inherited certain interests in shipping that his father had acquired on his own retirement from the sea. He was first on the board of shipyards that had built half a dozen steamers at Whitby during the 1880s. He had then moved from building to owning, becoming a partner in a shipping line that ordered ships from certain yards in the North East. These they would use to trade, or sell on directly. Many of these vessels were bought by mine owners or iron traders for the export of iron and steel, chiefly from Middlesbrough.

In 1906, Falconer had reduced his involvement in the business. He had removed, at the beginning of his old age, to The Cedars, a big house in the country half a mile outside Saltburn. But like the ironman George Lee, he'd kept an office in the commercial district of Middlesbrough, where it seemed that he had played at ship-owning and investing rather than pursuing the business in earnest.

It appeared that Falconer was a man of modest habits. He employed only one part-time slavey; he had no stables, carriage or groom. It was speculated in the police report that he 'preferred to walk', for Falconer was a great outdoorsman, and was often striding out to the moor in his tweed breeches, in pursuit of botany, bird-watching and other interests.

Falconer had also founded the Cleveland Naturalists Club, which met four times a year in a timber hut in woods near The Cedars (that sounded a rum do, I thought), and was president of

83

other fellowships of a similar tramping nature, and patron of the Whitby Seamen's Hospital. He was a churchman (Methodist), charitably inclined and therefore pretty well-liked despite being, according to the report, 'somewhat of a stubborn nature, not easy to manage'. He had been a bachelor lifelong.

A porter put his head around the door and announced the Whitby train. I left the refreshment room, and crossed the icy platform, still reading.

Taking my seat, I found the notice concerning Falconer that appeared in the *Police Gazette*. Going by the woodcut that accompanied it, he did not look like the sort of man who went missing, but the sort of man who *came back*: a strong man – a Shackleton of the moors.

The advertisement was headed 'Missing'; then came '£100 reward'. The meat of it was this:

Since December 2nd 1908, Theodore Falconer, aged sixty-five, afflicted by stutter. Medium height, hair and beard grey and abundant, eyes blue, complexion pale, suit of grey tweed, silver lever watch and chain, lace boots, black hard hat. Last seen walking towards his house, The Cedars, Saltburn district, at six-thirty pm on December 2nd. The above reward will be paid by John Mason, Solicitor, Flowergate, Whitby, to the first person giving information leading to the whereabouts of Falconer.

I read the date again. He had last been seen the day before Peters had been deprived of one of his two cameras. All the dates were bunching up, but I could not make sense of them. Certainly, Falconer had been wearing what looked like a grey tweed suit in the Peters photograph. But no doubt he wore the same get-up every day.

What did I know? That Falconer was last seen on 2 December; that Peters reported the theft of the camera that contained a picture of Falconer and the Club on the 3rd; that some time shortly afterwards he'd visited Stone Farm for the second time, there to be done in, and to have his second camera not stolen but ransacked; that nine days after the last sighting of Falconer, Lee had been murdered by Gilbert Sanderson . . . Had Sanderson done for the lot of them? But he was a thief, and nothing suggested that anything had been stolen from Falconer – he had simply disappeared. And there was the old man, Moody, who'd 'gone under a train' *after* Sanderson had hung.

Perhaps Sanderson's friends or confederates had pursued the Club after his conviction. But the Club members had not given evidence against Sanderson, and in any event Falconer had disappeared before the robbery at The Grange had taken place.

Through the carriage window, I saw the world in fragments: a furnace in blast beyond Redcar, lighting up a great circle of snow for half a mile around; the flash of an illuminated mine, rotary tipplers circling on wires. Saltburn came, and we reversed out as before. The Club members had been photographed at Saltburn. *They were all up by Saltburn.*

We next passed Stone Farm: nobody about on the platform, Crystal's passing loop lit up behind. At Loftus, where the murderer Sanderson had lived, I had a clear view through a window into a brightly lit hall where a silver band played. I could not hear them, though. The viaduct came, and we rolled slowly through the darkness a hundred and fifty feet up, the Flat Scar mine appearing as a lonely cluster of lights to the left and far below. As we neared the fishing village of Staithes, I leant towards the window again, trying to spy a homestead that might have been Lee's place, The Grange

But the train was too fast, and the world was too dark.

Sanderson had argued that he had never visited The Grange; that at the material time he had been in the company of a man called Baxter. But this Baxter could not be found.

I sat back and thought again of the white horse, Juliette by name.

It was always likely that such a notable animal would be traced back to its owner, so why did Sanderson take the beast with him on the robbery? Sanderson's story was that the nag had been stolen from him a day or so before the robbery.

My thoughts suddenly shifted away from this head-racking business and towards the York office and Shillito. I had failed to do what he asked, and it struck me that he really might try to have me stood down. I turned again towards the window, but it was impossible by now even to tell the difference between land and sea.

Chapter Twelve

I slept for a while, and when I woke up, a man was sitting over opposite in the compartment. He was reading the *Middlesbrough Gazette*. There was the blather about the calendar on the front page of the paper – 'Beautiful illustrations, showing the locality in all seasons' – and something else told the readers it was a red letter day, for the words 'Complimentary Calendar' were written in each of the top two corners of the front page. The two Cs were intertwined in an artistic way.

I stood up and reached for my topcoat, which lay on the luggage rack, and removed from the pocket the photographs of the Travelling Club. The youngest man held the *Whitby Morning Post*, a newspaper published in the next sizeable place south of Middlesbrough (leaving aside the middling-sized town of Saltburn). He held the paper folded, but I could see one of the two top corners. The artistic Cs were there as well.

The *Whitby Morning Post* had served Baytown (where I'd grown up, and which lay only eight or so miles south of Whitby), and I recalled that it too had published a complimentary calendar annually. It was at about the time when dad's shop (he was a butcher) began to take in the Christmas fowl – an exciting sign that Christmas was coming, along with the annual visit of my Uncle Roy, dad's brother, who always came over from the Midlands a couple of weeks before Christmas. Uncle Roy was a worried-looking bachelor, and it was as though he thought he'd better get his Christmas visit in early, before anything terrible might cause the *cancellation* of it. He would always bring me sugar balls.

Was the *Whitby Morning Post* connected to *The Middlesbrough Gazette*? I did not think so, but they used the same design for the advertising of their calendar.

Whitby West Cliff station appeared out of the darkness; I must change here for the Town station in order to make the connection for York. Sometimes the carriages were shunted down through the streets from West Cliff to Town station, which lay in the middle of Whitby. Whether that was about to happen this time, I did not know, but I climbed down, and made a walk of it in any event.

Whitby was cold and old: the streets were filled with grimy snow, and the harbour was packed with empty boats, as though everyone had given up on the outdoor world for the present.

The office of the *Whitby Morning Post* perched on the harbour wall, and as soon as I hit the waterside, I saw the lights blazing inside. I was in luck, but barely, for there was only one man left in the office at that late hour. Freezing though it was, he worked with the door propped open; seemed to keep open house. I walked straight in and pulled off my cap.

'Evening,' I said.

There were three model boats on the low window ledge that overlooked the harbour, and the office was ship-like: low, and with a great deal of well-varnished wood. And it was as if the ship had listed slightly, for all the desks seemed a little out of kilter. The man – a journalist, as I supposed – sat on a revolving chair with his feet up on a desk. He was actually reading the *Whitby Morning Post*, just as though he was an ordinary citizen who'd had no hand in its making.

He nodded back, and put down the paper.

'You looking for work?' he said, eyeing the camera that hung from my shoulder.

I showed him my warrant card, and said, 'I'm looking into certain events of late last year. To make a long story short, it'd be quite handy to know when you came out with your Complimentary Calendar for 1908.'

'Early,' said the man immediately, 'so as to beat the competition.'

He did not rise, but pointed towards a table that ran along one

88

wall, where lay a great mountain of past *Morning Posts*. The whole purpose of the office was to add to that pile.

'See for yourself,' said the man; and he went back to reading his own paper.

The papers were all slightly damp, from being kept so close to the sea, as I supposed. The one at the top of the first pile was dated 12 March of the present year. I pulled it and the ones below aside and kept going until I reached December 1908. I proceeded slowly through these until I came to the edition in which the usual top-corner advertisement for Bermaline Bread gave way to the intertwined Cs of 'Complimentary Calendar inside today'.

It was dated 3 December. This was the same edition held by the young man in the photograph taken by Peters; Falconer was shown in that photograph, and yet the last sighting of Falconer was supposed to have occurred on 2 December. I brought to mind the dates I knew. I turned to the journalist, saying, 'I'm obliged to you, mate.'

He barely grunted in response, being still lost in the doings of Whitby and district as described by the *Whitby Morning Post*. It said a lot for both town and paper, I decided, as I set off for the station and my York connection. But then again, I was in good spirits anyway, for I felt that I'd had a pretty good day of it.

Chapter Thirteen

At York, the police office was closed, but the parcels office was all go with the Christmas traffic, and two great stacks of parcels waited outside for booking. Under the gaslights of the forecourt, delivery vans waited: a dozen horse-drawn and two motors. They all trembled in the cold. I slung the Mentor Reflex over my shoulder, pushed the police papers into my inside coat pocket and pulled the Humber from the bicycle rack. My frozen hands were only good for a certain number of movements, so I did not trouble to light the lamps, but set off directly, half-pushing, half-riding the bike through the snow.

There was a mile of snowy darkness between the end of York's lights and Thorpe-on-Ouse, but the village itself was a deal livelier than usual. The windows of the church were all lit, and the door stood open. The wife, I knew, had planned to spend the afternoon in there with Harry, Christmassing the nave with holly and mistletoe. The Church and the housewifely socialism practised by the Women's Co-operative Guild were her main interests in life, and I often felt that Harry and me came a poor second. She loved that boy, but I felt on occasion that she'd board him out if she could – just for the odd time or two. Pushing the bike under the lights on the main street, I saw that the snow was on the left side of everything, including the sign of the Fortune of War, the pub that stood over opposite our cottage. Its curtains were closed, but I knew the place was packed, and wondered whether it was share-out night for the goose club. We were not in the goose club; we were to have a chicken, and the bird was to come from the Co-operative Stores.

I stowed the bike in the woodshed, and walked into the parlour, where the wife had her hair down before the glass. She was trying out new styles for the Co-operative Women's Guild party, which would take place the following evening, and which she had undertaken to organise. She'd been paid a pound on top of her usual part-time wages for doing so, and this had evidently not been enough since – to listen to the wife – the organising of this beano had made the Labours of Hercules seem like a few small errands.

'You look all in, our Jim,' she said, when I kissed her. 'Did you bring the man in this time?'

'No,' I said, moving over to the fire. In preparation for the festive season, she had black-leaded half the grate and cleaned the stains off some of the crockery – just the spoons, perhaps. I knew that some sort of mixture was on the go in the kitchen, but no Christmas fare had so far appeared in a finished form.

'Well,' she said, 'you're keeping the railway in business at any rate, with all your journeys up there. Why did you not fetch him this time?'

'He's innocent.'

The wife turned about, both hands holding her hair, and frowned at me. She looked more fetching than a person ought when frowning.

'How's Harry?' I said, thawing my hands by the fire. 'I'll go up and see him.'

'Leave him be,' said Lydia. 'He's just nicely got off.'

Her typewriter had been moved off the top of the strong table, and placed underneath to make way for some sprigs of holly, ribbons and her best bonnet and coat. There were also some papers, including one headed 'Terms for hire of the Ebor Hall'.

The Co-op ladies' party was to be held at the Ebor Hall, the Co-operative Hall in York having been reserved months since for a lot of men's parties, some completely unconnected – according to the wife – with the high aims of the Co-operative Society, such as York and District Rugby Club.

'Are you sure the Ebor Hall is big enough?' I said.

No answer. She continued at the mirror, her back to me. I looked again at the paper.

'Are you having a plain tea or a meat tea?' I asked her, looking at the scale of charges. 'A plain tea's half the price, but it is Christmas after all, so I would hope you'd be having a meat tea.'

'I know perfectly well that you're trying to make me anxious,' she said, 'so I'm ignoring you. I had a run-in with the manager of the hall today,' she ran on. 'A horrible man, and very well named: Hogg.'

'A row over what?'

'As you will see from their terms, no charge is made for use of the piano.'

'I don't see what there is to complain of in that,' I said, taking off my coat, and sitting down in the rocking chair.

'Today, Mrs Appleyard, who is to play the piano on the evening, came in to test it. She said it is out of tune to the extent of being quite unplayable. I passed on the news to Hogg, who said, "Well, the instrument comes free," and suggested that by discovering the fact of its being out of tune, we were, as he put it, "looking a gift horse in the mouth". I told him that a piano out of tune is worse than none at all, and would he pay for it to be tuned, or at least split the cost of tuning. He said we must bear the cost entirely; that the piano had been tuned only recently, but that the cold weather made it go out. I told him that rather suggested that the room had not been kept properly warmed.'

'And is that right?'

'Don't get me on the subject of the heating. It makes me absolutely livid. I will not discuss it. . .'

'The heating,' the wife continued a couple of seconds later, when she was back at the mirror, 'is provided by two radiators, which is not enough; and you can quite clearly see where there used to be a third – just by the door.'

'Do you suppose they removed it just to spite you?'

'I brought this up with Hogg, and he said they'd had to remove that radiator in order to fit the piano into its alcove. I said, "So we've lost a heat source in order to accommodate a piano we can't play because of the cold."'

'And what did he say to that?'

92

I was standing now, lifting the net curtain to look across at the Fortune of War.

'He said nothing to it, but had the nerve to remind me that proceedings will be stopped by the caretaker if there is any sign of damage to the fixtures and fittings or other violent or disorderly behaviour. I said, "We are the Women's Co-operative Guild – are we likely to behave in a violent or disorderly way?" He said, "I don't know what you get up to, but there'd better not be any rough stuff, that's all."'

When she turned round, she was grinning.

'How's that?'

'Beautiful,' I said.

'But you are looking at my hair. It is the skirt that's new.'

'Oh,' I said, 'that's equally good. I was a bit thrown because you've spent the past five minutes fixing your hair.'

'I'm only doing that to see how it sets off the skirt.' She glanced at me a little guiltily as she added, 'It's part of a suit, but Lillian Backhouse is making some adjustments to the jacket for me.'

'You bought it today?'

'I simply could not settle on an outfit . . . Look on it as an investment,' she ran on. 'My post is not secure, you know. Some of the ladies on the committee would be very happy to block the appointment if this party doesn't go like clockwork.'

'But your wearing a new outfit won't make the party go any better,' I said.

'It will,' she said simply.

She was looking at the papers I'd put on the tabletop, and now she caught up the photograph of the Travelling Club.

'Who are these men?' she said.

'A travelling club.'

'They look as if they do themselves pretty well,' she said.

'Yes,' I said, 'but they've very likely all been murdered –'

'Oh no,' said the wife, but whether this was in connection with the photograph, or the sound of Harry's voice that came at that moment from the room above, I wasn't sure.

'I'll go up to him,' I said.

He was sitting up in bed, just as though he'd woken from a good night's sleep. The fire burned low in his bedroom grate – he had a fire in his bedroom for most of the year, which was another expensive going-on.

He looked better, but coughed a little as I approached, so I gave him another spoonful of compound linseed, which was the cure-all of the moment. After taking it, he coughed some more, saying with a cackle, 'It must be working, Dad.'

He had the fixed idea that cough medicine was meant to *make* you cough, about which he was perhaps right. I tried to settle him on his pillows. Then Lydia took his hot bottle, to top it up with boiling water in the kitchen, and I looked at the window to make sure it was not iced. In cases of bronchitis, it is recommended that windows be kept slightly open. The used-up air must be removed.

He said, 'What's it like out on the moors, Dad?'

'There's been a great snow,' I said. 'The gales have blown it into huge mounds, and conditions are very dangerous.'

'Good,' said Harry. 'How high are the mounds?'

'About as tall as four men – no, taller. Mountainous. Thirty feet, I should say, getting on for.'

'Thirty feet – get away!' said Harry.

'At *least*,' I said. 'Nearer forty.'

'And how are the trains going on?'

I thought of a phrase I had heard during my firing days.

'Some difficulty may be experienced in locomotion,' I said, and Harry liked that, I could tell. He was pretty sleepy, and he'd drifted off again by the time I turned down the night light and left the room. Back in the parlour, a supper of pork pie, pickle and a cup of cocoa waited for me on the strong table. Lydia was stirring the fire. 'You'll be coming straight from work tomorrow, will you?' she asked.

'Aye,' I said.

I was required to show my face at the Co-operative women's party.

'And you will be in your good suit, won't you?'

'I will.'

'It starts at seven with a spelling bee,' she said, for the umpteenth time.

' . . . and you mustn't take a drink beforehand,' she added.

'I know,' I said.

'That's because I'm going to introduce you to Mrs Gregory-Gresham.'

'I know,' I said.

Mrs Avril Gregory-Gresham was the head of the York Co-operative Women. She did not drink.

' . . . and she might smell it on your breath.'

'So you keep saying, love,' I said, through a mouthful of pork pie.

I was contemplating again the photograph of the Travelling Club. The wife hadn't thought it worth pursuing the question of whether or not they'd all been lately and brutally murdered; or perhaps my reference to this likelihood had gone clean out of her mind, what with the big party coming up. It suddenly struck me that Detective Sergeant Williams had also shown very scant interest in it, all things considered, not even asking to keep a negative. Everyone lived in their own little world, and that was all about it.

'The thing about the spelling bee,' I said, rising to my feet having finished off the pie and pickle, 'is that I'm actually a much better speller after a few drinks. Three or four pints and I come into my own as an intellect –'

'No, Jim,' she said, 'you are *not* to.'

I picked up my coat, kissed her and said, 'I'm just off over to the Fortune. I reckon it might be the night of the goose club share-out.'

'But we're not in the goose club.'

'I know,' I said.

In the pub, I saw Peter Backhouse, with a great heap of holly branches on the table before him. His wife Lillian was the wife's best friend in the village. Backhouse had a ridiculous quantity of children – about nine – and he avoided them by practically living in the smoking room of the Fortune. Outside pub opening hours, he was verger at St Andrew's and dug the graves. He was meant to be distributing the holly about the village, but he'd never got beyond his first drop, the Fortune of War, although he told me as I sat down that he might yet deliver a load to his second drop, which happened to be the other pub in the village, the Grey Mare.

I asked Backhouse the news, and he said that the boiler had bust in the church school, causing the inkwells to freeze and a half-holiday to be given. But then the vicar, who had wanted the school kept open, had spied Tom Barley, who was the headmaster of the school, walking into the Fortune at two o'clock in the afternoon. Backhouse reckoned there'd be bother over this, but I was thinking of the dead men, and of Shillito, who I had to face the next morning. For the second time, I had failed to arrest Clegg. There was going to be a row all right, and a bigger one than that in prospect between the vicar and Tom Barley.

Chapter Fourteen

In the police office at nine the next morning, I was in the jakes draining off the remains of the beer from the night before when there came a fearful pounding at the door.

'Get a move on there!'

It was Shillito, just arrived in the office. In my agitation, I put the bung in sooner than I ought to have, and consequently pissed a few drops down my leg as I fastened up my fly. This annoyed me particularly, for I had on my good suit, of best blue worsted with turned-up trousers. I was also wearing my stiffest and deepest collar, which had been cricking my neck since seven in the morning. It was all on account of the wife's party to come that evening.

I glanced in the glass before quitting the jakes. I looked respectable enough, but I was no man for letting Shillito torment me. At any minute, he would want to see my notebook, and hear my account of the second encounter with Clegg.

When I stepped back into the office from the jakes, Shillito was writing at his desk, his big body all bundled up with the effort of it. With him in the office, I could not ask Wright to telephone through to Bowman for me. I had already tried to do so myself at eight-thirty, but the connection had been lost, and I doubted that Bowman would have been in the office at that sort of time in any case. Wright was saying, 'There ought to be a pound of tea maintained at all times.'

'Yes, but who's to maintain it?' said Constable Crawford, who was lounging at the mantelpiece, watching the fire smoke.

'Whoever finds the caddy short,' said Wright.

'But that's always me,' said Crawford. 'Whenever I go to make a pot of tea there's none left, and I have to go to the stores for more, which sets me back a tanner.'

'If you're the one who most often finds it empty,' said Constable Baker, who was leaning against the wall near the open door that gave on to the Chief's room (he wouldn't have been doing that if the Chief had been around), 'then that proves you must drink the most.'

'Let's have this right,' said Crawford, looking up from the smoking fire. 'You're saying that I never have the chance to drink tea on account of the large quantity of tea that I drink?'

'Yes,' said Baker. 'That puts it very nicely. But in my view the tea ought to be paid for out of the swear box.'

The two constables looked at Wright, who kept the swear box on his desk.

He was shaking his head, saying, 'I got the swear box up for the superannuation fund.'

Shillito looked up from his writing.

'Will you lot quit blathering and get down to some police work? Crawford,' he continued, pointing, 'fettle that fire instead of gawping at it.'

I knew that he was about to start in on me next, but he only eyed me for a moment, then rose smartly to his feet and stepped out of the door. Here was my chance to telephone Bowman. But no, there was a telegram form in Shillito's hand, which meant he'd only be gone for a moment. When Shillito wanted his business kept secret, he'd go out into the station, and give the form directly to the telegraph boy.

'What do you think, Jim?' said Crawford, who was now half-heartedly poking the fire in accordance with Shillito's instructions.

'Eh?' I said.

'Do you think the swear box should pay for the tea? Speaking as a regular contributor to the swear box –'

'– or a regular *swearer*, at any rate,' put in Baker.

But just at that moment Shillito returned, killing all amiability with his habitual order:

'Your notebook, Detective Stringer.'

The office fell silent as I picked it up from my desk, and passed it to him.

'I went to the Cape,' I said, 'but I did not arrest Clegg.'

My heart was galloping as I spoke, but I tried not to let him see it. This was the first time that I had crossed him in any serious way. He said nothing to my answer, making a show of reading the book for a space; but I could see the colour rising in his face.

He initialled the book and handed it back to me.

'I have sent you twice to bring in this man, and twice you have failed to do it, and for no good reason. Your book is once again full of this business of the – Club.'

I reached over to my desk, and handed him the photograph.

'This is the picture described in the book. It shows the Travelling Club. It was taken by Peters, who was murdered. I know for a fact that one of these men in the pictures has also been killed and another more than likely. One of 'em's Lee, who was done in the Lame Horse Murder – you might remember that. Burglary gone wrong. But everything points to all the blokes having met a very sorry end.'

Shillito had a dead look in his eyes; he was staring hard at the top button of my suit coat.

'I am placing you on report, Detective Stringer. I will speak to Chief Inspector Weatherill later today, with the recommendation that your application for promotion should proceed no further.'

'But the interview with Captain Fairclough is all arranged,' I said.

'One stroke of the pen will fix that,' said Shillito.

Suddenly, the end of my time in the police force came into clear view. I would not continue in any event if I did not achieve the promotion on Christmas Eve. Shillito spoke on. I hardly listened, but I saw in imagination the Gateshead Infant crossing the high level into Middlesbrough station, and the picture of it somehow reassured me. I was a railwayman through and through, where Shillito was not, even though he got his living from the railways. He hardly ever gave a glance to the traffic notices that were pinned up in the police office, and were meant to keep us in touch with the world out there on the lines. The Iron Roads held no romance for Ernest Shillito, and it was wrong that he should prosper in the North Eastern, and therefore he *would* not. I would win out over this double-gutted bastard in the end, whatever setbacks there might be on the way.

Shillito was now mentioning a name that was for an instant unfamiliar: Williams. He held a telegram in his hand. Detective Sergeant Williams had been in communication – letter sent express overnight, written in haste – forgive scribble, but Williams most unsettled as a consequence of his interview with Detective Stringer. Stringer, it appeared, had a bee in his bonnet about a case long since solved and closed: the murder of George Lee. A very vicious individual of proven bad character, Sanderson, had been hanged for this, a point seemingly not taken by Stringer, who had appeared, all in all, a rather curious sort of fellow, if one detective sergeant might so put it to another . . .

Williams, then, was a bigger bastard even than Shillito, for he presented himself as something else. Face to face, you'd take him for the whitest bloke that ever stepped, with his kindly manner and 'Do take the documents away with you, if you'd rather'.

'You are to return the files you took from the Middlesbrough office by the next post,' Shillito was saying, 'and then you are to go back to your normal duties.'

'What about the photograph?' I said.

But Shillito had gone back to his work.

I stood before his desk with my arms folded, photograph in hand, feeling like an ass. Shillito looked up at me, saying, 'I've done with you for the present, Stringer.'

I said, 'Do you want me to go back for Clegg?'

At this he gave a mock laugh, and set down his pencil.

He leant back in his chair and looked at me.

'Now that beats all,' he said. 'Do you honestly think I'm going to send you back so you can sup another few pints with your pal Clegg? Why, you'll be turning out for his blinking football team next.'

Nobody would be arresting Clegg, for Shillito had now realised that he would be in bother if the matter went any further.

I walked back to my desk, where I collected up the papers on Lee and Falconer, preparatory to posting them back to Middlesbrough.

'That photograph of yours,' Shillito called across. 'What does it signify? You might have a picture of any lot of men – the Institute Billiard Club for the matter of that – and if you came to look at it again a year on you might see that some of them had come a cropper. It's called damned bad luck, Stringer.' He said this last with impressive force, as if he really knew something of damned bad luck – and perhaps he did. After all, he'd missed his way in life, as I'd missed mine. My goal had been the footplate, his playing football as a professional.

I could not prove the importance of the photograph, and I had staked my future on inadequate data. Well, that was too bad. As Shillito got his head down again, for another hour of loud breathing and effortful writing, I got out my own pen, and composed, not a flash report, but a letter to a good fellow called John Ellerton. He was the shed superintendent for the Lancashire and Yorkshire Railway at Sowerby Bridge where, four years ago, I had driven a locomotive through a wall after a day of firing that engine in the company of an old boy called Terry Kendall.

Kendall, my driver and therefore my governor, had asked me to stable the engine at the end of the turn. It had been quite in order for him to do so, but he had also told me that the engine brake had been warmed, which it had *not*. As a result, the steam by which it worked condensed in its tubes instead of putting the brakes to the wheels.

It ought by rights to have been Kendall who was jacked in and not me. I had always known this, but had held off saying it. I would not say it now either, but it was the conclusion that I hoped would be drawn from my letter. In any case, Father Kendall, as he had been known, would be out of consideration by now, superannuated long since.

My letter began: 'My dear John, You will be surprised to read my name after such a long time . . .' and went on to ask whether he might see his way clear, if he could do so without entrenching on his own convenience (which expression was used, as far as I could see, by all police letters of a non-threatening nature), to inquire as to the possibility of my appealing against the decision to dismiss me, which I had always felt was unjust, and which over time might have come to seem so within the motive power office. With Shillito labouring away at his letters before me, I went on to say that my heart was not in railway police work, and that my experience in the force had only confirmed my decided inclination for the life of the footplate.

I closed with a few friendly remarks, and news of the birth of my son. I used police-office paper, but crossed out that address and wrote in my own at Thorpe-on-Ouse. I did not look over the letter on finishing it, because I knew that I might not have the brass neck to send it if I thought too hard about what I'd put. In fact, I was in such a rush to get it off that I swept my arm across my ink pot as I reached for an envelope, sending a tide of blue across the green leathern top of my desk, and towards the photograph of the Travelling Club, which I automatically tried to protect by making a barrier with my arm – with the *sleeve* of my good suit coat.

'Fuck!' I shouted, and Shillito's head rocked upwards.

I turned to see Wright, who, instead of shaping to help me mop the ink, was tapping the swear box with his pencil. I ran off into the jakes with the idea of soaking my coat sleeve, and when I returned, Wright *was* now blotting the ink, and Shillito had left. It was as though there *could* be fellowship in the office, but only with Shillito out of it.

'I'm obliged to you, mate,' I said to Wright.

'No harm done to your precious picture,' he said, handing it over to me.

It was on account of the picture that I had ruined the coat (for it *was* ruined), and I began to think the damned picture cursed. Perhaps it brought ill luck to every man connected with it.

My letter had escaped the ink flood, and I gave it for posting to Wright, who was pointing at the picture.

'I know this one,' he said.

He was indicating the distinguished-looking cove in black. But he was frowning at the same time.

'Can you put a name to him?'

He closed his eyes for a space, which, Wright being very old, made him look dead.

'No,' he said, opening them again. 'But I have a mental picture of him here in York – somewhere about the town.'

I looked again at the gent in the picture, contemplating the blank wall of mystery.

'Everyone thinks they know this bloke,' I said, at which Wright looked a bit put out, so I said, 'But thanks anyway.'

'I'd drop it if I were you,' he said, and he glanced at Shillito's empty chair, adding, 'Never mind missed promotion – he means to have you stood down.'

A mental picture came into view: the high wall that ran around the York Workhouse.

'That would be a shame, wouldn't it?' I said. 'I know what a lark it is for you to watch our battles.'

Then Wright knocked me by saying, 'It would be more of a lark if you stood up to him.'

I nodded.

'I always mean to,' I said, 'but when it comes to the touch –'

The thought of my own weakness shamed me, so I changed tack, saying to Wright, 'I'd like to telephone London again. Could you put me through?'

Wright took my letter for posting and wound the magneto for me.

A moment later, I was speaking this time to a very cheery bloke who worked on *The Railway Rover*.

'Editorial,' he said.

'Is Mr Bowman about?' I asked.

'Not presently,' I think he said, which was followed by something that might have been: 'He's been out of the office a good deal lately, and I haven't seen him all day today.'

The sound of what seemed like a gale blowing down the line took all expression out of his voice, so that he might have been delighted by Bowman's absence or greatly worried by it. I said I would call back; but the idea was growing on me that Bowman had bloody well disappeared too.

Chapter Fifteen

'Where's the Chief?' I asked Wright.

'Don't you know?' he said. 'He's at a shooting match.'

I struck out along Platform Four with the photograph in my hand.

A couple of dozen people waited there, huddled into their comforters under the station's sky – the great frosted-glass canopy. Passengers always looked lonely until the train came. A sort of Christmas lean-to, hung with tinsel, had been put up by the side of the Lost Luggage Office for the sale of nuts and sweetmeats. It was an assistant from the bookstall who'd been put to working inside.

I gave him a nod, thinking the while of the letter I'd written to Ellerton, and already wincing at the memory. It was all sob stuff. What did anyone at the Lancashire and Yorkshire care that I was miserable in my new employment; and had I really suggested that they might change their minds?

I saw the telegraph boy walking towards me – the Lad, as he was always known.

'How do, Mr Stringer?' he called out.

'How do?' I said.

'Where're you off to?' he asked, as we closed.

'Platform Thirteen,' I said.

'Good-o,' he said.

He was always cheerful, the Lad.

I jumped down off the edge of Thirteen, which was against regulations, and strode out over the sidings, on to which a few snowflakes that looked like bits of paper were falling. I was making for the old loco-erecting shop, which having been disused for years had lately been converted into a shooting range for the

Company rifle club, of which Chief Inspector Weatherill was the governor.

I pushed through the door of the great shed, which at first seemed empty as well as freezing, and then a shot rang out, quite deafening me for a space. In front of me were booths roughly made out of railway sleepers. Each booth corresponded to a target dangling from a wire stretching the width of the building at the far end, and the bullets flew to these targets through half a dozen columns of light from gas rings high in the roof. There was a balcony above the line of targets, and, set into the wall behind it, a vast clock with no hands, but the central spindle that had once held them remained, and it struck me that it must have made a tempting supplementary target for the riflemen.

I walked along the line of booths, and they were all empty but the last one, in which the Chief sat at a low stool, hunched over with the rifle on the stone floor beside him. Evidently the contest hadn't started yet – that, or it had just finished.

'Sir?' I called. 'Might I have a word?'

The Chief seemed not to have heard; he wore a cravat against the cold, but no topcoat or jacket (to allow free movement to his arms, as I supposed), and he was bareheaded, allowing me sight of his scant strands of dirty yellow hair, which fell across his head at intervals of about half an inch, like the lines drawn on a globe.

I heard a thin squeal of metal, and the targets fifty yards off began to moving to the right They were being winched towards a hut made of old boiler plates in the right-hand corner of the building. The target marker sat in there, I knew.

I called to the Chief again, and then I spied the ear defenders bundled into his earholes. He was still looking down at the floor, perhaps muttering to himself, but what he was saying I could not make out, just as I could never make out what the Chief was *thinking*. I couldn't make him out *full stop*, but I liked him, and I'd always felt he had a liking for me, though he'd given me the hard word on plenty of occasions.

I had taken the photograph out of my coat pocket, and was advancing towards the Chief when an electrical bell sounded from the far end of the shed. This made enough din to rouse the Chief, who looked up in a daze as I passed him the photograph.

'If you have a second, sir, I wanted you to see this.'

'Eh?' he said.

I passed him the photograph, and he looked at it with his ear defenders still in. Behind him, at the far end of the range, the marker had opened the door of his iron shelter, and was approaching us under the line of gaslights.

'It's the Club,' I said.

He knew the story of the Travelling Club in rough outline, but this was the first time he'd had sight of the photograph. He was studying it as the marker leant across the low timber barricade that separated the firing positions from the main part of the range; he passed the Chief a target that had been riddled with the Chief's bullets, and the Chief passed the photograph back to me as he received the target. It was about the size of a newspaper, and the Chief took a while getting to grips with it, which annoyed me, for it was a hard job to keep his mind fixed on a subject even without distraction.

Indicating the photograph, I said, 'I believe they're all dead, sir – murdered. This one's Lee.'

'Lame Horse man?' said the Chief.

'That's it.'

'Maybe the fellow that did for him did for all of 'em?'

I shook my head.

'Can hardly believe it. Sanderson was a burglar – no other burglaries have been reported touching the others.'

'I know the one on the left,' the Chief cut in, and my heart began racing, but he'd gone back to studying the target along with the marker, who was leaning over the barrier. Both were shaking their heads.

'My best bet would be to run at it with a bloody bayonet,' the Chief said to the marker.

'You know this one, sir?' I said, holding up the photograph, and pointing to the handsome man in black.

But the Chief was listening to the marker, who was grinning

and imitating the Chief's firing position, saying, 'You're too much *this* way.'

'Bloody left shoulder,' said the Chief, who was loading his rifle again from the kitbag at his feet.

I pressed the photograph on him for a second time, and he took it as the marker returned to his boiler-plate hut.

'Aye,' said the Chief, evidently a little riled at my persistence, 'this one. His name's Marriott, and I'm surprised you don't know him yourself.'

He passed the photograph back to me, took up his rifle and adopted the shooting position.

'Bloody left shoulder,' he said again, when he'd seemed to be set.

He was looking away from me now, towards the target. Before he could start blasting away again, I asked:

'Who is he, sir?'

'Brief,' said the Chief, still eyeing the targets. 'Barrister; defender mainly. Name's Marriott. I went against him a couple of times at the Assizes.'

'York Assizes?' I said.

'Course bloody York,' said the Chief.

'I don't see much of the Assizes,' I said, 'being forever in the police courts, prosecuting small fry.'

That made the Chief turn round, and I was worried as he did so, but as luck would have it, he was grinning. He could be suddenly friendly in a way that was quite as worrying as his distant moods.

'You put up a good show when you were last in the Assizes,' he said, and I coloured up with pride. The Chief was talking about the murder – my murder, the killer netted by my own efforts. I had been leading witness for the prosecution, and the Chief had twice taken me to breakfast at the Station Hotel in the course of the trial.

'You're like me, lad,' he said, finally removing his ear defenders. 'Better outdoors – firing at the *long* range. You like a challenge.'

'But Detective Sergeant Shillito wants me always in the office filling in reports.'

The Chief gave me a look that might have meant anything.

'Do you still see him about at the York Assizes?' I said, pointing to the handsome man.

'I don't,' said the Chief.

'I knew it, sir,' I said. 'Ten to one he's dead.'

'Well, he wasn't one of the regular ones,' said the Chief. 'I mean to say, he wasn't from York chambers. The fact that I haven't seen him lately could mean nowt at all.'

'Was he any good? Did you win against him?'

'Ended in a tie between me and him. He won one; we won one. Company official – fraud case. We got that bugger sent down. But Marriott got a chap off a wounding charge.'

'Wounding? What was the name of the accused?'

'You and your bloody questions,' said the Chief, shaking his head.

'Some of the fellows at the Assizes,' the Chief continued, 'they'll walk in holding the papers tied with the pink ribbon and you'll practically shit yourself. You'll think, "It's all up – might as well chuck it in now." Marriott was bright enough, but he wasn't in that company.'

The Chief smelt a little of beer, as usual; perhaps he'd taken a drop to steady his arm before the contest. At the far end of the shed, the marker was hanging up another target for the Chief.

'He was an arrogant sod, mind you,' said the Chief, who was picking up his ear defenders once again.

'How do you mean?' I said.

'I've nothing against barristers,' said the Chief, 'though they're all snobs and half of them are sodomites, but this bloke took the bun. Got up to the bloody nines. I mean, they're all that way, but I reckon half his money must have gone on tailoring – that and laundry bills. I was bloody determined to win both times we were up against him – just to take the gas out of him a bit.'

'Shillito's warned me off the investigation, sir,' I said. 'He says Middlesbrough won't stand for it.'

'They won't,' said the Chief. 'I've seen the letter from Williams.'

This meant Shillito had seen the Chief only an hour or so since.

'He's out to block my application for promotion as well,' I said. 'It's not right. It's not –'

'Sporting?' put in the Chief. But he wasn't smiling now.

It was disheartening to see the Chief fixing the second ear defender in place as he said this; or maybe it would be better if he hadn't heard, for it was all just more sob stuff, like the letter to Ellerton.

'Shillito's your senior officer,' said the Chief, turning away and making ready to fire. 'I can't interfere.'

'We don't get along,' I said, marvelling once again at the strands of hair dangling from the back of the Chief's head. 'He's always trying to check me.'

As he squinted along the sights of his rifle, I could have sworn that I heard the Chief say, 'Don't stand for it – lay the bugger out.'

I was about to say, 'Come again, sir?' when the first bullet was loosed, and I stood, quite deafened, watching the gas lamps swaying in the vast, freezing shed. After a moment, it came to me that the Chief was cursing, getting ready to fire again.

I pushed off before he could do so.

Chapter Sixteen

I was walking back along Platform Four a couple of minutes later when I saw what I knew to be the Pickering train at a stand. It was waiting at the bay platform just north of the police office, and I was closing on it even before I saw Davitt, the fare evader, climbing up.

He had snow on his cap and coat, for the stuff was now coming down thickly, and I marvelled at how this bloke would go to any lengths to get out of his house and ride on a train without paying. But he gave me an excuse to go to Pickering – home of Club member Moody's son. After all, Shillito himself had told me to put the collar on Davitt.

The guard was now holding out his green flag. I broke into a run, and was only half-way to the train when the flag was waved.

'Wait!' I shouted, but you can't unwave a flag, and the train was off. My hurtling progress took me past the open door of the police office, from where I fancied that I heard a man shouting after me – it might have been Shillito, might have been Wright. But I ran on regardless. I leapt up on to the footboard of the rear carriage just as that carriage came out from underneath the glass roof, and into the flying snow. I wrestled with the door – the train was now making a good thirty miles an hour through a blizzard, and there was only six inches of timber between me and the sharp track ballast. We were out of the station bounds, and running along by the back gardens of the Bootham district by the time I managed to fettle the door and get in.

Inside the compartment, a fearful-looking man sat in the semi-darkness: Davitt. He nodded to me over the top of the *Yorkshire*

Evening Press that he was pretending to read. He was a small bloke in a dinty bowler – shop assistant type or junior clerk in looks, but he rode the trains so often that his work must have required him to do it. Perhaps he travelled in some line of goods or other, but he was never seen to carry anything except a newspaper.

'You had all on there . . . Nearly lost your hat.'

I couldn't speak for a moment, but had to catch my breath, scattering snow on the compartment floor as I unbuttoned my topcoat. I took off my hat, and pushed my hand through my sodden hair, noticing as I did so that my coat sleeve had dried to a solid blue – just as if it had been patched with blue darning.

'I was just about to get up and let you in,' said Davitt.

Very likely, I thought. There was no doubt that Davitt knew me for a railway copper, but I fished out my warrant card in any case.

'Like to see your ticket, please,' I said and Davitt reached for his pocket book, looking pretty sick. I was just rehearsing the caution in my mind, when I looked down and saw that a great spray of black mud had been flung at my left trouser leg. I was fairly clarted with the stuff – it must have come up off the wheel. Then came an even worse lookout, for I saw the ticket in Davitt's hand. I didn't need to take it from him; I could easily make out the date and the words 'Pickering' and 'Third Class'. (We were in Third Class, so even that was in order.)

'I'm obliged to you,' I said, and quit the compartment in double quick time.

I found an empty one three along, where I fell into a seat. What the hell did Davitt mean by travelling on a valid ticket? Had he turned square? I looked again at the mud on my trouser leg. I would let it dry, then try to brush it off before the wife's 'do'.

The train ran on quickly, past white fields, deep white lanes. It was express to Pickering: a mid-afternoon fast train to a town that slept through every day but market day. If anybody in the traffic office had given it a moment's thought, the service would have been struck from the timetable immediately. I took out the photograph. The snow had stopped by the time I stepped out of the station, but it had done its job. Pickering, which was in the beginnings of the moors, was all white. The town beck was frozen like a photograph. On the main street, I passed the ironmonger's shop – the pails outside it were full of snow. I walked past the post office – a white clock-face gazed through the glass, but not a soul was to be seen inside. I continued past the bike shop, where each bike stood outside had its load of snow. It was amazing how much snow would fit on one bicycle saddle. Why did they not take them in? I walked in a dream, wondering whether I might be given the boot directly on my returning to the office, and hardly caring either way.

And then a man riding a bike came round the corner from the little road that leads up to Pickering Castle. He had the trick of snow riding, even though the stuff was six inches thick in the road. He looked like a machine, leaning first to the left and then to the right as he pedalled, and never varying this rhythm. His Dunlops made a crunching noise as they cut through the snow. He was the one man alive in Pickering.

'Do you know where a man called Moody lives?' I called out.

'I do,' he said. 'Aye.'

And he carried on rocking, pushing on down the high street. I fell in with him (he wasn't going at much more than walking pace).

'Where then?' I said

'First left,' he said, still rocking, and not looking at me. 'Keep going till you're out of town; then it's first on your right, over the beck.'

'Ta,' I said.

I turned down the street he'd indicated.

Here was another frozen beck, with many pretty little bridges crossing it, each belonging to a big house. In my dateless state, I fell to wondering about the exact moment at which the beck had frozen. Midday? One o'clock? At that very moment, whatever it was, it had become a Christmas card. Moody's was the last house, and the biggest and oldest, and the sharp roof gave it the looks of a chapel. In the garden, I half-expected to see graves.

A maidservant answered my knock. I took off my hat and held up my warrant card – and I half-hoped I was doing it for the last time.

'Is the master of the house at home?' I said.

'Oh,' she said. 'Hold on.'

She wasn't very polite, for she left me dangling on the doorstep, and with a very tempting hallway before me: wide and firelit and with no furniture but two small, thin dogs in a basket. One stood and looked at me for a moment, but neither could be bothered to risk a cold blow by making a move in my direction. You couldn't blame them: they were just skin and bone the pair of them – two whippets.

The maidservant came back.

'Go up,' she said, still not polite.

The staircase had been wide, but the room she showed me into was small. Not much in it but a fire. It held a card table, an armchair and an empty bookshelf besides, but they didn't signify. It was a very clean house, considering the money came from chimney sweeping. I took the photograph from my pocket and looked at the oldest Club member: Moody. I must expect a man who looked something like him only twenty or so years younger. I walked over to the window, and looked out at the pretty road. I then heard a single loud slam, followed by a great roaring shout. Looking down, I saw a trap pulled by two horses and containing two muffled-up men come racing around the side of the house, along the drive and through the gate. It turned left into the road and flew, at full gallop, along the snowy road.

The maid came back a long while later.

'The master's not in,' she said.

'He *was*, though, wasn't he?' I said. 'I mean, he was in until he bloody left. He was in when I arrived.'

'He's been called away sudden,' she said.

She was quite bonny, but a good blocker.

'I am here on important police business. When is he coming back?'

She said nothing.

'Does he mean to return today?'

'He didn't leave word.'

We walked out into a corridor, where a manservant stood; he was closing a door behind him, but he didn't do it soon enough to stop me seeing that there was a world of whiteness inside this house as well as outside – white sheets over every article of furniture. He knew that I'd seen; and I could tell that he'd been told I was a copper. You can always tell when people know that.

'Does Mr Moody plan to remove?' I asked him.

'I think so, sir,' he said. 'We've all been given notice.'

I could feel the agitation of the maid without even giving her a glance.

'Since when?'

'A week since.'

The maid stepped in.

'You'd best talk to the master about that.'

The man said, 'If you leave a telegraphic address . . .'

I wrote out the telegraphic address and the telephone number of the York police office, and gave it to the man, who was the more amiable of the two; or the more scared. The dogs and the two servants watched me go and, as I ambled along by the frozen stream, I turned and saw the two of them closing the great gates. I thought they were speaking to each other, but the frozen snow took away the sound.

Back in the high street, I saw that even the town hotel was called the White Swan, which seemed to be so in keeping with the whiteness of the place as to be ridiculous. I felt a powerful fancy for a pint of John Smith's, but I'd given my word to the wife, so I tramped on towards the station as afternoon changed to evening. All I was doing was sinking ever further into a kind of despairing dream; and all I had so far proved was that the Mystery of the Travelling Club certainly *was* a mystery. That house of Moody's was the sort of place in which a wealthy man saw out his days. It was the final prize for a lifetime of toil or luck. He ought not to be haring away from it at such a great rate in terrible weather on account of questions about his father. And who had been riding with him? Was the second fellow just the coachman? Or was he another member of the Travelling Club?

We stopped at the little town of Malton on the way back, making only a small disturbance in my tangled dreams.

Chapter Seventeen

Shillito was writing carefully. Baker and Crawford were in, and Crawford was reading a paper, evidently a comic paper, for he was saying to Baker, 'Here's a good one. What is the relation of the doorstep to the doormat?'

Shillito said, 'You and I must have words, Detective Stringer.'

'A step *farther*,' said Crawford. 'Do you see?'

But Baker had lost interest; all eyes were now on Shillito and me.

'I particularly wanted you in this afternoon,' said Shillito. 'You're still a good deal behind on your paperwork, and Davitt was seen earlier on at the bookstall.'

'He boarded the Pickering train,' I said, leaving off the 'sir', but looking at my boots, which I knew took away the *force* of leaving it off. 'I decided to have it out with him. I boarded the train, and asked to see his ticket.'

'And?'

'He showed me it.'

'He had a ticket?'

'He did.'

'And not just any old ticket? Not a last year's bicycle ticket for Poppleton with the date altered and destination disguised?'

Poppleton was the nearest station to York in any direction. A bicycle ticket for that stop was known to be the cheapest available at the York booking office.

'No,' I said. 'He had a valid ticket.'

'Davitt?' said Shillito, and his voice rose to such a pitch of disbelief that it sounded almost like a girl's. It worked on me like an electric jar, and I suddenly knew I could no longer be either the doorstep or the doormat. Well, I don't recall the moment, but only afterwards, with Shillito lying on the floor next to his desk, and skin split across my knuckles. He was looking up at me from just next to the ash pan of the stove, which somebody had half pulled out, and that was the best bit: the puzzlement on his face, the *newness* of the look that I saw there.

I picked up my topcoat and hat, and walked out of the office with my handkerchief over my hand. I was in search of a bottle of carbolic, and a pint of beer, but I didn't walk fast, and Shillito didn't come after me, or didn't see me in the crowds, for the station was like one colossal club now. It was five o'clock, rush hour, but there was something more. It was 16 December, and Christmas had started. There was all sorts going off in York: concerts and parties and plays, which all meant more top hats for the men and fancy bonnets for the women, fur collars and meeting off trains and kissing and laughing. I was not part of it. I had blood on my shirt, which had somehow flown there from my hand, and I was out of a job or as good as. But I had paid Shillito out, and that made up for it.

In the booking hall, the Salvation Army played and the decorated tree finally looked right. I walked on – out into the latest snowfall. I walked over the bridge that crosses the lines joining the old and new stations; even the old station looked picturesque, with its lamps all lit, and snowflakes flickering down over the crippled wagons kept there. I cut down Queen Street, heading for the Institute, where there was tinsel over the doorway, and paper chains in the corridors. I followed one of these past the reading room and the bars until I came to the caretaker's office. He was in there as usual, smoking by the hot stove. He was called Albert, and he was the idlest bugger that stepped.

'Now I know you've a bottle of carbolic in here, Albert,' I said.

He pointed with his pipe towards a cabinet, taking in my hand as he did so.

'What's up?'

'I clocked Shillito,' I said.

'Get away,' he said, but he wasn't really interested.

Albert had a nice set-up. Cleaning equipment arranged in a barricade all around him, and very seldom touched. A broken basket chair by the stove to sit on and a pint pot placed underneath that he filled up from the Institute bar – regular like.

'I've just nicely sat down,' he said. 'We've half a dozen dinners here tonight if we've one. Every function room to be swept and fire made – no two seating arrangements the same, and all to be set out by Muggins here – Passenger Clerks we've got coming in, Railway Reading Circle, League of Riflemen, Angling Club. I don't know why they don't just form the Society for Making Work for Caretakers, and have done – You crowned Shillito, did you say? He's a big lad, twice your size.'

There was an ambulance box in the cabinet. I took out the carbolic, and a roll of bandage. As I splashed on the carbolic, I made a face at the sting.

'Hurts, does it?' said Albert, grinning. 'It's Christmas that brings it on, you know – scrapping, I mean. You should be here after hours on party nights. One minute it's "Should Auld Acquaintance be Forgot", next thing they're braining each other with iron bars down in the siding.'

'I can't believe the Reading Circle acts like that,' I said.

'Them?' Albert replied. 'They're the worst of the bloody lot.'

'I'm off to the Women's Co-operative Guild annual beano,' I said.

'You'll need a drink,' said Albert. '*Two* drinks – you're never going in that suit, are you?'

'Why not?'

'Because it looks like nothing on earth.'

I did not want to be reminded of that.

I asked Albert, 'Which floor are the riflemen on?'

'Top,' he said, taking another pull on his beer. 'Nice drop of punch they've got up there.'

I climbed the four flights to the top, where the room was packed. The Chief's team were in there, and the opposition. A shield was being passed around; everyone looked very happy, but only one side could have won it. A red-faced shootist came up to me, and said, 'We've finished top of the league table in number one district – fourteen points!'

I moved away (for he looked minded to kiss me) and circled the room, keeping an eye out for the Chief, and not knowing what I would say when I saw him. I'd tell him about Pickering and how Moody had fled, and then about what had happened in the office. I would give him my side of it, but what was my side of it? I'd belted the man, and that was all about it. I'd had my reasons, but the Chief knew those of old. I moved over to the tall windows. They looked down on the Lost Luggage Office and the small siding that stood next to it. The snow was streaming quickly on to both, as if to say, 'Let's get a load down while no one's looking.' I knew a young fellow who'd worked in the Lost Luggage Office, and met a bad end. I turned towards a better sight: the long table in front of the window that held the big silver punchbowl. I pushed across to it and looked inside – the stuff was orange, and there were many fruits floating in it of a kind not normally seen in York.

Somebody passed me a glass – the stuff was, or had been, hot – and then I saw the Chief, and so had to drink it. I downed the punch and things were different straightaway, which was just as well.

The Chief held the shield in his arms, and was receiving congratulations from his fellows, which meant that his lonely practice of the morning had paid off.

The Chief didn't seem surprised to see me, but then he was canned.

'Can you shoot straight?' he said, coming up to me.

'Probably not after drinking this stuff,' I said, showing him the empty glass.

He passed me another one.

'You've something to say to me,' he said, and it might have been a question or not.

'I went to Pickering to see a man connected to the Travelling Club,' I said, 'but he made off while I waited in his house. Then, later on, there was a bit of set-to with Shillito. It came to blows. Well, on my part.'

The Chief was giving me a queer look.

'There's been bad blood between the two of us, as you know sir, and –'

He continued with the queer look: he was making a decision – I could see him doing it. He would ignore what I'd said.

'Why do you not shoot?' he said.

It took me a while to adjust, but I eventually said, 'I always think I'll end in the army if I take it up.'

'It's not a bad place for a young lad to be,' said the Chief.

I began to say something, and he cut me off with 'When trouble comes, you must be master of your rifle.'

He shot me the funny look again; then he gave me the road – moved off back into the crowd.

What the hell had he meant? That Shillito would come after me with a gun, and that I ought to be ready? That the Travelling Club business would end in bullets fired? Or was he saying that, since I was done for as a copper, my only remaining hope was to take the King's Shilling?

I would take another bloody drink, at any rate.

Chapter Eighteen

The Ebor Hall was packed and very brightly lit. I'd have felt a little dizzy entering it even if I'd not had such a peculiar day and drunk the Rifle League's brain-dusters.

I could not see the wife, but I could see her hand in almost everything. The holly that hung from the gas mantles and all about the stage – that was her doing; and the piano was not in its alcove but at the side of the stage – so she'd managed to get that shifted. A lady was playing it, and ladies were in fact doing everything, especially collecting up papers or passing out cups of tea by the gross. I knew what was happening: the spelling bee had just come to an end. Half the ladies were sitting on clusters of chairs under gas mantles and half were moving about. *All* the ladies were talking, and it was all to do with the Movement and its stores.

'Have you seen the new York store? Plate glass and electric light to show off the loaves.'

'There are better things in the old store, I think.'

'We had a very nice visit to the warehouse . . .'

I caught sight of one of the ladies looking at my suit and at my bandaged hand; she turned to point me out to the woman sitting next to her, but she was talking fourteen to the dozen with a third woman. I walked on through the hall; half wanting to see the wife, half not. I could trust myself to speak; the only trouble was that I was not as concerned about my appearance as I knew I ought to be . . . and the only *other* problem was that my head seemed a long way from my shoulders. As I looked about, the piano came to a stop, and that somehow left me feeling as though every woman in the place was eyeing me, and not in a way I would have liked; but in fact they were all now facing the stage, where a very well-spoken woman was calling for quiet.

She was bonny-looking, though fifty years old at least. I liked the way her grey hair set off her dark eyes. She was upper class, but a socialist – there were more of that sort about than you might have thought, and they were given to speech-making

She was making a speech now.

'Co-operation is not merely about buying goods at a community store, and then waiting for the dividend . . .'

'I wonder if she takes cock?' said a man who was suddenly alongside me. He lurched as I turned to look at him. He was a sight drunker than me, and had evidently been given up as a bad job by whatever woman had brought him.

'We must apply our principles of co-operation to every aspect of our existence . . .'

'Your missus in this show?' asked the drunk.

I nodded.

'Mine 'n all. She knows the price of grate polish in every Co-op in Yorkshire, but I say, "Buy the bloody grate polish; *clean* the bloody grate."'

Behind him I saw another of the few men in the place, and after a moment of disbelief I realised that it was Wright, the police-office clerk. He must have a wife who was a Co-operator. He was coming up to me fast; and curious as usual.

'What the heck are you doing here?'

Before I could answer, he said, 'I've been hunting for you all afternoon. The man Bowman from London – he's been –'

But the wife had stepped in between me and Wright, and was blocking him out.

'Hello, baby,' I said.

She sort of slid away, and the woman who'd made the speech had replaced her. She was holding out her hand to me. In shaking hands, she had to touch the bloody bandage.

'Avril Gregory-Gresham,' she was saying. 'Lydia's told me so much about you.'

The wife, slightly behind her now, close to Wright, was looking murder at me. It made her look beautiful in a different way. But Mrs Gregory-Gresham didn't seem quite so bothered about the state of me. She was more like Wright – a curious type, and she frowned quite prettily as she said, 'You look rather –'

'Pardon my appearance,' I broke in; and it was as if a different man was speaking. 'I've been in a fight.'

The wife was still there; but I did not like to meet her eye. Mrs Gregory-Gresham was frowning more deeply.

'I am a policeman,' I explained

'Yes,' she said, 'I know that,' and she was leaning towards me, not away, which was good.

'The fight,' I said. 'It was much –'

I couldn't speak for a moment.

'Much of a *muchness*?' suggested Mrs Gregory-Gresham.

I had meant to say that what had happened had been much less bad than it looked or sounded – or *something*.

'Are you quite all right?' she said, and the fact of the matter was that she was trying to help. 'Forgive me, but you do smell rather strongly of –'

'Yes,' I said quickly, 'carbolic.'

'You were arresting a wrongdoer?' she asked, and I at least had enough off to say, 'That's just it. I am investigating a murder.'

'The man you arrested was a *murderer*? But this is fascinating.'

'The business was *pursuant* to a murder,' I said, or that's what I'd meant to say, but I'd never even tried to speak that word *sober*, so I suppose it came out wrongly. As Mrs Gregory-Gresham looked on, I fished in my pocket for the photograph of the Travelling Club. As it emerged, I saw that it had become quite crumpled after the adventures of the day, and I thought of it as being like the calling card of a man who travels in some goods that nobody much wants.

'Most of these men are certainly dead,' I said, 'and so is the man who took this picture. Nobody knows why.'

Least of all me, I thought.

'You think,' she said, taking the photograph, 'that one of them killed the others.'

'Yes,' I said, '– or that someone else did.'

There was quite a long pause, after which Mrs Gregory-Gresham asked:

'What is your surmise about the murderer?'

'That he did not want this picture seen, that he will stop at nothing . . . that he is not a member of the Co-operative Movement.'

She laughed at that, but only for a second.

'But I know this man,' she said.

She was indicating the *young* man.

'Phoebe – that's my daughter – she knew him at the University. They had a jolly at the river; a day of . . . rowing, you know, and she introduced me to him.'

'What's his name?'

'I can't remember, but I know the face; oh, now I *know* it. He was from the north,' she said in a rush, 'Middlesbrough way – and he'd won a prize for speaking.'

'Speaking about what?'

'Anything. It's the hair that I recognise, and he was sweet on Phoebe, I distinctly had that impression. I also think she was rather taken with him, although of course she never let on.'

A long bar of silence; then the piano started up again, just as Avril Gregory-Gresham said, 'His family had a place in Filey – on the Crescent, and they would summer there. Well, we have a place there too, and Phoebe had been in hopes of seeing him over the –'

'Last summer?' I put in.

'Last summer, yes.'

'She looked in the register every week. It's a ridiculous thing, but any fairly well-to-do visitor is listed in the local paper there.'

'Did he not come?' I said, thinking how strange the words sounded.

Avril Gregory-Gresham shook her head.

'He did not. I will speak to Phoebe, and I will get his name to you directly. I will speak to the girl next week, and pass on the name to Lydia, who will give it to you.'

I took this to mean that she would after all be giving the job of secretary or typewriter to the wife, who for the present stood in the background, still looking very doubtful. A moment later there was a switch, and in the fast-changing strangeness of the Co-op ladies' social, the wife was before me.

'Well, Mrs Gregory-Gresham found you fascinating.'

More tea was being distributed.

'*I* found you drunk,' added the wife.

'Yes,' I said. 'Well, you're both right.'

There was a new Co-operator speaking from the stage.

'What's going off now?' I said.

The wife half-turned her head towards the stage.

'Blind man's buff,' she said. 'What do you flipping well think?'

More speeches were taking place.

'Some speak of the *sections* and *districts* of our organisation,' the woman was saying. 'I say we are the moon and the stars . . .'

They applauded that, did the Co-operative ladies.

'What happened to your suit?' enquired the wife. She was nearly but not quite angry.

'It's been a very long day,' I said. 'But I'll tell you this. I think you have secured your position.'

'I think you are right,' she said slowly; and she nearly smiled into the bargain.

I held the photograph in my hands, and she was looking down at it.

The woman on the stage was saying, 'Until the King himself hears our message . . .'

'I've got into a few scrapes on account of these chaps,' I said, indicating the photograph. 'It's murders in the plural, looks like, and I had a bit of a row . . . not with a man I was trying to arrest, as I said just now, but with another officer.'

'You were fighting with another policeman?'

'One blow started and ended the matter.'

'You should have told Mrs Gregory-Gresham,' said the wife. 'She's had many a fight with a policeman herself.'

'I daresay,' I said, nodding, for of course the Co-op ladies went all out for the women's cause.

'I had to take a drink with the Chief,' I said. 'I saw him this afternoon at the shooting gallery –'

'He was at a funfair, was he? I wouldn't put it past him, from what I've heard.'

'Shooting *range*,' I said, 'if you want to split hairs. It was necessary for me to take a glass of punch in order to keep in with him.'

'Does he take your part against the man you hit?'

It was a cute question, but I gave a nod, just as though the matter could not possibly be doubted.

'You must have your promotion, you know,' she said. 'Otherwise I will not be able to take up my own.'

Wright was signalling to me from behind her.

'I must see this chap,' I said, indicating Wright.

The crowds of ladies pressing in from all sides were threatening to part us in any case. I cut through to kiss the wife, and moved towards the old clerk, who looked very anxious at the strangeness of being overwhelmed in this way, and very curious.

'I didn't know your missus was in the Movement,' he said.

'Aye,' I said. 'Well, what's up?'

'The London friend – Bowman –'

Wright was eyeing my suit.

'He's been coming through on the line every hour.'

'I thought he was dead.'

'Not him. You look half-dead yourself. What's up?'

'I crowned Shillito.'

We were walking towards the door of the Ebor Hall.

'You crowned Shillito?' he repeated in a sensational whisper.

He'd repeated it twice more by the time we were out in Coney Street, with the Co op ladies' piano becoming faint in the background.

'I gave him a damn good hammering,' I said.

Wright was fairly bursting with questions, and the one he eventually gasped out was: 'When?'

'Four o'clock time,' I said

'I was out of the office then,' said Wright, and I could tell he was cursing himself for that. He then started in on a hundred other questions, but I checked him with one of my own for him:

'Where are we going, mate?' I said.

'You're going to telephone this Bowman fellow. He told me he's stopping late in his office, and I said I'd let you know if I happened to run into you.'

I was going to telephone, and old Wrighty was going to *listen*.

Ten minutes later we were in the empty police office, and the snow was dripping off our coats as Wright wound his magneto. The cold air had sobered me somewhat, though I still felt queer as Wright passed me the mouthpiece and did not move away. We were elbow to elbow as I said into the instrument, 'Mr Bowman? It's Detective Stringer here.'

But he didn't quite take that.

'Jim?' he said. 'It's Steve here.'

He might have been moving fast on a train from the sound of him – an Underground train.

'There's been a bit of a turn-up over the Peters business,' he said. 'A man has been stationed outside my house every morning and evening for four days.'

'What's he doing?'

'Watching the place. Watching me.'

'All the time – morning and night?'

'Not quite. He comes and goes. He must've taken lodgings roundabout.'

'Do you know him?'

'Certainly not.'

'What does he look like?'

'Big, wide – not over-pleasant, strange stockings.'

'How do you mean?'

'Yellow. Nobody wears yellow stockings in Wimbledon.'

'How do you know it's touching on the Peters business?'

'Well, isn't it?'

The line went and then came back, swallowing what might have been a moment of fear on Bowman's part.

'Look,' he said, as the connection came back, 'this man's not your Wimbledon type, and it's a little anxious-making.'

Bowman was an intelligent man who was not at that moment in drink. He was speaking to me as though I was the same, and I was galvanised just as I had been at Stone Farm. Bowman was not an adventurous sort himself, but he brought adventure to me. Here was movement in the mystery, and I heard myself say, 'I'll come up to London directly – come and see you tonight.'

'Tonight?' he said.

But even as I spoke, I was thinking: I'll arrive in the early hours, too late for the Underground . . . I didn't fancy the cost of a cab across London.

'Well, I've got to look into the timings – that might not be on. But I'll run up to *London* tonight, put up somewhere near King's Cross and meet you first thing in the morning.'

'Then come to the office. But it can't be first thing – it's press day, and there's a lot of copy to get off. We'll meet at midday underneath the big clock at the Royal Courts of Justice on Fleet Street. Do you know it?'

I did – from my Waterloo days.

'I could spare an hour before I'd have to be back here,' Bowman continued, 'but we can sink a few pints and I'll put you in the picture.'

'Scrub out the beer if it's your press day,' I said.

'No fear.'

'But now you're going to have to go through another night of being watched. You might contact the Wimbledon police.'

'I've thought of it, but that would mean alerting Violet, which I'd rather not – and then again, what do I have to complain of? There's a man standing in the street. Well, it's not *my* street.'

Wright stepped back and marvelled at me as I put down the receiver.

'What now, then?'

'He's being followed.'

'It's to do with your photograph, is it?'

'You're beginning to believe there's something in it, aren't you?'

'I didn't say that.'

Wright was holding the door of the police office open for me. We stepped out and he locked up behind us.

The cold wind of Platform Four was cutting like no other.

'You can't go to London,' said Wright, as he followed me into the booking hall where the timetables were pasted up.

The last London train was nine thirteen. I knew the one. The night stationmaster turned out to see it off, then everything went quiet until six in the morning. I had no need of a ticket; my warrant card would see me to London.

'You'll be for it, you know,' said Wright, as we walked back to Platform Four. He had evidently decided to wait and see me off, being in no great hurry to get back to the Co-op ladies.

I was looking in my pocket book: two fivers might be in there, or one and a quid. I couldn't bear to look. I had a bit of silver besides, but that was all I had until payday – if there would ever *be* another payday. And there was still Harry's aeroplane to be bought, amongst many other Christmas items.

'You know my missus, don't you?' I said. 'Will you go back to the Ebor Hall and tell her I've gone to London in connection with a case – with *the* case, for she'll know what you mean – and that I'll most likely be back tomorrow?'

'Most likely!' exclaimed Wright. 'You've belted your superior officer, and now you're making off without permission.'

There was nothing to say to that. Above our heads, the great minute-hand of the station clock shuddered to the mark of half past ten.

It was a shame I had to go to London with my suit in such a state, for they were all dapper dogs down there. Further along the platform, a lass in a cape stood singing 'God Rest Ye Merry Gentlemen'. I'd seen her on the station before; she sang with a toy dog on a decorated box at her feet with an upturned straw hat placed alongside. By rights she was loitering and liable to a forty-shilling fine. Wright looked on as I walked up to her and put a shilling in the hat.

'Why d'you do that?' he said, as I returned to where he stood at the platform edge.

'For luck,' I said

'I'd say you'll need it,' said Wright, as the London train came into view behind him.

PART THREE

The Railway Rover

Chapter Nineteen

As I took my seat in an empty Third, I realised that I had boarded the London train partly in order to get properly warm. Even with my topcoat on, it took a good half-hour for the steam heat turned to maximum to thaw me out. Wherever there were lights beyond the window, they showed snow scenes, but the track was clear – at least the main line along which I travelled was. I saw gangers just before Doncaster, burning rags in the points of the branch lines, fighting the ice. On the platform at Doncaster, a tea wagon pulled up alongside my compartment. I opened the window and bought a cheese roll, a long bottle of water and a basket of chocolate biscuits off the boy, and these together killed the last of the Chief's rum punch. Then I cleared the stuff under the seat, kicked off my boots and stretched out. I watched the telegraph wires rise and fall against the dark blue of the night sky.

What were the chances that I would be returning the following day with the whole thing knocked and the case closed? Nil. For a start, I was most likely heading in the wrong direction. This was a northern matter, somehow tangled up with the iron-mining industry of the Cleveland Hills; it was in the slice of moon over Stone Farm; the lonely pit tops; beacon fires burning on the cliffs; the mineral train going between the legs of the Kilton Viaduct like a mouse between table legs. I watched the telegraph wires rising and crashing into the telegraph poles at an ever greater rate as we sped towards Peterborough, and somewhere on that stretch I fell asleep, waking on arrival at London King's Cross.

I walked along Platform One, going by a long line of trolleys piled with mailbags. A barrier had been erected around the parcels office so as to make extra space for working through the Christmas rush. Everybody who worked in that station looked in need of a good night's sleep, and the ones not moving about were shaking with cold. I stepped across the road from the station. The constant flow of traffic had turned the snow into black slush, but some remained on the pavements. I bought an orange from a bloke with a white beard who sold oranges and chestnuts – he looked very Christmassy, but wouldn't have thanked you for pointing it out. I looked along the Euston Road: it roared with life. I glanced upwards, at the giant white face of the clock on the Midland Grand Hotel, and it looked wrong for a moment. One hand had fallen off. But no – midnight.

I would not be spending fifteen bob on a night in the Midland Grand. Instead, I walked north to the small house-sized hotels that served King's Cross. The first was called the Yorkshire Hotel. Well, London was anybody's, and this place got custom by reminding folk of the places the nearby railways went to. A notice on the door of the Yorkshire Hotel read 'Respectable Persons Only', and I wondered whether that included me. For instance, I was probably out of a job at that very moment, but I'd brushed most of the loose mud off my suit, and it passed muster with the not very respectable customer who ran the place. He showed me to a sooty room at the top that had no fire, but two beds, and he advised me to take the bedclothes from one and pile them on top of the other. That was the Yorkshireness of the place, I thought: the bitter cold. But after putting my boots to air on the windowsill, I got my head down and slept through until ten o'clock, when I pulled back the curtains to see a bright, bitter day.

I was too late for the serving of breakfast in the Yorkshire Hotel, so walked to a stall near the station and drank a cup of Oxo and ate a bacon sandwich. I then rode the Inner Circle line to Charing Cross. There were faster ways of getting to Fleet Street, but I had time to kill until my midday meeting, and I liked the Inner Circle. They'd put on electric trains since I'd seen it last, but it was still a railway in a coal cellar; you were still looking up from below the streets at the towering, blank backs of the buildings, many of them covered with giant posters for Lipton's tea.

I stepped out of Charing Cross Underground into muddy snow, and the black shadow of the Hungerford railway bridge. Having taken my bearings, I put up my collar and walked north up Villiers Street, turning right on the Strand. I was under the clock a quarter of an hour before time and I felt a proper ass for standing still in that weather. Nobody else in Fleet Street stood still. They pushed on fast in their good suits, clicking canes and highly polished boots – all the dapper dogs, with many straw hats worn even in the extreme cold. Everyone walking was really *working*; there were no loafers in Fleet Street.

And the ones in the shiniest boots and hats were the lawyers – the thoroughbred black horses among the London nags. They were an exquisite lot, which made you suspicious of them. As I watched, they came and went from the ancient alleyways opposite in capes or fur-collared coats, and I thought of Marriott, the barrister of the Travelling Club who was known to the Chief. Every brief in the country came from that ancient place opposite – from it or other, similar places near by. They came to York for the Assizes, and I pictured them riding into the city like a pageant.

At twelve o'clock, about a dozen clocks struck, driving the people on to faster walking, and the vibration of the air seemed to bring on snow, for it started again now – just the odd, accidental snowflake, escaping from the dark, moving clouds above. Where was Bowman? I tried to recall his looks: the red, ridiculous face, the nose at once too big and too small. His head put me in mind of a teapot, somehow. He was strange-looking – and as a clever man, he *knew* it. He didn't like to be stared at and would seldom meet your eye. It would be wrong to take against him on that account.

I watched the road. I had the feeling that Bowman would cross it to get to me. Fleet Street contained as many cabs as the pavement did people, and they could only fit on to the road as long as they all kept moving – if one of them stopped, they all would. None did stop, though. Anybody in a cab in this weather would be inclined to stay in it, while the omnibuses, being open to the snow, ran empty.

A hand touched my shoulder and I whirled around.

He'd already had one or two, I could tell. The cold had made his face extra-red. Same green topcoat, same flat sporting cap, which was like a saddle on a donkey, for he was not at all the sporting type.

'Good to see you,' he said, and his eyes settled on mine for longer than at any moment during our time at Stone Farm, but even so, not for very long.

'This way, Jim,' he said.

'Where are we off to?'

'Licensed premises,' he said without looking back. 'He was there again last night. Looking at the living-room window when I sat in the dining room, then at the bedroom when I went upstairs . . .'

There were pageboys everywhere, dashing about with great piles of newspapers – fresh batches, newly made.

'Snowing up north, is it?' Bowman asked me, looking ahead.

'It was bitter when I left,' I said.

We were passing newspaper offices: the *Yorkshire Observer*, the *Irish Independent*, the *Aberdeen Free Press*. The grander ones hung out a clock, just as a rich man will show off his watch.

'"Truro as a Railway Centre",' Bowman was saying. 'That's the masterpiece I've been slaving over this morning. Truro, you know, is one of the largest towns in Cornwall . . . which is saying absolutely *nothing*. The station is *quite* modern; there is still *some* tin traffic.'

He was talking more than he had at Stone Farm – still sounding worried, but in a different way. A newspaper placard read 'African Doctor Cooked and Eaten By Natives', and the hundreds of people and the hundreds of cabs just flowed on by. It took more than that to cause a sensation in Fleet Street.

'In the end I decided on leading off with the fact that every train on the main line stops there, but then Fawcett walked up – he is the leading railwayac of the office – and he told me of two that don't, including one that stops everywhere *but* Truro.'

He had stopped walking, and was standing before two pubs, weighing them in the balance.

'It's champagne or beer,' he said.

Both pubs had black windows with white writing on them:

'Saloon Bar and Buffet', 'Luncheons and Teas', 'Dining Rooms First Floor'.

'Will you take a glass of champagne?' Bowman asked, pushing at the door of one of the pubs. 'No thanks,' I said, as we entered, 'I had a skinful last night, and I'm a little –'

But Bowman had already moved off towards the bar. It was a good-sized, jolly wooden hall in full swing with a decorated tree just inside the door and giant beer barrels end-on over the bar, like locomotive wheels. The customers stood at tall tables – or just anywhere. Bowman was giving good morning to a man at the bar; he held two glasses of champagne in his hand. As he turned away from the man and approached me, I said, 'I didn't want a drink, thanks', at which he just frowned.

'It's on expenses, for heaven's sake,' he said. 'You'd better force it down because I'm getting you another in half a minute.'

He emptied his glass and folded his arms.

'I don't want to over-dramatise, but do you carry a gun?'

'No,' I said, downing the champagne.

'What do you do if someone fires at you?'

I shrugged.

'I get shot, I suppose.'

'Well, that's heartening,' he said. 'This fellow who stands outside our house always has his right hand in his coat pocket. I'm sure he has a pistol there. I'm sorry, but I can't talk about this without a drink . . .'

He was about to move off to the bar again, but I checked him by asking, 'The man who keeps watch – he was definitely there again last night, was he?'

Bowman nodded. 'From eight to nine-thirty.'

'Did Violet not notice?'

He shook his head. 'We spend most of our time in the drawing room – at any rate, the room that she *calls* the drawing room – and that's at the back of the house. Fortunately, she's gone off to her mother's for two nights.'

'Where's that?'

'Environs of Hampstead Heath.'

'Eh?'

'Strictly speaking, it's Tufnell Park.'

And he went back to the bar again.

He returned with two more glasses and a bottle of red wine. The cork had been taken out and put back loosely. It was 'finest Algerian wine' according to the label.

'This fellow outside my house obviously thinks I know something about the death of Peters,' he said, filling the glasses, 'and of course he's right. I'm sure the only reason he hasn't acted is that the street's been busier than usual, what with all the Christmas coming and going . . . You said there'd been developments in the case.'

I produced the photograph and explained how I'd come by it; told him as much as I knew about it.

'Is the man outside your door one of these?'

Bowman looked, shook his head and saw off another great gulp of the Algerian red, and looked again.

He said, 'You think Peters was killed for that picture?'

I nodded. 'I'm sure it's the one his killer was after – only it didn't come from the Stone Farm camera, but the one stolen at Middlesbrough.'

He handed back the photograph, pulling a face, and saying, 'It looks just like something that might appear in our magazine: an interesting new sidelight on First Class travel.'

'Well, that's what it was meant for, wasn't it?' I said.

'Of course,' said Bowman. 'I'm not thinking straight.'

I was not surprised over that. Bowman's glass was at his lips, and the bottle was half-empty. I myself had not yet tried the Algerian wine.

'How can you write, shipping all that stuff?' I said, pointing to the bottle.

'You might ask that of any man in here,' he said. 'I mean, it's all scribes in this place. Every paper in London's carried into print on a wave of booze, you know – it accounts for a lot of the rubbish you read and a lot of the best stuff too.'

Silence for a space.

'Well, I'll come back to Wimbledon this evening with you and have a look,' I said.

'What will you do?'

'Well, I'll quiz him as to what he's about.'

'Do you have authority here in London?' he asked.

'It's a matter that began on North Eastern Railway lands,' I said. 'It would be a poor lookout if all any villain had to do was flee the territory.'

He sighed.

'One more ought to do it,' he said, looking at the empty bottle. 'Will you not join me in –' He was squinting at the label on the bottle, '– in Algeria, then?'

But he was already at the bar.

'Do you not take wine at luncheon?' he said, returning. He never so much as grinned, but sometimes it was there in his voice; and I could tell that the wine was now working in him.

'I don't take luncheon for a *start-off*,' I said.

'I will generally have a wine,' he said, pouring out two more glasses. '*One* wine, that is,' he added.

'One *gallon* is that?' I said.

'One wine means half a bottle in Fleet Street,' he said.

'That's handy,' I replied.

'I drink because my nerves are strung,' Bowman continued. 'I mean to say, is that unreasonable? Whoever is behind it all has killed Peters, a young lad, so obviously they'll stop at nothing.'

'We must identify the man following you,' I said. 'It will all come clear then. You've not seen him about round here as well, have you?'

Bowman frowned and looked about the pub.

'Not so far,' he said. 'Of course, most of the blokes in here would kill for this story – "Curious Affair of the Body in the Snow", "Travelling Club Men Disappear". It's a detective yarn, ready made.'

'You could write it up,' I said.

He shook his head.

'It's a sight too interesting for *The Railway Rover*. It lacks the necessary *boredom*.'

'Do it for someone else. *The Times?*'

He nodded once quickly.

'I've had articles in *The Times*, you know. I did some comical railway pieces for them – byline "Whiffs". A layman's guide to the railways. That was their idea. The series was stopped in '06 to make way for the General Election, and never put back.'

'I'm a *Yorkshire Evening Press* man myself,' I said. 'I don't want *The Times*. I want, you know, the *lighting-up* times.'

I'd had four glasses by the time we pushed out into the snow again, with the consequence that my own barometer had swung a bit further towards 'fine'. The programme was that we would go back to the office of *The Railway Rover*, where Bowman would do another hour's work while I drank coffee, filled out my notebook and telegrammed to the wife to say that I would be returning by the last train of the day, or the first of the morning. Then we would go to Wimbledon and challenge the mysterious man. There had to be *something* in it all, and if the fellow cut up rough, that would only prove me right. It was all quite above board – an almost routine bit of police work. I told myself that I was not some child playing truant from school; I'd had no choice but to come to Bowman's aid – anything else would have been a breach of duty. I had the solving of one murder to my credit; if I solved another, I would be invincible. They could not then stand me down, or refuse me promotion. What could Shillito show to match the solving of a murder? He spent all his time chasing folk who'd pulled the communication chains without good reason, or defaced notice-boards, or failed to shut gates set up alongside railway lines.

We were back on Fleet Street now, into the great tide of men and traffic. They moved in all directions, like the snow. We were passing the *Yorkshire Observer* once again, and I was glad that my home county had a footing in Fleet Street – it made the north seem nearer. I would make sure I was on the last train of the evening rather than the first of the morning. I hadn't seen Harry in what seemed like ages, and I still had his present to buy.

'I'm after a toy aeroplane for my boy,' I said to Bowman, as we marched on. 'Any likely shops hereabouts?'

'In Fleet Street?' he said. 'Only *paper* aeroplanes here.'

I thought of the way the letters would swoop through into our parlour at Thorpe-on-Ouse. Might there be one waiting from John Ellerton, governor of the Sowerby Bridge shed? All the wine in Algeria couldn't make that a likely prospect. And the picture of Shillito flat on his back in the York police office *would* keep coming to mind, but the Chief would see my side of it. Shillito had been putting in the poison for three years . . . And hadn't the Chief *told* me to clout him?'

We'd turned off Fleet Street into a dark, narrow road with buildings that were too high: Bouverie Street. We passed a single black door, and a brass plaque six inches square. The *Railway Magazine*, it said, and it was hard to believe it came from such a small place. The windows were lit with a greenish light, and I could see men moving about inside. None looked like a *Railway Magazine* type.

'Would you credit it? They're all back from the pub,' said Bowman.

He was down on the *Railway Magazine*, all right. Probably sour grapes, for *The Railway Rover* was located further along, where Bouverie Street became darker and narrower, and subject to the river winds, although the lane kinked, so you couldn't see the water, but only hear it. There was no plaque on the door either.

'I've put in my three years here,' said Bowman, pushing at a narrow door. 'I'll be moving on shortly, I suppose.'

'Where to?' I said.

We were climbing cold stone stairs.

'Another paper,' he said with a sigh.

'I think I'll be moving on as well,' I said, 'or moving back.'

He stopped and looked at me.

'Back to what?'

'Firing engines,' I said, and I only did so to see how it sounded.

'You did that before, did you?'

'Aye,' I said, 'but I got stood down – unfairly.' Again, I was trying the word out for size.

'I wouldn't go in for that,' Bowman said, as we continued our climb. 'I'd stick with the collar and tie job. The governors are very hard in that line, from what I hear.'

'They can be with a young bloke,' I said. 'There's a good deal of leg-pulling: "go and fetch a bucket of steam" and so on.'

'What a lark, eh?' said Bowman, as he pushed through double doors on the first landing. The office of *The Railway Rover* looked so much like a school form-room (being over-lit with white gas flares and with the desks all in a row) that it was surprising to see full-grown men in there; and to see that one of them was laughing out loud.

'That's Randall,' muttered Bowman. 'He does the obituaries . . . decent man, but he holds a BA from London University, and you'll never hear the last of it. And that's Fawcett,' he ran on. 'Go up and ask him about trains that don't stop at Truro.'

'Afternoon, Steve,' the one he'd pointed out as Randall called. 'You all right?'

'Quite thoroughly chilled, thank you,' Bowman replied, at which there was some muttering between Randall and the man sitting next to him. A few of the blokes nodded at me; nobody seemed to mind a stranger in the office.

The desks stood in rows, but were not all the same. Bowman's was tall – counting-house style – and it seemed that he wrote by hand. Some of the other blokes had flat desks with typewriters on. Bowman had got down to his work straightaway, but a lad of about sixteen – assistant to the editor – was put to looking after me. I wrote out a telegram form, and he went off to another room to get it sent to the post office in Thorpe-on-Ouse. I made it as reassuring as I could, given that such fun and games as might be in wait had not yet started. The wife would have it within two hours, and it seemed *The Railway Rover* would stand the cost.

The assistant then brought me a cup of coffee from a small spirit stove on a table by the mantelpiece. The man I took to be the boss – the editor – sat inside a glass-walled cubicle. Alongside the main office hearth were some ordinary fire irons for home use, and a set of the eight-foot-long irons used on any locomotive: dart, pricker and paddle. They'd never seen a day's work, and were highly polished, being kept no doubt as trophies or symbols of what the magazine was about.

As Bowman wrote, I walked about the office, looking slyly at the work going on. Over the shoulder of the man called Fawcett, I read: 'It is with pleasure that we advert to the introduction, in November, of –'

He was the one better up on railways than Bowman. 'Don't put me out, old man,' he said, waving me away without looking up.

Then the jolly obituaries man, Randall, called across to me: 'Go and see old Hicks there. He has plenty of time to chat.'

I walked over to the bloke indicated, who was drawing lines with a ruler, a rusty bowler perched on his head.

'I'm Hicks,' he said, without looking up. 'Known to the readers as Querio.'

I knew what he was about: he was the puzzle-page man, and he was setting out a shunting problem for the readers. He had drawn two train diagrams, a curved line running between. Sidings stretched before each train; a signal was indicated at the beginning of each siding.

Hicks (or Querio) said, 'Two trains with sixty vehicles – fifty-nine wagons and a van – meet at a bank situated on a single line. The thirty-first wagon from the engine on both trains has unfortunately been brought along by mistake. Are you with me?'

I nodded. 'Happens all the time,' I said, grinning.

'The two trains are required to pass each other,' he continued, 'and at the same time transfer the two wagons referred to, so that they may be taken back again, likewise in the thirty-first position from the respective engines. Now then – are you still with it?'

I nodded.

'With these exceptions,' Querio continued, 'the trains will depart with the wagons in precisely the same order as before they met.'

'Right-o,' I said.

'Sidings B and C each hold an engine and thirty-one vehicles,' Querio continued. 'An engine cannot move more than sixty vehicles on the level, cannot take more than thirty up or down the bank and must not propel or stand vehicles between the signals – still with it?'

'Yes,' I said, although I was now not.

'Care to demonstrate?' he said, passing me a pen and paper.

I looked across to Bowman, hoping he might interrupt us, but he paid me no mind, and his pen kept up its steady travel.

'I'll turn it over in my mind,' I said to Hicks or Querio, 'but I must speak to Mr Bowman.'

I wandered back over to that red-faced fellow, who muttered, 'I'm writing up my northern experiences just now. Should be done in a minute, and we can get off. I've been speaking by telephone to your ex-governor, Crystal . . . I'm making him Man of the Month in "Notes by Rocket".'

'He'll like that,' I said. 'Will you be talking about the Peters business? I thought you didn't mean to?'

'No fear,' said Bowman, now looking up from his page. 'As far as that's concerned, I'll just put that Stationmaster Crystal's capable of dealing with the many strange eventualities that have come to hand, or some rubbish of that sort.'

'Will it make a long article?

'A hundred words,' said Bowman with a shrug.

'A hundred words?' I said. 'That's heaps.'

But when I thought on, I knew it couldn't be.

'How many words are in a book?' I said, and the man called Fawcett looked at me strangely. But Bowman had his head down again, writing away like mad. Beside him, a man sat typing at one of the low desks. He was faster even than Lydia, and much louder. It was like a train smash every time he returned the carriage to the starting position. But Bowman didn't seem to hear him.

I watched him write on, until he caught up some papers and walked quickly into the editor's greenhouse. He consulted there, and I wondered whether he needed to show the editor everything he set down, just as I did with Shillito. I walked over to the window, and looked down. The wet snow on the ground contained all the greyness of the day. A man was walking along Bouverie Street. He was heavy set, but there was no fat on him; he was a wide block of muscle.

He wore a wide brown tweed coat, and tweed trousers tucked into thick yellow socks.

Chapter Twenty

He wore a sporting cap like Bowman's, but it suited him better. He looked like a rambler, out of place in Fleet Street, or a rough sort of motorist suddenly deprived of his motor car. He was not quite bearded, but wore white sideburns that became a moustache, flowing over the top of his mouth like a snowdrift. He carried his head tilted backwards, as though taking exception to everything he saw.

I looked towards the editor's cubby-hole. Bowman was stepping out of it, papers in hand.

I indicated to him that he should join me at the window, and we glanced down at the man standing in the dirty snow. Bowman stepped back from the window and said, 'Christ, it's him.' He then returned to the window, and began wrestling with the catch, making to open it, at which the man in the street looked up. He turned in the street, somehow like a man trying to make up his mind about something.

'What are you doing?' I said. 'He'll see you.'

The man writing nearest to us was looking up:

'It's cold enough just as it is, old chap,' he said to Bowman – who now let the catch alone and stepped back again, saying, 'I only meant to call down to him and ask what he meant by skulking about in Wimbledon at all hours.'

The man in the street then turned smartly and began walking north with boots turned outwards, heading back towards Fleet Street.

'He's going back . . .'

Bowman was moving towards his desk, just as though he meant to start writing again.

'Let's get on his rear,' I said.

'What's that?' said Bowman, with a strange look on his face.

'We must follow him,' I said.

Somebody in the office cried out, 'Copy!'

Bowman stared at me with his mouth open.

'He's only going to Wimbledon,' he said. 'He'll take up station outside my house again.'

'It makes no odds,' I said. I had my topcoat in my hand, and the office was waking up to the agitation in our voices; I was through the door and down the stone stairs in an instant. In Bouverie Street, I looked north towards Fleet Street. The man had made the junction, where he wheeled his wide body to the left. I followed him, as snowflakes fell in the darkening sky – and it was something dangerous now, like the first flaking of a ceiling.

I stood at the junction with Fleet Street. Bowman was coming up – a lonely man struggling to join the crowds. I shouted 'Run!' and he did his best, but I thought his hot head would explode.

I pointed left so that he would know the way, and set off directly. I was fifty yards behind the man, keeping him in sight without difficulty. Most people on Fleet Street wore plain black and were thin; but this man was a tweed-coated cube. He never once looked back, and did not seem in any hurry. He walked with the swinging step of the outdoorsman. Where was he heading? I tried to put up in my mind the Underground map. Was he heading for a station that could take him to Wimbledon? I hoped not, for I knew about his Wimbledon connection, and I did not want to go there. I did not like the place: high, thin red houses like guardsmen in a row – a fucking prison of a place. No, this one would surely be making somehow for the ironlands of Yorkshire.

I looked behind. Still Bowman came on, though with a few pavement collisions on the way. I struck the billboard again: 'Doctor Killed and Eaten by Natives of Nigeria'. The man ahead had not given it a glance, but kept his great head tilted upwards, as though to receive the refreshment of the snow.

Gaslit advertisements flashed as we came towards the Strand; a huge church stood in the road, blocking traffic. I did not remember it being there in my Waterloo days. My eyes flickered back towards the path ahead, and the man had gone.

Bowman came panting up beside me.

'Lost the bastard,' I said, but Bowman was shaking his head, gasping out a word I couldn't hear and pointing directly left, to one of the theatres. No, it was a new Underground station – Aldwych – that he was indicating. We walked into the booking hall followed by a blow of snow. All the signs in the place showed arrows, but which one to follow?

The man was in the lift looking out – one of half a dozen occupants. The attendant drew the steel mesh across, and down they all went.

My eyes moved right: there were two lifts and the second was ready to go. The attendant had the mesh dragged half across, but I stopped him and pushed my way in, dragging Bowman behind.

'Ticket,' said the liftman in a sour voice.

As we went down, I held up my warrant card – he might make of it what he liked. Bowman he ignored.

'Did this fellow ever get a good look at you?' I said.

'I don't believe so,' said Bowman. 'I had my comforter up and cap down every time I saw him – at first just on account of the weather, later on by design.'

The doors clashed open at the bottom, and I was out of that lift like a rat out of a drainpipe, with Bowman panting along behind. The sight of the man in tweed slowed us, though. He was only ten feet ahead in the passageway, walking slowly, checking the people behind him like the church in Fleet Street. He certainly seemed to have no notion that he might have been followed, for he'd never once turned about. He was gazing up at a swinging sign that hung before the point at which the passageway split into two. The sign was an electrically lit glass box, and it showed two hands, each with a pointing finger. One was marked 'North', the other 'South'. He slowed further, approaching it. He did not know London, and that was because he came from the ironlands of the Cleveland Hills. Or was it simply that he hadn't decided where to go?

He hadn't quite stopped by the time he made his decision. He chose the northern passageway, and we followed at a distance of twenty feet. You couldn't get to Wimbledon this way.

There were perhaps fifty people in between the man and Bowman and me as we all lined up on the platform. The adverts on the tunnel wall were for Lipton's tea, but, looking sidelong, I saw that the man was looking above them all, gazing at the tunnel roof.

The train came in, and we boarded the carriage behind the one into which the man stepped, but we could see him clearly through the windows at the carriage end, and the bright electric light seemed to bring him too close. I turned away from him, towards Bowman, who had removed his sporting cap and was wiping his head, dragging the few hairs on his head hard to the left.

'I'm in need of a dose of wine,' he said. 'Where do you think he's heading? The Cross?'

He meant King's Cross.

'Must be,' I said. 'He's going north.'

If we stuck with the man, we would end back in Yorkshire, and that was fine.

As we came crashing into Russell Square station, I tried to picture the place he might run to earth: one of the little iron-getting towns on the Cleveland cliffs – Loftus or some such. The carriage doors opened. A third of the passengers got off; a new third got on. The man remained, and it seemed to me that the new third avoided standing near him, just as the old third had. It was his great width, and that strange rig-out with the yellow stockings – a challenge to all-comers. The train started away again with a jerk, and it jerked a thought into my head: I knew the man.

I turned to Bowman, who was fixing his cap back on his head.

'It's Sanderson,' I said, as the black brickwork thundered away beyond the windows.

'Who?'

'The man we're following is Gilbert Sanderson,' I said. 'He was hanged last year for the murder of George Lee.'

Bowman gave me a narrow look.

I fished in my pocket for the Club photograph, pointed to Lee. 'This man was done in as I told you. It happened in the course of a robbery committed by Gilbert Sanderson. It's him,' I went on, tipping my head back to indicate the man in the next carriage. 'I've seen his woodcut.'

Bowman was shaking his head as the train seemed to gain speed before suddenly seizing up. It had stopped at the Underground station called King's Cross St Pancras. And here of course the man who was Sanderson, or the spitting image of Sanderson, turned and stepped off.

'Identical twin?' asked Bowman, as we again fell into line twenty paces and twenty people behind the man. 'Or is he a ghost?'

We stepped off the train behind the man, merging into the moving crowd. He was through the ticket gate. I held my warrant card up to the ticket checker, who said, 'What the hell's this?' as we went by, but he was grinning as he said it. In the passageway beyond the barrier, the man was slowing once again. His choice now was King's Cross or the passageway connecting with its rival, St Pancras.

'It's King's Cross for my money,' I said. 'He's heading for Yorkshire.'

But the man followed the *St Pancras* direction, his open coat swinging.

'That's rum,' I said. 'What the devil is he up to?'

I tried to think it out: the man had come to Bouverie Street half-intending to do something – and then had decided not to do it. Had he seen me at the window, and suspected I was a copper? Or then again, had he seen Bowman there, and decided, looking at his terrified expression, that he had succeeded in putting the frighteners on, and that his job was therefore done? But Bowman had told me that the man didn't know him; that he wouldn't necessarily be able to pick him out away from his known haunts.

And who had told the man of Bowman's haunts? Who had put the man-who-looked-like Sanderson on to Steve Bowman?

He walked along the passageway, up another flight of stairs and out into the great wide roaring of St Pancras Station. On the pillars and roof arches, the red colourings of the Midland Railway looked like Christmas decorations. The man paused again, and turned right around in the circulating area, taking sights, or just letting everyone have the benefit of his biscuit-coloured suit and bright yellow woollen socks.

'The glass of fashion, isn't he?' muttered Bowman.

It would have been a comical sight but for the brute power that obviously rested in the man. He walked towards the booking hall, and we followed. We stood away from him as he queued at the window marked 'Bedford and All Stations North Thereof.'

'He's not going to Kentish Town, then,' said Bowman. 'I rather hoped he would be.'

Kentish Town was the next stop on the line.

As the man moved towards one of the pigeonholes to make his ticket purchase, I looked at the tile map of the Midland territories that was fixed to the booking-office wall. You *could* go to York from St Pancras and other points immediately north of York. You *could* do it, but this wasn't the regular London station for Yorkshire. I pictured the man alighting at Derby, Trent, the Midland towns. But they were not in the *case*.

He was buying his ticket now, but we could not risk moving closer to hear the destination stated. He gave his request in the shortest amount of words possible, I could tell that much. Having done so he stood back, looking upwards again. It was as though his moustache was a false one, held on with gum and in danger of falling off unless he held his head in that particular grand and arrogant way.

The ticket was pushed out under the window, and the man paid over his gold: pound notes – at least two by the looks of it. This was a bad lookout. At Third Class rates, each of those pound notes represented about three hundred miles' distance, and I did not think my North Eastern warrant card would pass muster with a Midland ticket checker.

The man came out of the ticket hall, and swung away towards the waiting trains.

'We've struck a trail here all right,' I said.

'Why don't we just let him go?' said Bowman. 'He's given up hounding me, at any rate.'

'Then we'll be left with the mystery,' I said.

'Yes,' said Bowman, 'and left alive as well.'

As we stepped out of the booking hall, we saw the man take up position once again in the middle of the circulating area. He was gazing towards the trains this time, then glancing at his watch.

'If I were him, I'd go for a stiffener just now,' Bowman said at length, and the fellow was indeed within striking distance of the refreshment rooms, but he didn't so much as glance that way.

I looked to the left: the platform behind the ticket gate at that extreme – Platform One – was beginning to fill with people. A line of baggage trolleys waited there. A pageboy was towing a heavily loaded tea wagon across the circulating area towards it. The wagon flew a small flag that bore the word 'Sustenance'. As I watched, a red tank engine came wheezing into view on that line, drawing more carriages than it could easily manage.

'It's the bloody sleeper,' I said. 'The bugger's off to Scotland.'

Chapter Twenty-one

I ought to have guessed. What other ticket would have set some-one back two quid? The man was approaching Platform One, coat swinging as he strode behind the tea wagon, feet splayed wide.

I looked at Bowman.

'The missus is not expecting you to go off on a jaunt, I suppose?'

He made no reply, but adjusted his specs in a nervous fashion.

We followed the man to Platform One; there was no ticket checker at the barrier but we were delayed by the people ahead – a party of a dozen or so, struggling with trunks and portmanteaus. When we stepped on to the platform, our quarry was gone from sight.

'Well, he's got to be on the train,' I said. 'You get us two seats and I'll walk along.'

Bowman was standing forlorn next to the little tank engine that had drawn in the rake of carriages, and was now continuing to simmer, pumping out the steam-heat for the carriages.

'Maybe he'll get off at Trent,' he said.

Trent was the first stop of the sleeper, not more than a hundred miles from London.

The first carriage was the dining car: there were only railway chefs in there, making their preparations. We climbed up into the next carriage – an ordinary Third Class marked, like most, for Edinburgh – and Bowman took a seat in an empty compartment. Telling him I'd return once I'd located our man, I carried on down the corridor.

I did not see the man in that carriage, so I walked on, pushing through the press of people boarding the train, gazing in at the compartments and trying to look like an interested tripper rather than a policeman. All were either Firsts or Thirds, for the Midland had dropped Second. Most of the passengers would sleep sitting down; there was only one carriage with bunks. It was First Class, and I came to it next. My footfalls were muffled, the red carpet being thick, hotel-like. A man stood in the open door of one of the sleeper berths, smoking in shirtsleeves. Inside, on the red blanket of the bed, his things were all a jumble – but it was an expensive jumble. He eyed me narrowly as I went past, as if to say, 'You're never First, clear off out of it.'

I approached the final two carriages with a fast-beating heart. Here, the labels pasted on the windows read 'Inverness' – a fresh engine would carry them to that far northern point from Edinburgh. I began walking slowly along the corridors of these, which were not bustling like those of the others.

He was there – in the last compartment of the last carriage. Nobody stranger would be joining him in there, I thought. He took up the best part of two seats, with stout legs spread wide, and yellow socks bristling. As before, he seemed to gaze at vacancy, with head tilted upwards. For all his size, he seemed to live on air. There was no food or drink with him, and he carried no bag. It was seven hundred miles to Inverness. Would he sit like that all the way?

I had just stepped beyond his compartment when a bang and a violent jolt sent me stumbling against the window. Righting myself, I stepped down once again, and saw that the train's engine had coupled on at the 'down' end, and an assisting engine was backing on to that. We would be double-headed to Edinburgh. The first of the two blew off steam as the second one hit, and the great white column was like a flag of distress. Snow flew about beyond the engines, beyond the platform glass, as if it too was in distress; but the line ahead was evidently clear.

I looked again at the engines. Two 4-4-0 compounds they were, fitted with both high- and low-pressure cylinders for fuel economy and better torque. They were handsome too: the 'Crimson Ramblers' to the Midland men. I saw the fireman of the first working the injector with what seemed like a look of fury, but when he saw me watching, he gave a grin. He wouldn't go all the way to

Edinburgh. There'd be an engine change at Leeds or thereabouts.

I walked back along the platform, glancing quickly into the last compartment. The man sat there as before, looking ahead. He didn't *have* to go as far as Inverness; he might have favoured that carriage simply because it was the emptiest. He was a very independent unit.

'Don't tell me,' said Bowman, when I re-entered our compartment. 'Inverness.'

'Bang on,' I said, sitting down.

'It's the law of sod,' said Bowman. 'And I'm sure he'd go further north if he could – just out of pure spite.'

'He might well be doing,' I said. 'Inverness is the connection for the Highlands, don't forget.'

'He's Scots, I suppose,' sighed Bowman. 'Something about those bloody socks of his should have told me that.'

'I can't see any Scottish connection in the whole business,' I said. 'I mean, Paul Peters wasn't Scottish, was he?'

'Londoner,' said Bowman, shaking his head. 'Born in some tedious spot like – I don't know – Pinner.'

Bowman had moved into the corridor, and was leaning out of the window, looking along the platform.

'Where's the dammed tea wagon?' he was saying.

'I'll fetch you a tea,' I said. 'I'm just off to the telegraph office.'

'You've called my bluff,' he said, turning around and almost smiling. 'I'm after a bottle of red, to be perfectly honest.'

There were fifteen minutes before departure. I jumped down next to a gang of porters who were all pasting labels on trunks and jabbering about the weather. The tea wagon was rolling up, so Bowman would have his wine.

I strode over to the telegraph office, where I took up a form and joined the queue. While queuing I wrote 'HAVE PROCEEDED TO SCOTLAND', but when my turn came for the clerk I realised that was ridiculous, so I changed it to 'GONE TO SCOTLAND'. I was going to add something, but the clerk was agitating for the form, and there were half a dozen people behind me so I handed it over as it was, together with the fee of one and six.

I climbed up into the Third Class Edinburgh car again, and Bowman said, 'Sent the wire?'

'Aye.'

'What did you put?'

'Gone to Scotland,' I said.

'Little peremptory,' he said. 'That was to your wife, I suppose,' he said after a space. 'Did you not telegraph your governor?'

I shook my head – but now that he'd mentioned it, I started fretting about whether I ought to have. Bowman had at last removed his hat, and he was now unbuttoning his topcoat. There was a certain delay in his movements, which told me to look about for a bottle of wine, and I spied it on the compartment floor, just below the window, with two glasses alongside and nearly half of the stuff already gone.

'You didn't get any grub?' I said.

'Dinner baskets available at Derby, apparently,' he said. 'And there's always the restaurant car.'

'I didn't cable the office,' I said, sitting down opposite Bowman. 'The fact is that I'm in bother with my governors. They haven't given me leave to be here.'

'Well . . .' said Bowman.

He seemed embarrassed for me; but then he was always red.

'My aim is to go back with the mystery of the Travelling Club solved,' I said. 'I must bring the killers to light. Nothing else will serve.'

Bowman took a long drink of wine, and then sat forward in a curious, hunched way, looking down at his boots, face flaming.

'Of course, it's odds on I will fail,' I added, 'and then I'll be on the stones.'

'Where does your office *think* you are?' asked Bowman, looking up.

'Well, since things aren't running on so smoothly for me just now, I daresay they think I've just – you know, bolted.'

I thought of the high brick wall at York, the word 'Workhouse' running along it.

The doors began to slam shut all along the train. On the platform, a new army of porters stood back from the carriages alongside a barrow piled with mailbags. They were waiting for the next train to come in. As far as they were concerned, we were ghosts, already gone.

At six-thirty on the button, the bell rang piercingly; our carriage seemed to lean towards the buffer stops for a moment, and then we swung forwards and we were off, gliding out from under the glass and into the snow.

Bowman sipped wine as we watched the house-backs roll away in the darkness, and we kept silence until Leagrave. I stood up as we drummed through that station.

'I'm off up front again,' I said. 'It's best we keep on the nose.'

I walked along. The narrow corridors were full of bustle: people talking, smoking, making ready for dinner, all full of Christmas plans. I did not walk quite as far as the last compartment of the last carriage, but stopped short of it so that I could just see the right side of the lower half of the man. I saw his right leg – the orange boots and yellow socks. It was quite still, but his right hand was moving. The hand was bringing something out of his coat pocket. He placed the object on the seat to his right, and reached out quickly to pull down the compartment blinds.

It was a revolver that had been in the man's hand.

Chapter Twenty-two

The jollity of the corridors seemed very strange as I returned to our compartment – where Bowman slept. He had a look of concentration. The wine bottle, one inch remaining, was placed in the corner of the compartment, steadied by his coat. I sat down opposite, and watched him. Presently, he began to groan, and I imagined all the men in Wimbledon doing that every night, trapped in their neat red houses.

It was just as well that he slept. I did not need to tell him about the gun until Inverness, where matters would have to come to a head. No, that was quite wrong. I ought to warn him earlier, for we would be joining the man in the Inverness carriage at Edinburgh, and so moving within shooting range.

We did not stop at Derby. It was a beautiful, bright station, but it spun away from us at a great rate. I finished off the wine as we raced on. I was ravenous by now, and I thought about the restaurant car. It seemed odd to have an appetite when I knew that there was a bullet waiting for me at the far end of the train.

The restaurant car was all life, though; full of chatter and the clanking of the pots in the narrow kitchen. I stood by the door, reading the menu of dinner. Ten bob, it cost. Mock turtle, halibut and so on. 'Passengers are earnestly requested not to pay any money without a bill,' I read. Well, chance would be a fine thing. The waiter skirted past me twice, but said not a word. At busy times like this, you had to be a First Class ticket holder to get a look-in.

I returned to the compartment to find the ticket inspector – and Bowman paying his fare: single to Inverness. I did not try it on with the warrant card, but just paid over the coin. I took a return: four pounds and five bloody shillings. I would get it back, I supposed, if I ran the killer, or killers, to earth.

When the ticket inspector had gone, Bowman took his glasses off and looked at me, but his eyes were not up to the job without specs.

He looked towards the window, saying, 'It seems tempting fate to buy a return.'

I made no answer, but thought of the gun. What was Bowman looking at without benefit of his specs? The scene beyond the window was a blur to begin with. He put them on again after five minutes, but only in order to go to sleep again.

We were at Trent for nine forty-two, and Bowman slept on. It was a gloomy place, with smuts floating under the gas lamps and a loud crashing out of sight. On the other hand, three tea wagons stood waiting for us. I pulled down the window, and a pageboy dragged his trolley up. I had it in mind to buy one of the five-shilling baskets. I asked what was in them and the kid shrugged, saying, 'Pot luck.' Then it seemed that his conscience got at him, for he added, 'Chicken or beef.'

I asked for one of each, and he had to open the baskets to look: bread, salad, cold meat, cheese and a small bottle of wine.

'Can I pay you for an extra one of those?' I said, pointing down at the bottle. 'My friend likes wine.'

'Aye,' said the kid, 'don't we all?'

And he gave me an extra one gratis, saying, 'Never a word to the governors, eh, mister?'

That wouldn't have occurred had my suit been in better nick.

I sat back down; the cold air had wakened Bowman.

I said 'Chicken or beef?' and we fell to, still not speaking, save for Bowman's muttered thanks. We were half-way through the supper when a man in sombre black joined our compartment. He looked just the sort to have boarded in the gloom of Trent.

Bowman drank his wine in silence, looking just as anxious as if he already knew about the revolver. On and on, swinging violently on. The rhythm of the wheels over the rail joints was steady until a mass of points were hit, and then the train swayed and rolled, and there'd come a sound like a brick wall collapsing, but still we kept on. The man in our compartment got down at Leeds; we didn't give him goodbye. The dining car was taken off there too.

I thought it was promising that the man in the yellow stockings was armed. It was another proof that I was on to something. I looked through the window at empty fields. Such lights as came and went showed the ground as black and white with melting snow. In some fields the snow cover was complete, and these were perfect, like jewels. They appeared with greater regularity as we approached the heights of the stretch to Carlisle: the summits and viaducts came and went, with the snow gangers out in strength, watching us from the wilds of the night.

We came to Carlisle, the mighty Citadel station, with a skeleton staff of laughing men larking about on the platform. It was half past one in the morning, and they had the run of the place; that's why they were happy. More banging as the Midland engines were taken off. The North British company would take us on.

I dozed as we rolled towards Edinburgh. Twice I was woken by ringing bells in signal boxes sliding back away from us in ever thicker falls of snow, but both times it was the three bells that are rung for 'line clear'. At three-thirty a.m. I saw the ticket inspector walking past the door.

'How long before Edinburgh, mate?' I asked him.

He looked at his watch.

'Twenty minutes.'

Bowman was asleep again, groaning again, a litter of bottles and glasses at his feet. I tapped him on the knee, and he jerked forwards, his glasses nearly tumbling off his nose.

'The Inverness carriages will come off at Edinburgh,' I said.

'Eh?' he said, in the confusion of sleep.

'We must join it then,' I said.

Bowman caught up his coat, and stumbled behind me towards the front of the train. The first compartment in the first of the two Inverness carriages was free, and Bowman said, 'Where is the fellow?'

'End compartment of the next one,' I said.

Bowman nodded and sat down as I walked along a little way.

The corridor blinds were still down in the man's compartment. On returning, I put the blinds down in our own.

At Edinburgh, the two Inverness carriages were cut loose, and a new engine banged into us. It was more like a smash than a coupling, but Bowman just took the jolts and stared straight ahead, all conversation gone. We both slept over the Forth Bridge – must have done, for the next thing I knew was Perth at five o'clock, and another change of engine, evidently conducted by invisible men, for I heard shouts but looked out on an empty platform and one stationary baggage wagon, dazzlingly lit for no good reason.

We were approaching Inverness, and I woke again to see sleet flowing through the greyness beyond the window. It was nearly nine. For all the freezing weather, there had been no schedule slacks. In a goods yard to the left of the ticket gate stood a row of wooden letter As: snow ploughs to be fitted to the engine fronts. I stepped into the corridor. Our man was waiting at the head of the short queue for the door at the end of the carriage. I counted the queue – nine people – and I thought of all the effort the Midland company had gone to for this.

The night on the train had not put a crimp in the man in the least: breeches and socks were perfect as before, coat swinging open, cap pulled low over the great boulder of a head. He climbed down, advanced along the platform and stood still for a second, breathing the cold air of Inverness, taking the sleet. I thought: he likes this – this must be his home. He had a barrel chest, legs a little too thin and bandy. He might have been a boxer once – a boxing farmer. His white moustache was like the handle of a pail.

We walked the length of the short train, and we were right behind the man at the ticket gate. I thought: there is nothing out of the way in this – the three of us were all on the same train, and now we're heading for the same ticket gate. We had no *option* but to follow him; the only thing that marked us out was our lack of luggage. The man crossed the booking hall. He was standing before a wall panel showing the timings of Highland Railway trains.

'He's going on,' I said.

Chapter Twenty-three

But then we watched from the ticket gate as the man crossed the booking hall and left the station.

'He's *not* going on,' said Bowman. 'He's done with trains.'

He cut diagonally across the square that lay beyond the station, and walked into the Station Hotel. A five-second battering from the icy wind, and we were in the hotel ourselves – soft carpets, soft fires, beautiful warmth. There was a bar or lounge directly opposite the reception desk. The man who looked like Sanderson was carefully folding his coat, and draping it over the arm of a chair. As we looked on, a waiter approached and asked to take his coat. The man refused with a quick headshake. He then said one very short word to the waiter, which, as I worked out a moment later – when the waiter returned with a silver tray – must have been 'tea'. When the waiter placed the tea before him, the man did not seem at first to notice it, but then he took the silver tweezers, and moved four sugar cubes from the sugar bowl to the cup. He drank one cup, stockinged legs akimbo. There was more in the pot, but he left it. He did not smoke.

He then repeatedly shot his cuffs while sitting in the seat: left, right, left again. There must be just the right amount of shirt linen extending beyond his country coat sleeve. His clothes were not quite of the best quality, I thought. He was not, by his looks, a rich man, and there was something tired about his clothes, as if he tyrannised over them.

He now fell to stroking his moustache, coaching it forward, as though conjuring for himself an ever-longer top lip. Suddenly he stood up, put some silver on the table and walked smartly out of the hotel. Another blow in the square – where stood the snow-topped statue of some kilty fellow from times past – and we followed the man once again through the booking hall of the station, and on to a bay platform. Here another short train waited – but there was a powerful engine at its head. I sent Bowman to buy biscuits and water bottles and climbed up. As I did so, the man looked for the first time directly at me. He sat right by the door. His head was tilted back, and he inhaled slowly through his white 'tache as he saw me, as if to say, 'Now you're a bit over-familiar. What's your game?'

I took a seat two along. It was a Highland Railway carriage, flimsy as a cricket pavilion, and with no compartments but open seating – and with no *heating* either. Bowman came up by the same door, and gave not a glance at the man but coloured up even more deeply as he brushed past him. He carried a paper bag in which were bottles of mineral water, bread and cheese.

'You might've picked up a couple of footwarmers,' I said with a grin, to which Bowman made no reply. He had barely spoken since Edinburgh. Only two other passengers joined the carriage – two men. They were discussing church matters but were not vicars. Their accents made them sound mechanical, as though driven by clockwork: the words 'rector' and 'kirk' came round again and again. I could only see the backs of their heads, and it bothered me that they did not move more.

We came out of Inverness by a great grey stretch of water. A single ship sat miserably in the middle of it. The line was single, and there were many pauses for other trains to pass, and many stations. We heard them before we saw them, for we approached to the sound of a bell rung by hand by the stationmaster. I recall the strangest of the names: Beauly, Muir of Ord, Foulis, Nigg. It was odd to see ordinary-looking – by which I mean English-looking – working people standing about near such station nameplates. Not that there were many outdoors in the sideways-flying sleet. All the stations were church-like, made of heavy stone. They had what looked like low fonts projecting from the station houses, and I fancied these must be for the dogs to drink from. The stations were not meant to look beautiful; they were meant not to be blown away.

One of them would come up, and it was as if the town supposed to go along with it had been mislaid. Or there might be a few buildings – more of a camp than a town. There was a sawmill by one station; a blacksmith's by another; sidings here and there, with horses being loaded; some wagons with a word written in a giant letters – 'HERRING'; great tanks of lamp oil. Well, the people went to where the fuel was. Every platform showed a simple sign with one arrow pointing in a direction marked 'Inverness', and another marked 'Wick and Thurso'; no 'up' or 'down' here. We were way beyond all that.

At most stations, one or two climbed up into our carriage, and one or two got off. Our man remained; the two ministers remained. I wanted as many up as possible, for every person aboard was a guarantee against the man loosing off a bullet from his pistol.

We were now somewhere beyond a spot called Dingwall. When would the bloody man get off, and what would I do when he did? I had no notion. We'd been on the go for more than an hour. I looked at Bowman, and he seemed to be asleep. Had he even noticed the great mountains to our left? You could mistake them at first for great banks of clouds, until you worked out that they were not moving. I peered forwards: our quarry sat still as before. I could see the top of his wide cap.

One of the ministers was saying, 'It's all to the guid, it's all to the guid . . .' and I cursed his ignorance. It was *not* all to the good.

I turned again to the window. The sound came of another bell floating through the sleet, another station rolling into view. A curiosity on the platform: a smoking stove attached to the base of a water tower – against ice, as I supposed.

There came a clattering of a door in the next carriage as I read a poster on the station wall: 'Further North! Further North! Fortnightly Passes for Visiting the Northern Highlands', and then, underneath, in smaller print: 'Summer Only'.

I looked at the seat opposite; Bowman was eyeing me from the depths of his coat. The turned-up collar had skewed his glasses.

'Who comes up here in winter?' I asked him.

'Juggins like us,' he muttered.

Huddled in his coat, he did not meet my eye; he had hardly the will to speak. He hadn't taken on alcoholic fuel for a long while, and he had now reached the point of being made tired by the cold – which was a dangerous point. He belonged in an office, not a Highland train; an office or a pub, of course.

I looked out at two winter diehards in the fields, following a hay wagon as we moved on.

I was almost asleep myself when a jolt of the train brought me up sharply. Bowman was eyeing me again.

'The wild sea disclosed,' he murmured, and he nodded to the right. Great grey waves were rising and coming at us. The line was practically on the beach.

'When will he bloody get off?' I said, nodding along towards our friend; but Bowman had gone back into his own world.

I had hoped the man might step down at Helmsdale. This was a seaport with a slightly larger station. For once, grey houses blocked the view of fields and sea. But while everyone bar the two ministers got off there, our bastard sat tight.

After Helmsdale we were rocking along in a valley by a fast black river – one-sided trees and tumbledown cottages, all snow-covered. It seemed a great impertinence for the engine, which was green, and its carriages, which were greener still, to intrude upon this white world, which was a kind of fairyland, not real, not Britain. I could not believe they had the Royal Mail here; or even newspapers. There were telegraph poles and wires, but they were all askew and snow-loaded.

We stopped at a place called Kildonan, and hastened down on to the platform. I needed a piss, and there was no WC on the train.

A man in railway uniform stood before the station house.

'Good day,' I said.

(That was a laugh, with the wet snow flying at us.)

'Could I use the jakes in the station house?' I continued.

'The *whit?*' he said, making the sound of a cane going swish through the air.

'The station lavatory,' I said.

'Aye, aye,' he said, and jerked his thumb at the open door behind him. It was half booking hall, half living room with a good fire going and three pot dogs on the mantelpiece. The lavatory was in a door leading off. I pissed and came out, lingering by the fire. I then turned, nodded at the man and climbed up into the train as he blew his whistle. The ministers had gone, and Bowman was standing up at his seat.

He was talking in low tones to the man we had been pursuing.

The stationmaster slammed the door behind me, and the train jerked into motion as the man we had been pursuing turned towards me, gun in hand. With perhaps the beginnings of a smile, he motioned me towards him, motioned me into my seat. He sat down opposite me, and Bowman sat down beside him.

Bowman would not meet my eye.

He was in on it.

Chapter Twenty-four

'In five minutes, ye'll alight the train,' said the man.

'Will I now?'

'Aye, ye wull,' he said, with a glance down at the revolver in his hand.

Juggins like us, Bowman had said. Juggins like *me*. The business of the photograph was never meant to come to any good, and I should never have taken it up. Shillito had been right. I knew hardly anything, but it was too much for this Scotsman. Was he Sanderson? Had Sanderson been Scottish? I asked him outright:

'Are you Gilbert Sanderson?'

'Sanderson's deed,' he said. Again, the half-smile came. He had the smooth kind of Scottish accent, making the most of the Rs.

Down below us to the left, the black water seemed to be in a panic as it rushed towards two mighty boulders. We and it were the only things moving in the valley. Looking up at the mountains, I thought for some reason of hymn-singing in church, the search for the Beyond. This was an almost heavenly, life-after-death place where everything was different. I would not see my wife and child again, and all that was left was curiosity.

'Where is this place?' I said, and it was Bowman who answered, looking down and away. It took me a while to make out what he'd said, which was: 'Strath of Kildonan'.

Well, it sounded like a place in a book.

I looked back at Bowman, but he could not meet my eye.

The train began to slow, and a station rolled into view, but there had been no bell, and there were no people.

'Oot,' said the Scotsman, and I stood up. We climbed down,

Bowman slamming the door behind us, and then immediately huddling up into his coat again. The train went on. This was not a station, but a halt. The place was not named. The platform was of wood, like a theatre stage, and there was no station building, but only the two pointing arrows for 'Inverness' or 'Thurso and Wick'. The Scotsman must have requested the stop miles since.

I could not keep my eyes open in the floating snow, but I knew that the clattering river was near by, that mountains rose all around; and that a high-wheeled dog cart stood waiting at twenty yards' distance.

'Tae yer left', said the Scotsman, and I could not make out the words.

I turned in the snow towards Bowman. The lenses of his spectacles might have been painted white. He looked like a red-faced blind man.

'He means you to go to your left,' Bowman said.

The snow-covered heather leant across the path so that, as I came up to the cart, my trouser legs were soaking. It wasn't weather for a forty-shilling lounge suit.

Two men waited in the cart. Their collars were up, and their hats pulled low, but I knew them. They had stepped from the photograph in my pocket and up into the vehicle. They were the barrister known to the Chief and called Marriott, and the youngest man of the five, the one who'd been missed in Filey over the summer. Had I run them to earth, or they me? The young man was speaking to the Scotsman in what seemed like a friendly way, but the barrister, who was in the driving seat, stared straight ahead at the miserable horse. I was placed on one bench; the young man, the Scotsman and Bowman sat facing me. The revolver lay in the Scotsman's hand. He did not wear gloves; the gun would freeze before that hand of his did. He was made for this weather, born to it.

'Ye've the photograph about ye?' he said, and I gave it over.

Marriott the lawyer cracked the whip, and we started to roll as the Scotsman said to the young man, 'Would you no say I was better to look on than yon Gilbert Sanderson, Richie?'

The young man said something I didn't catch.

'Aye, he's the same high foreheed as me,' said the Scotsman, 'I'll grant ye that.'

Again a remark from the young man that I did not hear, to which the Scotsman said, 'Nay, nay, he was *bald* – I'm towsy-haired compared to the leet Sanderson.'

He pulled off his cap to show his smooth brown skull; there was not a hair on it. He didn't crack a smile, but he was jesting with the younger man, who smiled a little uneasily. The Scot seemed to have a liking for that young man, who looked maybe a couple of years shy of my own age.

Of course, the Scotsman's identity of appearance with Sanderson had been the key to the whole scheme. He had stolen Sanderson's horse and lamed the beast in the garden; he had then entered the house to do the murder, made sure he was seen by a servant and made off on foot. Was the Whitby–Middlesbrough Travelling Club a band of robbers then? I could not believe it.

The young man, evidently called Richard, stood in need of a shave, and there was a deep red cut on his forehead. He had come a long way from garden parties at Filey. The road was rising up above the railway line now. We were passing a broken-down stone house, and a sign reading 'DANGER', warning travellers off the land at certain times when shooting would take place. I glanced up again at the mountains, but could not make out the tops. On the hills were four-pointed shelters, like crossed swords.

I looked across at Bowman. He had found the horse's blanket and wore it over his shoulders, so that he looked like an old woman. Had he made the plan to net me? Who was the true governor here? The Scotsman? Or the man in the driving seat – the silent lawyer?

A thought came: *I* had been the one to suggest giving chase when the Scotsman had walked away up Bouverie Street. How could Bowman have known I would do that? But it was not really a mystery. Bowman had been on the point of making the suggestion himself. He had played with the window of the magazine offices. There had been no reason to open it on such a day of cold; instead, it had been the signal to the Scotsman to set off.

I looked up at this fellow who had led me such a dance.

'What are you *called*?' I asked him.

'Haud yer tongue,' he said, head tilted back. He was still staring as Bowman muttered, 'He's called "Small David".'

'Why are you called Small David?' I asked the man.

'Dae ye have any objection to the name?'

'It is not accurate.'

We were coming to a fork in the road.

'You're about the largest man in this cart,' I said, and again the half-smile seemed to develop underneath that moustache.

A white cottage marked the junction; deer antlers hung on the end wall. The Scotsman did not give a glance, but continued staring at me.

'He's called "Small" because he's big,' Bowman said.

'It's humour,' said someone; and I realised that the lawyer in the driving seat had at last spoken up. Having done so, he evidently thought he might as well continue.

'County Sutherland,' he said, half-turning around towards me. 'A country very different from the levels of the North Riding, Detective Stringer.'

He was as handsome as he had looked in the photograph, but strangely rigged out: half poor farmer in looks, half gentleman. Beneath his ulster he wore a good black suit, but with a dirty black guernsey under *that*. At his throat, he wore a black comforter and a green silk necker. And he had the wrong boots on for this place: town boots of thin leather. His face put me in mind of somebody. I looked quickly between him and the young man, Richie.

The lawyer was the father of Richie.

Beyond the white cottage, we turned on to a higher road. A white cloud was rising slowly behind the mountains ahead as the snow came down fast. The railway was out of sight below, but I knew it must be blocked by now.

A few seconds beyond the house, we had to pull into the hedgerow to let another cart by that contained another lot of muffled-up men. They looked respectable enough, but none of us raised our hat. The way was now becoming rougher; the stones

167

rolled under our wheels, and underneath the snow.

After another few minutes of being shaken to bits in the cart I realised that the Scotsman, Small David, was staring at me again.

I said, 'Why are you looking at me like that?'

In reply he spat out something that sounded like: 'Why are *ye*?'

'What's the programme?' I asked the company after another long interval.

No reply from anyone.

Chapter Twenty-five

At first, I took the cottage we were approaching to be nothing but a wide stone wall. It was some way up a mountain, part of the grey blur beyond the snow.

'I know you're watching the chimney, Small David,' said Richie Marriott.

'Why's there nae smoke, laddie?'

'We're low on firewood and peats, Small David.'

'And ye're low on brains,' he said, but there was perhaps some affection there; these two were cronies, who conspired over the heating of the house.

'I can't manage that flue in the scullery, David, and that's all about it,' said the son.

Everyone jumped down; I followed. It was not so much a garden, more like an island in the sea of heather. Two rusty long-handled shovels leant against the low stone walls; a rain barrel stood at one corner, barely higher than the wall. You'd call it a one-storey house, only it was lower than that. As we approached it, the Scotsman nodded from me to Marriott, saying, 'He stays here the neet if ye insist, but then it's o'er the burran wi' him.'

The lawyer was walking the horse towards a broken-down barn a little further up the track that had brought us to the house. The house looked over a white, misty valley – threatened to roll down into it. Whether this was the same valley we'd run along in the train or another, I couldn't tell, for I could not see. I could just make out through the blizzard a steeper hill rising above the one on which we stood; black clouds flowed across the tops like a spillage of oil. The day was nearly done, and the world was closing down to this house and these men. The snow was a foot thick as I stepped out of the cart, and I knew that I was held prisoner by the weather as much as the revolver. I suddenly thought of my interview for promotion at Middlesbrough. I would not be there after all, and the fact was a very good demonstration of the strangeness of life.

Small David walked up to the door of the cottage, on which a note was pinned, reading: 'Shut this door after you. This means YOU', with the last word underlined.

He kicked it open with bullet-like force, and entered the house.

'What's "over the burran"?' I asked, following him in.

In the smoke-filled scullery we had now entered, he turned sharply about towards me:

'Ye spoke just now of Gilbert Sanderson,' he said. '*He's* o'er the burran.'

'Steady now, David,' said Marriott, who stepped in behind the two of us, having settled the horse.

Small David was at the stove that squatted in the centre of the room, cursing to himself, and trying to fettle the fire. The lawyer held a pitcher of water; he stood at the stone sink – which was as big as a horse trough, and took up about a third of the room – washing his hands as thoroughly as circumstances permitted. Then he turned to me:

'I am currently negotiating to save your life, Detective Stringer.'

If nothing else, his beautiful lawyer's voice had survived whatever decline had brought him to this house.

'Negotiating?' I said. 'Who with?'

Bowman, now also alongside us, cut in, saying, 'With Rob Roy there, of course', while nodding towards Small David, who was still crouching at the stove. 'And I want you to know that I hope he succeeds.' He was addressing me in the haze of the cold kitchen, but not looking at me. He knew he had done a low thing. He had stopped short of friendliness ever since I'd known him; he'd always been cagey, and he'd been all wrong on the chase from St Pancras. If he'd been straight, he'd either have jibbed at the business or got keen on it; he'd done neither.

'I had no choice but to bring you here, you know,' he said, as though the whole disaster was somehow my fault. There was one small window in the scullery, and I craned to look through it. Seeing what I was about, Marriott said, 'Don't try a breakaway, Detective Stringer. Or Small David will be upon you in an instant.'

I remained at the window, but it was only a bluff: the glass was thick with ice and I could see nothing – and the sight of that blankness made me feel I could barely breathe.

I turned around, and saw that none of the company had removed his hat; yet all the hats scraped against the grimy roof beams that swooped low across the room, which was more like a *cave* than a room. Small David now opened a door leading to a sitting room of sorts, and it seemed that I was free to follow him in.

The stove was black and cold here too. The young man, Richie, was in the room already, lighting greasy, evil-smelling paraffin lamps at either end. It was a long, low place with several truckle beds pushed against the three stone walls away from the fire. Filthy tab rugs were placed anyhow on the floor, and stacks of papers, books and journals were placed around the fireplace, whether to be burnt or read, I could not say. Richie then began remaking the fire, and he proved a shocking bad hand at doing so. Instead of cleaning the grate, he poked at it with the tool, which constantly rang against the iron of the door, striking a high, unpleasant note. He had obviously lit it earlier on in the day, but it had gone out because the draught was not properly created. As he poked and prodded, I wondered whether he had ever lit fires before he came to this place. I doubted it of a man who was a barrister's son. He got a burn going eventually, but I could see that it might not last.

'The trick of keeping a slow burn,' I said, 'is to close the top flue a little more – the lever wants tipping another ten degrees.'

'And who're ye tae tell him?' Small David called out.

I had not seen him enter the room. He carried a bucket in place of the revolver. For all his size, I ought not to be held off by a man who wore yellow socks and carried a bucket, but my thoughts would keep going back to that revolver of his, evidently close at hand in one of his coat pockets.

'I'm trained up as a fireman,' I said.

'Fireman?' said Small David. 'Ye are a dirty polis.'

'I was first trained up as a railway fireman,' I repeated.

'But he was *fired*,' said Bowman, who had also entered the room, and whose speech was now slurring.

'Sorry, Jim,' he added, as he sank down on one of the truckle beds. He'd got a bottle from somewhere, though I couldn't make out the contents.

The stove was warming up after a fashion – it would keep me at close quarters as surely as any manacle. I claimed for myself one of the beds, but Small David ordered me off – I guessed from what he said that it must have been his. He then quit the room, and a moment later, I thought I caught sight of him walking past the one tiny frosted window that served the sitting room. Bowman sat silent on his bed, perhaps asleep, while Richie occupied another of the beds, reading a paper. He had never passed a word to me, and come to that, I had not seen him speak to his father or to Bowman. He only ever seemed to speak to Small David, who had evidently taken the place of his father in his affections. He seemed very young for his years, this fellow, but he must be in – or rather he must have *been* in – employment himself, otherwise he wouldn't have been in the habit of riding up to Whitby with the Travelling Club.

We had all kept our topcoats on, and all sank into them; and the room was quite silent now, save for the crackling of the fire. I could hear no stream rushing by, but only the baaing of sheep, which were at very close quarters.

Why were they all *here*? My thoughts raced in a circus. They'd fled Yorkshire after the disappearance of Falconer and the murder of their Club confederate George Lee, but why had either been killed in the first place? Not for the few silver candlesticks that had been taken from Lee's house. I looked again through the tiny window, where I saw that the lawyer Marriott had joined Small David; they were holding a conference in the falling snow, which seemed to muffle up their words, but I heard my own name mentioned twice by Marriott.

He came into the room a moment later and stood before the

stove for a warm. He had removed his topcoat, and he managed to cut a handsome figure even in that old black guernsey. He then moved over to one of the two vacant beds. This, I saw, was better ordered than the others, with the blankets properly folded, and the papers over there were in better order than in the other parts of the room. As far as I could see, they were mostly shipping-line brochures. He caught up one of these, and read it for a few minutes before impatiently leaving the room once more.

I turned to the son, Richie, and repeated my earlier question.

'What's the programme?'

He just gave a shrug, and went back to his reading matter. The arrangements of the mean lamps meant that the shadow of the page he read covered the whole wall behind him.

I glimpsed Bowman, who now stood in the doorway, watching me with bottle in hand. I glanced that way, and he turned on his heel and disappeared. He could not bear to be in my company, now that he had betrayed me. I looked down at the crumpled papers under my boots. They seemed to have come from a holiday agent: 'Winter in the Cornish Riviera'; 'Railway Map of the British Isles'; 'Bournemouth, the Land of Pines and Sunshine.'

'Can you see us in Bournemouth, Detective Stringer, taking tea in an hotel?'

It was Marriott, standing by me and looking down at my reading matter. The householders would keep coming and going, but much as they wanted to keep clear of one another, they were all drawn back to the fire before long. The lawyer held a small glass in his hands – quite dainty by the standards of the cottage. I imagined it might be valuable to him; an object saved from his earlier life. From the kitchen came the smell of food, and I wondered how many more meals would be left to me.

'I cannot bear to see the daylight lost as early as it is here,' Bowman said, moving towards the fireplace, 'and so a flight to the south *is* contemplated – but a good deal further south than Bournemouth.'

'A flight?' I said.

'The trip has been in prospect for some time, Detective Stringer, but I would not have called it a flight until I heard about you.'

Small David entered the room, saying, 'Where's yon bottle, man?' Receiving no answer, he called out, 'Hey, Bowman!' at which Marriott turned on him.

'Don't shout so, you fucking Scottish hooligan!'

I had never heard swearing in such refined tones.

'You see,' said Marriott, turning towards me again, 'I must get out of this quagmire . . . And I must make a satisfactory arrangement about you before I do so. I brought you here to save you, don't you see that?'

'Strikes me this is a good place to bring a fellow if you wanted to do him in.'

'Now Small David would disagree with you there, Detective Stringer,' Marriott said. 'He holds that the best place for that business is the Cleveland Hills.'

'You pitched Theodore Falconer down an old iron shaft,' I said.

But then another, and better, thought hit me like a thunderclap.

'No, you put him into a blast furnace. His body was never found, and that's because it was melted away to nothing.'

Small David was watching me from the doorway. Marriott kept silence. He stood before me with his arms folded – a good-looking man with too much on his mind.

'Richard's a good fellow,' he said suddenly, nodding towards his son.

The boy looked up at him. 'Stow it, father.'

'But he has a poor physique – a defect on his mother's side, I suppose, for she died young herself. Small David, now –'

Marriott indicated the Scotsman, who had sat down on the last remaining free bed.

'Small David is a practical man, if not a very great hand at conversation.'

The Scotsman muttered something, and Marriott made a show of cocking an ear.

'Did you get that, Detective Stringer?'

I shook my head.

'I didn't either. He's not a great one for talk, as I say.'

'Wi'oot me,' muttered Small David, picking up a newspaper, 'ye'd be deed – and ye stull could be.'

Marriott rolled his eyes at me, saying, 'I just can't help wishing that fellow was a little more – just ever so slightly *English*.'

Small David put down his paper, and closed on Marriott, saying, 'Haud yer tongue or I'll gie ye somethin' for yersel' –'

Marriott turned once more to me, saying, 'He is not a *university* man, you know.'

I had a quick impression of Marriott in the position of an old-fashioned boxer, with fists high and chin lifted for Queensberry Rules, but the scrap itself was a wild affair lasting not more than a few seconds.

And it was Marriott who was bloodied – and almost knocked on to the stove. Steadying himself against the wall, he again turned to me, saying, 'Small David was not on the Classics side, Detective Stringer, but then again he was not on the Modern side either. On the face of it a black mystery, until you remember this: Small David was *not at the University*.'

The Scotsman stood for a moment, as though deciding whether to give this latest provocation the go-by, and he evidently decided not to, for he clouted the lawyer a second time, sending him sprawling amid the newspapers and journals on the floor.

'Look, I know this is all fun, but can we drop it?' said Bowman, who'd had his hands over his glasses as the blows had been struck. Marriott was finding a shaky pair of legs, blood running freely from his nose. He did not look strong, being so thin, but there again he was not the sort of man you expected to see felled.

'I'm not a university man either, if it comes to that,' Bowman was saying. 'Not by a long chalk.'

The lawyer was now standing in silence before the stove, occasionally giving a flick of his head so as to send the blood from his nose away from his mouth. He would not raise his hand to it, for that would show weakness. He was all ablaze inside, but still no colour showed in his face, and he paid no heed as his son stood and walked out of the room, preferring, as I supposed, to sit in the poorly warmed scullery rather than hear more of his old man's ravings.

'The boy is not vigorous like me,' Marriott said, 'and he cannot scrap, as I can. I learnt to take a punch in the boxing club, Detective Stringer . . . it was at *the University*.'

He shot another quick glance at Small David, who did not rise to the bait this third time, but sat back down on his bed. Marriott then removed the photograph from his coat pocket and looked it over, nodding the while.

'It proves you were all on the train that morning,' I said. 'The newspaper in your son's hand proves it.'

The lawyer turned and opened the stove door with the fire tool, placing the photograph carefully on top of the burning wood within.

'I have another print,' I said, '. . . and the negatives, of course.'

The lawyer looked at me and sighed, brushing his hair back once again. And now at last he raised a handkerchief to his bleeding nose.

'You are not helping the case I am trying to make for keeping you above ground, Detective Stringer.'

At which the Scotsman, who had his head buried in one of the newspapers, muttered something like: 'Aye, that's right enough.'

'You killed Falconer,' I said to Marriott, 'but why?'

The lawyer looked at me fixedly as he dabbed at the blood – almost with real curiosity.

'You killed Lee as well,' I added, 'though I daresay not with your own hands.'

I turned towards Small David, who was still reading, and making such a great show of coolness that I almost believed he wasn't listening.

'Or did you pay *him* to do it?'

The Scotsman read on.

'You are of a questioning humour,' Marriott said, rocking on his feet before the fireplace, quite composed again. 'It is the mark of a good pleader. Have you considered the Bar? There's a good deal of reading to put in, much burning of the midnight oil with your Stephens's *Commentaries*, your Hunter's *Roman Law*, but it's quite a democracy, you know. There's no 'mister' at the Bar, still less any 'sir'. In fact, it's not at all such a toff's profession as you might suppose, Stringer . . .'

I was plain Stringer to him now, which meant I had riled him, about which I was glad.

'Any man with brains might aspire even to the silk gown of the King's Counsel – army officer, actor, schoolmaster. A *university* training usually precedes the call, but not necessarily. Fluency of speech is the chief requirement, you see, thinking on one's leg – although of course you must also become fashionable, and in that, I confess, I never succeeded . . .'

'Now I winder why not?' put in Small David, looking up from his paper.

Marriott ignored him, saying, 'I did well enough for a time, mark you. Three or four cases a day was nothing to me – not all of them jury cases, of course, but still: seven guineas for a thirty-minute consultation . . . Five shillings to the clerk, yes, but even so . . . Unfortunately, I did not put in the hours flattering the important men of my acquaintance. Rather than dine with the benchers in my evening at the Temple, I would go off to the German gymnasium at King's Cross, Stringer.'

He kept saying my name. The man was speaking only for my benefit.

'I worked at my boxing night and day at that gymnasium,' he went on, at which Small David, turning the page of his paper, muttered, 'And much guid it did ye.'

I thought that the lawyer might fly at Small David for a second time, but instead he touched the handkerchief to his nose again, saying, 'Unfortunately, I did not generally like the judges. I knew many of them, Stringer, and I knew many that were inclined to hanging.'

At which he fell silent for a space, during which time I watched Small David turn two further pages of newspaper.

It was the *Sutherland Gazette* that Small David was looking over. Bowman, as far as I could make out, was now asleep, the bottle at his feet, but he righted himself a moment later when the boy Richie walked in with two bowls of steaming broth. He gave

177

the first to his father, who began sipping from the bowl directly, and somehow doing so in a mannerly sort of way. The other bowl went to Small David – so that the two governors had been fed first.

The boy returned a moment later with a bowl for Bowman, who, after staring at the concoction for a while, said, '. . . Looks almost good enough to eat.'

The last bowl was given to me. A spoon rolled in the brownish stuff; a hunk of bread floated on it. I nodded thanks, and the boy nodded back – which was the first communication between us. I tasted the soup, which was like slow Oxo – Oxo slowed by flour and something that might have been potatoes. But I hadn't tasted food for hours, so it was nectar to me.

But just after I'd taken my second spoonful, something made me glance up towards Small David, who was eyeing me narrowly.

'Ye ken ye're gaun to dee, don't ye?'

Well, I could *not* believe it; I seemed to be living in a dream, as we all ate in the dimly lit room on the hillside, while the blizzard wind made a repeated low note, like the sound of a ship coming into harbour, as it blew across the chimney top. Presently, Richie went around the room again, this time collecting up the bowls. The lawyer drained whatever was left in his small glass, and put it on the mantelshelf. He did not seem in need of another dram. He watched after his son as the boy left the room, and turned towards me again. He seemed minded to talk, and I had the powerful notion that he wanted to tell me as much as I wanted to know.

Chapter Twenty-six

'As I say, the boy and I are not constructed at all on the same lines,' Marriott began. 'For example, I do not take a constitutional, Detective Stringer . . .'

(Perhaps the supper had put him in better humour. At any event, I had regained my title.)

'I do not take a constitutional,' he repeated, 'and never let it be said that I take a stroll. I *walk*, Detective Stringer, and I would walk with Theodore Falconer for quite hours – right over the tops and all about Whitby. Do you know Whitby at all, Detective Stringer? A very fine old seaport, beautiful ships . . . Do you know about ships? The parish church at the top of the steps is quite exceptional, and Falconer and I would make a wide circuit from there on Sunday mornings in all weathers. I was in fact a member of his rambling club for a spell, and a very strange grouping they proved to be. They met in the woods, you know – an almost pagan confederacy.'

'I had met Falconer at the University,' he continued, again looking keenly at Small David, hoping to reopen the quarrel, but the Scotsman read on, so Marriott continued addressing me. 'We were not of equivalent rank, socially speaking, but fell in with each other while tramping on Christ Church Meadow. Almost every Sunday for two years, we'd tuck into our mackintoshes and have a blow. He'd enjoy that, and the rougher the weather, the better he liked it. We continued in the same way when I removed, with Richard, to the Middlesbrough district – to the village just south of Saltburn, which was Falconer's home territory. We rode into town in the Club car, and on Sundays we tramped. High up on the tops – he would never keep to the paths but would battle his way through the heather singing Methodist hymns and booming on about the wonders of nature.'

And he nearly smiled, adding, 'Quite the fresh air fiend was Falconer.'

Small David was looking up from the *Sutherland Gazette*.

'We've come to' t now!' he said in a strange, fluting tone.

'The virtues of fresh air are well attested,' Marriott went on, 'and the cramped, stifling rooms of the suburban house are to be deprecated . . .'

He spoke with agitation, fairly shaking now, and not from the cold. I knew that the truth was approached as Small David, leaning further forward on the edge of his truckle bed, said, 'Spit it oot, man, spit it oot!'

The lawyer seemed in a daze now, gazing at vacancy and shaking his head. In an under-breath that I had to crane forwards to hear, he spoke the words:

'But to open the window on a day of heavy snowfall –'

'There y'are, it's oot!' cried Small David, rolling backwards on his bed, as the lawyer continued to shake his head, speaking a Latin phrase whose meaning I did not take at the time, for I am not well up in the language:

'– that was the *reductio ad absurdum*.'

The Scotsman was falling back on his bed, cackling, saying over and over, 'It's oot, it's oot!'

What was out?

Bowman was looking directly at me, red face at boiling point.

'Don't you see? Falconer opened the window in the saloon, and caught his death as a result.'

The lawyer went on, in the same head-shaking, sorrowful way. 'It was against the rules of the Club.'

Richie, the son, was standing in the doorway now; he gave a cough.

The truth was coming to me by degrees.

'Falconer opened the window in the Club carriage –' I said, eyeing Marriott, 'and you murdered him for it?'

'Yon dunderheed's got there in the eend!' came the cry from the

Scotsman's bed, and it was followed by a long bar of silence. Then Marriott spoke up again.

'He drew down the window, Detective Stringer. I put it up again; he drew it down a second time; and I struck out – one blow of the cane, Detective Stringer. I did not mean to kill. The word on the indictment would have been "manslaughter".'

The Scotsman snorted.

'But others have gone the same way,' I said. 'He was not the only one killed.'

The boy Richie was in the doorway.

'The kitbags are packed and stowed on the cart, father,' he said. 'All ready for the morning . . . but we must leave your books behind.'

Small David was drawing the bed that the boy had sat on closer to the stove; he then did the same with his own. He opened the door of the stove, and began putting on logs. There seemed to be a deepening of the darkness beyond the window.

'You're pushing off tomorrow?' I said to the room in general.

'Aye,' said Small David at the stove, 'and so are ye.'

'Planning on taking me with you, are you?'

The Scotsman paused about his work.

'A little o' the way, aye.'

'Another big snow's coming, you know?' I said, and Small David rotated his wide body to face me.

'It'll nae matter either way to yersel',' he said.

Chapter Twenty-seven

We all stepped out into the blizzard for a piss. This seemed to be a nightly routine around the house, for each man went to his own wall nook to perform. Small David pointed his gun at me as I unbuttoned my fly and kept it on me as I tried to start.

'Y'are awfy slow at this,' he said.

'Fuck off,' I said.

'– as y'are at everythin' else,' he added, and as I cursed him again and turned towards the wall, I realised that I could see the outline of his wide shadow very clearly against the stones, and that the falling snow was lit by a grey glow.

The moon was full.

In the living room, Small David fed the stove again, and set the draught for a slower burn. He then walked into the scullery, and I could hear him locking the front door. He might then have had a sluice-down in the great sink, for I could hear the swishing of water. He returned to the living room and put out one of the two lamps. A moment later every man was lying in his bed – each, as far as I could make out, with all his day clothes still on.

Whether any man slept, I don't know, for there were constant shiftings and half-muffled groans that put a kind of electricity into the atmosphere of that terrible smoke hole. I thought of Marriott, and how he had lost all by one moment of anger. The cane had been there in his hand in the photograph at the start of the journey. He had made no attempt to hide it. This crime was made ridiculous by the simple fact that half an hour before, or in fact one *second* before it had occurred, it had not been meant to happen. There was a double shame to it on this account, it seemed to me, and I was sure that Marriott thought of it in the same way. His crime had not been a manly one; and now he and his son were members of a different club. It seemed that I had joined this one.

My mind raced on in the darkness, and I fell to thinking that it was highly convenient they should have had a spare bed for me, and I wondered whether it was meant for Moody, the chimney sweep made good, who had perhaps survived for a while after the first killings, but had then threatened to speak out. Perhaps his son in Pickering knew all.

But many mysteries remained. How had Bowman fallen into the clutches of the band? He was kept there, I knew, by fear of Small David, but how had the thing begun? The connection was Peters, obviously, but exactly how? And where had Marriott dug Small David up from? My guess was that he was somebody he'd defended in a court of law.

Small David had done a good job with the stove, and it came to me presently that I was properly warm for the first time in days. I thought of little Harry, and I hoped that he was warm. I thought of how he would stand in the road at Thorpe-on-Ouse for minutes on end, and then suddenly go skipping off, as if he'd at last got hold of the answer to some very troublesome question. He was eccentric, like his mother.

Well, they would go on in their own way. It was better that I should die in the course of an important investigation than lose my job through my own foolishness and leave them with a loafer at the head of the family. I turned over on the narrow bed many times, back and forth until finally I knew that sleep would come. I was certain on that point, and I believe I spoke out loud the words, 'I have lost all my doubts', but there must have been the complication of a dream somewhere, for I now heard those words repeated directly into my ear by another.

'I have lost all my doubts.'

I felt the firm press of a hand on my shoulder and opened my eyes to see Bowman leaning over me.

He was changed.

'We're going to make off,' he whispered; and for the first time since I'd known him, he smiled. If he'd had any hair to speak of, it would have been tousled; his glasses were askew on his nose, but I could see by the one remaining lamp that there was more purpose about him than ever there had been before. He wore his topcoat; he held his sporting cap tightly bundled in his hand.

'Collect up your boots,' he whispered as I rolled upright. 'I know where Small David stows the key.'

The other men were still rolling and groaning in the darkness, like a restless sea. I picked up my boots, and followed Bowman into the scullery, where the air was just as cold as if we'd been outside. As I stepped into my boots, I could just make out that Bowman was kneeling at the grate. He came up with the key in his hand.

'Still warm,' he whispered. 'He keeps it in the ash pan.'

He walked over towards the heavy front door, and there came a great cymbal crash as he did so. All the breath stopped on my lips, as I looked towards the other door, the one leading into the sitting room, which we had left ajar behind us. It did not move.

'Kicked the damned ash pan,' said Bowman, who now placed the key in the front door.

He was straining at it.

'Won't turn,' he said, a little too loudly.

I looked again towards the living-room door.

'Can't get the trick of it,' he was saying.

I went towards him, stepping carefully, for I didn't know where the ash pan had been kicked *to*. I motioned him aside, leant hard on the door and turned the key.

Nothing doing.

I pulled it towards me by the handle – again nothing.

'Take the key out and try again,' said Bowman.

I did so, and the key went in further this time – it had not been properly lodged by Bowman. But as I turned the key, the wrong door was moving. With every degree of twist that I gave it, the *sitting-room* door was moving inwards. The key gave a click as I continued to look over my shoulder, at the door behind. A figure stood there: Richie, the son. A blanket was around him like a cape, and he might have been sleepwalking, or he might have been thinking hard. Above the blanket, his face shone white in a new light. The key had done its work as I looked at him. Before me, the door was open, and the Highlands seemed to rise like a drop scene at the theatre: the valley falling away before me; white clouds moving across the tops in succession, like a train, and all lit by a magical grey light. The snow had stopped, for all its work was now done.

We were through the door, and crashing through the drenching, snowy heather in an instant. I looked back at the house. Richie Marriott had not emerged from it, and nor had anybody else.

We moved with long, comical strides, stepping out, and then down and nearly over-toppling at every stride. We could not afford to take the track by which we'd come up in the cart – that was too slow and twisty. 'Had to get out, and had to take you along,' Bowman was panting behind me. 'I couldn't dodge it, having brought you up here.'

He'd shown himself a man at last, and it gave him new life.

I looked back at the house – still no sign of life.

'I'm obliged to you,' I said.

We crashed on, but the ground did not play fair. The snow and heather sometimes hid black, brackeny water; we might at any moment be stepping on to heather that hid a twenty-foot rocky gulf, and there were many streams running down towards the one that had made the valley. Over the next five minutes of headlong descent Bowman fell over twice behind me. After the second fall, he said, 'Glasses gone.'

I turned around, and saw that his small eyes seemed to have sunk further into his head, as if in retreat from the job of looking out at the world unaided.

I felt around in the heather near his feet.

'Give it up,' he said.

'Try to step in my tracks,' I said, and we carried on.

'How's your boots?' I asked after a while.

'Pretty well sodden,' he said, and it struck me that he had said it happily.

'Good old moon,' he said, after a couple more falls.

185

'The boy saw us,' I said.

'He might not let on,' Bowman panted out behind me.

'He's great pals with Small David, though,' I said.

'Small David's taken a fancy to him,' said Bowman. 'I don't know how far it works the other way. The boy's the one I feel sorry for in all this – apart from myself, of course,' he added, laughing.

'What does he work as?'

'Solicitor – only been at it a couple of years.'

'Up in Middlesbrough?'

'That's it.'

'I think I have the matter straight now,' I said, as we battered on through the drenching heather. 'The rudiments of it, anyway.'

'Well, Marriott's given you most of the tale. He has some kink in the brain that makes him always talk of it.'

But it seemed to me that Bowman's own kink was straightened out.

He was fairly skipping down the hill, in between falls. And he was not juiced, either.

'Marriott crowned Falconer,' said Bowman. 'And of course the whole Club knew it directly. It happened in the saloon, and half of them saw it. The body was put off the train at a spot near Marske, which is a little way north of Saltburn – it was just pitched into the snow at trackside, but they were lucky over the weather because the stuff was coming down fast, and Falconer would have been covered over in minutes. It bought them time,' Bowman continued, righting himself after another tumble. 'Well, you can imagine the discussion that went on in that carriage as it neared Middlesbrough – the *heat* of it. I think it would have been like a courtroom on wheels, with Marriott making out that it had been an accident, that he didn't deserve to swing for it or do thirty years, or whatever the turn-up might be if the police were called in . . .'

Something was moving along the hillside towards us; like a great brown cloud, only it came with a fast and dangerous rustling noise. It stopped twenty feet off, and the picture composed.

'Deer,' I said.

We both stopped and watched the herd for a second. Their eyes shone like new shilling pieces.

'Rum,' I said. 'They're looking at us as if there's something *wrong* with us.'

'That's because we're not firing on them,' said Bowman.

We crashed on.

'Richie stood by his father,' Bowman was saying. 'It was his notion of honour, and would be a lot of other people's too. Moody –'

'The old chimney sweep.'

'He was just scared. Scared and greedy – rather like me, in fact, but we'll come to that presently. Marriott struck a deal with him immediately. Moody would keep silence in return for gold.'

'But they did for him too – pushed him under a train.'

'I'm not sure about that,' said Bowman, stopping briefly on the hillside. 'I believe the whole business affected the old boy very badly . . . He might've jumped, you know.'

He stopped on the hill behind me, getting his breath. The heather was up to his waist; the cottage, our late prison, out of sight behind him.

'I thought I heard something,' he said.

There was a hidden roaring, as though of something under the ground.

'We're near the river,' I said, and we carried on.

'George Lee was different,' Bowman said, as we moved off again,' . . . would not be bought. At the same time, he couldn't quite bring himself to go to the coppers. There were days of . . . negotiations, I suppose you'd say, during which the Club carried on. They carried on using the saloon for a good week after the murder of Falconer, I believe. But I think that Lee eventually got wind of what had happened to Peters, and that decided him to go to the police. He made the mistake of *stating* his intention, though.'

'But before Lee could split,' I put in, 'Marriott sent Small David after him.'

'Small David and the horse,' said Bowman, 'Gilbert Sanderson's horse. The plan was Small David's, I believe. Marriott resisted it at first, but Small David worked his will. You know, I sometimes wonder whether he went to the lengths of removing his yellow socks, the better to impersonate Sanderson. That would have been a big sacrifice for him, I think. After it was done . . . well, the club was finished, of course. Moody gave out that he was simply retiring from his business. Marriott wrote to the railway to explain that as a result of an extraordinary series of misfortunes, the special carriage would no longer be required.'

'Where did Marriott find Small David?'

'It seems that Small David has a brother,' said Bowman, still stumbling along in my wake. 'You might want a go at hazarding his profession –'

'Villain,' I said.

'Lately released from gaol. He killed four men in a street fight in Newcastle and Marriott got him off the capital charge – sentence of ten years' hard instead of the drop. He argued that it was an accident – the same accident four times over. Didn't know his own strength, you know the line of contention . . .'

'Small David was paying Marriott a debt of honour then?'

'It would be nearer the mark, Jim,' Bowman gasped out, 'to say that Small David immediately started robbing Marriott blind. He has nearly all his money now, and the less money Marriott has, the less power he commands in the whole set-up – I miss my specs,' he ran on breathlessly. 'It's not so much being able to see that I miss as taking them off to rub on my sleeve.'

He was alongside me now and he was all in: sodden, and quite *white* in the face, for once.

'It's interesting about Small David's brother,' he panted. 'He lives in Middlesbrough, or somewhere that way. Small David sees him pretty regularly but he'll never speak of him – not that he speaks of anything very much, of course. The brother's a maniac from what I can gather. You might say that of Small David too, but he's quite careful. You can see that in the yellow socks.'

'How do you mean?'

'The way they're always kept pulled up.'

'Well, he wears garters. There's no mystery there.'

'But he tries to cover his traces. Takes a professional pride in –'

I held up my hand to silence him.

I was listening again to the rushing noise . . . and now distinct sounds of human voices came with it. We were within sight of what must have been the road: a smoother run of snow under the changing grey light.

'The river's down there,' I said, pointing forwards, 'and the railway line hard by.'

' . . . which won't be operating,' said Bowman, catching his breath.

The roaring was coming closer in the mysterious dawn, and the voices made real words. Then there came the sound of cartwheels too. It was Small David in the driving seat and I could make out, even in that explosion of snow, that his revolver was in his hand as he whipped on the frozen nag. He was alongside us in a moment, making mock of the three-mile stride we'd just completed.

'First ye're a traitor to *hum*,' he said, addressing Bowman and pointing the gun towards me, 'and then ye're after selling *us* doon the river. Well, it's awfy cauld, so here's somethin' to warm yer Sassenach guts –'

The gun had swung back to Bowman, and the bullet was loosed at that moment, but in the same instant I fancied that I saw a flash of Marriott in the old-fashioned boxer pose, and he and his son fell on Small David as he fired. Marriott and Small David fell to scrapping in the cart; I was right by the horse's head, and that beast looked at me while the vehicle rocked behind him, as if to say, 'Look what I have to put up with.'

Marriott was now standing in the cart, steadying himself like a man riding a raft over rapids, even though the cart did not move. His face was a wall of blood held up proudly to the floating snow (for the stuff was coming down again). He held the revolver in his hand, and Small David rolled in the well of the cart at his feet.

Marriott did not use words. He was beyond that; he spoke with the gun. He waved it to mean that Bowman and I should climb up; then once again to get Small David back in the driving seat. Even though he'd lost hold of the revolver, the Scotsman was in a better way than the lawyer. In fact, he looked just as he had done before the set-to, with his indestructible country suit, and his great calves smoothly enclosed in the yellow stockings.

He muttered a little to himself as he started us away, but did not seem too downhearted. He'd lost that particular round of the match, that was all. And we did not gallop; instead, the horse trotted along the track, as Marriott swabbed his wounds with a handkerchief, and Richie sat with head in hands, watching the bags belonging to the three rolling against his boots. There was more of blue in the Highland greyness now, and the tops of the hills were becoming clearer, just as though they had lately taken up their habitual place around us.

It was an alteration that passed for dawn on that day.

Bowman sat over opposite Small David; I in the same relation to Richie. We were going back the way we'd come the day before. Every turn of the wheels brought us nearer the railway station, and I was glad of that until I remembered that it would most likely not be working on such day, and that it was not manned in any case. When we'd been riding for ten minutes, the lawyer spoke directly to his son for the first time in my hearing.

'Richard,' he said, 'you have the key, I take it?'

Richie removed his gloves and began hunting through the pockets of his topcoat, but he was shaking his head even as he did so.

'I don't believe so,' he said.

'But I told you to bring it.'

Richie shook his head very sadly.

'Nothing was said about it, father.'

Marriot was hunting through his pockets as he drove the cart.

'It's all right,' he said presently. 'I have it here.'

As I wondered what the key was for, Small David turned about, and I saw that he was grinning, even though the gun was on him.

Chapter Twenty-eight

We drove on through that white world, until the stone house with the antlers on the walls floated into view, and then I understood the talk of a key. The snow had drifted against the house's walls, and I could not make out the door. It looked the part of a prison, and that is what it would become.

Marriott ordered Small David down from the carriage, and he passed him the key.

Small David approached the house with the gun on him. On the way, he kicked a heather bush, shaking off the snow and disclosing a small yellow flower, which set him cursing anew.

He found the door, and opened it while looking in my direction.

'Polis!' he called. 'Dree yer ain weird.'

That's what it sounded like at any rate.

The gun in the lawyer's hand wavered my way, and I climbed down.

Small David called again, 'Ye'll bide here too, bottle man,' and Bowman followed me through the door, which Small David clapped shut behind us without further speech. I could not hear the cart rattle away, for the stone of the walls was too thick.

'Had a moment of alarm back there,' said Bowman. I could hear him but not see him in that freezing tank, for there was no light at all.

'Came within half an ace of being shot.'

'It's one bloody turn-about after another,' I said, not over-kindly. 'Where are you?'

'I don't know,' he said.

There was a strong, sweet smell of old hay – the place was something between a barn and a house. I crouched down. The floor was made of stone flags, horribly cold to the touch. As the darkness began to resolve, I made out a low line of whiteness to my right.

'Well, I've found the door again,' I said, making towards it.

'Always a useful preliminary to making an exit,' said Bowman, and I could somehow tell from his voice that he was sitting down. He spoke in a level voice – he was even amused by the fix we were in. Before, he'd been as nervous as a cat. Now he was a new man.

'Are we "o'er the burran"?' I asked him.

'No, no, that was Small David's scheme. This is Marriott's doing.'

'What *is* "o'er the burran"?'

'A stream in Scots is a burn. There's one near the cottage. Beyond it is a black bog. He meant to put you in there.'

'I wouldn't have liked that,' I said.

'I hardly think that would have influenced him one way or another – and there'd have been a bullet in your head in any case.'

'But Marriott stopped him, not having the stomach for a murder.'

'He doesn't have the stomach for *another* murder. It's a point of pride with him that he can achieve his ends without further killing.'

'And now they're off.'

'The object is to go to France. Dieppe. Do you know it? And then on. They have a passage booked for tomorrow night.'

'But first they have to get to Inverness.'

'You have found the flaw in the scheme.'

'Why doesn't Marriott see it?'

'He's living on hope. He thinks there might yet be a train that way today.'

'I'm going to have a run at this door,' I said.

'I doubt you'll succeed.'

I charged, shoulder first. The door barely gave an inch.

I did it again; and again.

I sat down on the stone flags, nursing a sore shoulder.

'They build a good ruin, these Scots,' said Bowman.

We sat in silence for a space, listening out for any passing cart or pedestrian.

'How do the Club come to have the key to this place?' I said, after a few minutes of frozen silence.

Bowman sighed.

'I'm going to tell you everything I know,' he said, and as we listened out for any passing cart, he disclosed most of the remaining mysteries, the tale beginning December last in Saltburn, the model seaside town that lies between Whitby and Middlesbrough. As Bowman began, I pictured the place in winter: the sea wind blowing through the wide streets; the few people about looking like so many tin miniatures, positioned about the place to show how the amenities of the town worked.

Bowman and Peters had booked into the Station Hotel – being required by the limited expenses available to share a double room – in late November 1908. Bowman had then taken up residence in the hotel bar, made miserable by the weather, and the failure of some plans he'd entertained to turn novelist. On 1 December Peters had made his breakaway, darting off in all directions in search of artistic interpretations of railway scenes. He'd been very taken by Middlesbrough railway station, and by the passing loop-cum-marshalling yard at Stone Farm, which had lately been illuminated, creating many interesting effects of light and shade.

He made his first visit to Stone Farm on the 2nd and there met the lad porter, who'd tipped him off about the Club train. He'd shot back to Middlesbrough, but missed the Club.

That night, back at Saltburn, he'd explained to Bowman the fascination of the lamps at Stone Farm and mentioned his pursuit of the Travelling Club. He'd discovered that they would be coming through Saltburn the next morning – the 3rd – and woke early on that day to take the photograph, about which the Club were quite happy, for the row over the window lay ten minutes in the future and a couple of miles down the line.

Peters was a dead man after that, for Marriott's story would be that Falconer had never boarded the train at his customary boarding place of Saltburn or anywhere else. But the photograph – and the newspaper in Richie Marriott's hand – told a different story.

The lie Marriott attempted was not as wild as it seemed, for Theodore Falconer generally walked alone from his house to the station, which was all but deserted on that bitter day. The Club did not use the services of a porter, and were not troubled by ticket inspections; no steward served their tea or champagne – they helped themselves from the supplies laid on. It was quite possible for their journeyings to go unnoticed by any railway servant, or by anyone save the other Club members.

That afternoon Peters was robbed of his camera by two station loungers of Middlesbrough. They did not want the photographs the camera held; they wanted to get bread. Peters reported the theft and returned to Saltburn, where he told Bowman of the day's occurrences.

The next day – the 4th – was Peters's last. He left Saltburn at mid-morning with the expressed intention of returning to Stone Farm and its viewsome siding. At midday Small David – having been discovered in Middlesbrough or thereabouts by Marriott – pitched up at the hotel reception asking for Peters. He was directed to the hotel bar, and to Bowman. A conference occurred.

At first, Bowman had refused to give any information about Peters. But Small David had been given the first of his wages by Marriott, and he was in funds. Bowman was offered ten pounds for information. He turned it down. He was offered twenty, and they closed on that. A condition of the deal was that he would let Small David search the hotel room that Bowman shared with Peters. Small David's tale was that he wanted to make sure of the identity of Peters with a certain party to whom he owed money.

'I blame Wimbledon,' said Bowman in the gloom of the stone tank. 'The wife had seen photographs of new villas there in some picture paper. Well, she had to have one, would not let up on the subject. I'd say, "What's wrong with the present place?" We were in East London at the time, nicely situated for walks in Victoria Park. Yes, the Great Eastern Railway ran along the bottom of the garden, but we had five shillings a week off the rent on that account. "And I'm a railway journalist," I would remind her, "so it's all grist to my mill."'

After an interval of silence, Bowman continued, 'The money meant we could make the down payment on the new house in Lumley Road.'

Another pause.

'It is not near the railway line.'

I scrambled to my feet. The floor was too cold to sit on.

'I walked for hours about Saltburn when Small David had left the hotel,' Bowman was saying.

'Conscience,' I said.

'I was on the lookout for a pub.'

'They don't run to 'em there,' I broke in. 'The place is built on temperance lines.'

'I suspected some such infernal lunacy. I went back to the hotel and drank off half a bottle of whisky while staring out to sea.'

'You weren't to know they meant to harm Peters.'

'If you want to tell a man he's come into money,' said Bowman, 'then you don't need a fellow the size of Small David to do it.'

A long beat of silence.

'Peters was delayed setting off for Stone Farm that morning,' Bowman went on. 'He'd been buying film in Saltburn. He rode on the same 'up' train as Small David, who began talking to him; told him there was something of interest in the woods beyond the station. Small David went for the camera. Well, that camera was everything to Peters, so he fought back.'

Silence for a space, before Bowman added, 'He was killed as a consequence. Strangled, if you ask me; and then strung up to cover the traces. A clever notion, you'd have to agree. Small David's quite cute, you know. For example, he gave over the money to me right in front of the steward of the bar, making a big show of what he was about, and of course I was lost from then on: aider and abettor, accessory after the fact, accomplice – every damn bad thing beginning with A. If they were discovered, I was discovered.'

The rest of the tale came to me quickly across the few feet of darkness that separated us.

'Falconer's body was recovered from lineside – it ended in a blast furnace somehow,' said Bowman. 'Lee was done a little while later.'

Not many days after *that*, the Scot had pitched up outside the offices of *The Railway Rover* and taken Bowman to the Highland cottage, our late prison. Marriott had taken the place not so much to avoid the police as to avoid *questions*. It seemed he had the idea that, while the Middlesbrough railway police were not pursuing the matter, the town police might well do.

In the cottage, Small David had put the frighteners on Bowman, so as to make him see the sense of walking carefully. He had then been permitted to return to Wimbledon and Fleet Street, and to the pubs of both districts.

The two Marriotts stayed mainly in the Highland cottage; Small David came and went. He kept a place in Middlesbrough, where he was known in all the low places. Marriott had opened a banking account in Helmsdale, and Small David would accompany him there once a month so that he could receive the money directly it was withdrawn. He had already received most of Marriott's fortune for his part in the killing of Lee, for that had been dangerous work.

The first special edition on the North Eastern Railway having been abandoned, it had been Bowman's suggestion that *The Railway Rover* try again. Like Marriott, he had a kink that made him always return to the matter of the murder. He had been through Stone Farm on the train many times before the occasion of our meeting, horribly fascinated by the place, but never having the brass neck to get down and look about.

'That was all terrible enough,' said Bowman from his own part of the darkness, 'but it wasn't until I met you that matters began to really disintegrate.'

'Don't mention it, mate,' I said, moving towards the strip of light at the bottom of the door.

I took a flying kick at the door; then another.

Nothing happened, and the first inklings of a thirst were on me. I was hungry too, but that did not signify.

How long could a man survive without water?

Chapter Twenty-nine

'Small David would happily have shot you in your own house, your place of work, anywhere' said Bowman. 'He's very free and easy like that, you know. It was Marriott that wanted you brought up here.'

A beat of silence as I sized up the door.

'He did it to save you from Small David.'

'Well, he has a funny way of saving people,' I said, and I ran at the door again.

'I suppose he thinks he's given us a sporting chance,' said Bowman.

'The only thing for it,' I said, 'is to dig underneath.'

'To think that we're here just because a man opened a window,' said Bowman.

I moved towards the line of white light, and began feeling about for any loose stone that might serve as a tool. Bowman gave a hand. There was no loose stone, but I found the edge of the giant flagstone placed at the foot of the door. Its edge was about level with the edge of the door, and I began trying to work away the earth around it, but as this was frozen solid, it was no easy job. I could only chip away with my finger ends. There wasn't room for Bowman to help, so he sat back against the wall.

The stone was fast; I was scraping away only a few crumbs of mud at a time; and even if I got it out, I'd only have six inches of daylight under the door. A crawling space would need to be three times that.

Bowman's voice came out of the darkness.

'I could use a drink, you know.'

I worked on.

'Not *that* sort of drink,' Bowman ran on. 'If we get out of this fix, I mean to stop that lark for good and all.'

I would have to stop digging shortly; it was agony to touch the cold stone, and when I pressed my fingers to my cheek they trailed the fast-drying wetness of blood.

Bowman was saying, 'I think I'll go back to writing "Whiffs", if anybody will have it. Simple facts, simply put over. I enjoyed that.'

I pulled at the stone.

'"How does an engine re-water?"'

I pulled again at the stone and it gave slightly.

'"The secret of a travelling lavatory."'

I could prise it up a little way now . . . But I must have a rest.

'"Why do locomotives have two whistles?"'

I rolled away from the doorway.

'Any joy?' said Bowman.

'I'll go at it again in a minute,' I said, breathing hard and flexing my hands.

'Want me to try?'

I shook my head, not realising that he couldn't see me. It came to me then that Bowman must be in a double darkness, having lost his specs.

'It'll be Christmas soon,' he said.

'Six days,' I said.

'Jesus was born in a manger,' said Bowman. 'Did you ever hear of anybody dying in one?'

'I expect there've been plenty,' I said. Then: 'I've no bloody gloves.'

'Here,' said Bowman, 'take mine. I'm holding them out before me just now.'

I found his hands, and I found his gloves.

I went back to the scraping and chipping around the stone with a will.

'It's coming up,' I said, after a few more minutes.

I pulled at the stone and it rose up. I could feel the size of it: about two foot by two foot. I worked it away from the door and felt the space I'd created: an area of cold snow and cold air. I'd done nothing but create a draught. I pressed down, and for the first time felt it was all up with me, for there was another wide, smooth stone underneath, and no room for further digging. I rolled away from the door again.

'I've a powerful thirst,' said Bowman.

I put my hand in my pocket, and there was the orange I'd bought outside King's Cross. It had been through a lot. I took off the gloves, and peeled it with numb fingers, and it seemed to give a little warmth as well as the promise of food and drink. As I peeled it, two drops of its juice landed on the palm of my hand and, when licked, they weren't there, which seemed a disaster.

'I have an orange here,' I said into the darkness. 'There are ten segments – five apiece.'

I reached out once again, meeting Bowman's hand.

'That's kind of you, Jim,' he said.

'I'll tell you what – it's a good job there weren't eleven,' I said.

The orange gave the most beautiful drink ever supplied to anyone; but it was a small drink.

'I've given up with the door for now,' I said presently. 'Let's have another listening go.'

'Just as you like,' said Bowman.

I could half-see him moving about four feet away – his body made a deeper darkness. There came no sounds. After what might have been half an hour, might have been three hours, I divided up the orange peel and gave half to Bowman.

After another unknown time, Bowman said, 'It was pretty foolish of you to follow me up from London, you know.'

'I was bored in my work.'

Silence.

'You acted your part well,' I said. 'I kept thinking you might be a bit – fly, but I remembered that at Stone Farm you'd volunteered a good deal of information – told me that Peters had had his camera stolen, and so on.'

'I told you only what I thought you'd eventually discover for yourself.'

'Yes, I thought that later,' I said.

'I wouldn't say you'd been quite as stupid as me over the whole business,' said Bowman.

'Thanks for saying so, mate,' I said.

Silence again.

'I flattered the stationmaster at Stone Farm – the man Crystal. I thought: if I keep in with him, he'll tell me how the investigation proceeds . . . How's your wife?' Bowman added, suddenly. 'How do you get along with her, I mean?'

'Well, she's my lifeblood, mate.'

'A notch above you socially?'

'Aspires to be,' I said.' . . . and is in fact.'

'That supper on the train,' he said after a while, 'it was good; cheap, too.'

Another long silence, and he said through chattering teeth, '*Marriott* thought he was a cut above. It's all nonsense about the sudden loss of temper if you ask me. Marriott felt he had the right to crown the man.'

'But they were both toffs really,' I said.

'Well, it's all relative,' said Bowman, who after a space added, 'It's all r-r-r-relatives,' but he could hardly get the words out for shivering.

Silence again. My hands and feet hurt with an almost burning pain. I tried to tell myself that it was only cold; that we were indoors after all, but it bothered me that I could not stop my arms from shaking. A man ought to be able to command his own arms. I thought again of little Harry, in the middle of the dusty road on a day of heat. I loved the boy, and I nodded to myself at the thought.

I found, a few minutes later, that I was still nodding. The cold was making an imbecile of me. This was the worst way of killing: to lock a man in a room without food or water. It was the method a weak man would choose. I might have dreamt, then. At any rate, I saw in my mind's eye a dark herd of deer coming down a dark hillside. The antlers made them like a moving forest, and the notion slowly struck me that they were coming towards me.

'We would like our property back,' said the leader, and he spoke to me as the governor of the house with the antlers on the walls.

'But you already have them,' I said, and I pulled up sharp at the knowledge that I had spoken the words out loud. My legs were quaking now, along with my arms. My whole body was going away from me. I wanted to stand, to test my limbs in that position, but I couldn't be *bothered* to stand, couldn't be bothered to live.

'Hello there,' I said, while flat on my back.

No reply.

I tried 'Steve.'

No answer. I rolled upright, and all my body was saying, 'No, no, time has stopped, don't try and start it again.'

I could not hear Bowman. He had disappeared into the darkness. I dragged myself about the stone hut like a man on a wild sea. Twice I slammed into the walls, gashing my head each time. I rolled back towards the middle. I wanted to vomit, but my headache wouldn't allow it. I was slowly upended by the constant lurching, as it appeared, of the floor, and I found that I had fallen on a soft mass.

My hands were on Bowman's face, but it was far away. It ought, from memory, to have been red and hot, but it was as cold as the stone under my boots.

Chapter Thirty

I slapped the face twice, hard. I was trying to make it red again: the face red and the nose brighter red still – that was the correct order of things with Bowman.

There was a rattle at the door, which rose and fell.

The cold had become an illness with me: it was dragging me to the place where Bowman was – some great white land further north than anywhere.

And I needed water.

The rattle at the door again. Was I making that rattle or was there another person in all this? That I could not credit; I was finished with *people*. The door was coming towards me, and the light lifting with it. The door was opening, but caught on the stone I'd lifted.

'Who's there?' I called, in a weird voice.

'Ah've come tae dae ye.'

The light had brought Small David with it.

'Where's Marriott?' I called.

He was shaking the door, trying to get it past the upraised flag.

'Hum? Deed.'

It was his favourite word.

'Dead?'

'Aye, kulled.'

'Who killed him?'

'Husself.'

Small David was now revealed in the open doorway – the full width of the man. Small particles of snow flew about behind him, as though playing a game, and beyond them lay all the white, beautiful Highlands. The revolver was in his hand. He stepped forwards and fired, and I thought: that sound was pretty loud, and then it struck me that I was enjoying the luxury of hearing the sound die away. I was still alive, and the bullet had given life, not taken it away, for the soft mass underneath my hands was rolling again. Bowman raised himself up quickly and without a word. But Small David, over by the doorway – the snowlight was flowing in over the top of him, for he was down on the ground. The small hole I'd dug had been enough to trip him, and now it was his turn to scrabble on that stone floor as he searched for the gun he'd dropped.

I stood, still shaking, and thinking: what do you do with a man when he's down? Why, you kick him, and I knew I could give a kick for all the queer feeling in me. His big brown head was football-like, and I got him squarely on the temple. He went down further and I was across the floor, spider-like, searching for the revolver.

Bowman lurched towards the doorway.

He turned there, and said, in a dazed sort of voice, 'That's the second time today I've come within an ace of dying.'

I couldn't find the gun; I gave it up. Small David was breathing heavily on the stone floor like a man sleeping off drink.

'Is it the same day, though?' I said to Bowman, as once more we half-walked, half-fell down the hillside towards river and railway line. The light was changing: a mysterious smokiness was brewing over the white-covered fields, but whether it was increasing or decreasing, I could not have said. Small particles of snow flew about us – just the odd one or two, racing each other or circling in a dance.

We walked as before, moving forward and down with each stride, looking back fearfully to the house that had held us. But there was no sign of Small David.

'I might have put his lights out for good,' I said.

'Let me get alongside you,' said Bowman. 'I can't see my way.'

The walking had warmed me somewhat, and I kept scooping up snow from the heather tops as we walked, drinking the stuff. That stopped me thinking of water while giving no satisfaction. I took Bowman's arm. He was shaking very violently with cold, and I thought his face was becoming the same colour as his eyes: a pale blue. I fumbled the gloves back to him as we pressed on.

'Wear these, and you'll be able to pick up snow,' I said.

'What time is it?' I asked, and he held up his watch for me to see.

It was coming up to five o'clock, which was, perhaps, no more surprising than any other time. It must be five in the evening; we had passed the entire day – a full twelve hours – in the deer shack. I looked down and saw a railway signal, with a small gangers' hut nearby.

'We've struck the line,' I said.

But the track was invisible under the snow, so that the signal, which was giving the all-clear to nothing, looked a very ridiculous article. In both directions, the line curved away into rolling whiteness.

Bowman stood at my side, breathing steam; and then I saw to my left, beyond him, what seemed to be snow whirling upwards – snow making a ghost of itself, and rising for a haunting.

Instead, it was an engine.

'See that, Steve?' I said, but the engine was in earshot now.

It was doing its beautiful work in a world of whiteness: white steam, white snow. It ran over tracks only dusted with snow, and was now, as we watched, running at the thicker stuff. The soft crash of the snow plough was almost silent, and then the plough ran on, through the snow, looking for a marvellously exciting few seconds like a boat moving through rough water. But then the snow checked it, and it began to reverse, ready for the next go.

We were stumbling down towards it now.

'It's the first time I've seen a proper snow plough at work,' I said to Bowman, who gasped out, 'I'm thrilled for you, Jim.'

I had before only seen the small wooden ploughs attached to the buffer bars of ordinary engines. This engine – of some Highland make unknown to me – pushed a snow plough *vehicle*: a hollow steel wedge on wheels, a great metal arrowhead – and there was a man inside, I saw now, for he was leaning out of it and waving, calling on the engine driver and fireman for another try. That man was part lookout, part team captain, for what he gave was *encouragement*.

I was moving ahead of Bowman now.

'Push on!' I called back to him. 'I want to be up there for the next run. If they break through, we'll be clear away from that Scots bastard!'

The driver and fireman first noticed our approach; then the caller-on who rode in the plough spied us.

'We need to come up!' I called, wading on through the snowy heather.

We approached the beating warmth of the engine, and driver and fireman stepped away for us to climb up, and just gawped at us for a while. The man in the plough was hanging out of his cab, monkey-like, watching us. Bowman warmed himself by the open fire door, and then he turned about, and said, 'I need to sit down.'

The driver pointed to the sandbox, where Bowman perched. He still looked very seedy.

'There's a lunatic on our tail,' I said to the driver, while glancing over his shoulder to the darkening hill beyond.

But he didn't seem to take what I said.

'Where are you *for*?' he asked, just as though we were ordinary passengers

'We want to connect for Inverness,' I said. 'Do you reckon that's on? Tonight, I mean?'

'Don't ask me,' he said. 'Our job's to break through to Helmsdale.'

'Is it drifted all the way?'

He shook his head.

'We're at the worst of it now. Couple more goes and we should be through.'

He was a small, pale bloke, and he seemed to speak without force, and then the reason came to me: he was not Scots. He spoke with an English accent of no particular sort. Also, he seemed in a baddish temper. At first I thought this must be on account of our arrival, but he now turned and addressed his fireman, saying, 'Front damper's closed now, is it?'

If you left the front damper open while charging at snow – why, you'd put the bloody fire out. The fireman was not up to snuff, and the driver was out with him.

The snow plough man was calling to us from up front. *He* was Scots all right, to the point where I couldn't make out a word he said, but his meaning was clear enough. We were to get on with it.

The driver put on full back gear, and we reversed a little further; the fireman was labouring away all the time, swinging with his shovel between tender and fire door like a clock mechanism. A good thick layer of coal was needed, for each charge would suck a great hole in the fire. By the paraffin lamp that hung behind the gauge glass, I saw that we had our 220 lbs of steam pressure. The light was going fast, and it was already too gloomy to make out the height of the snow wall a hundred yards off that we were about to charge at.

The driver held on to the cabside; I gripped the mighty wheel of the hand brake, and motioned Bowman to do the same. The driver gave a tug on the regulator and we began to steal away, then there came a shout from the front man; the driver pulled harder, and we began to fly. We swayed backwards with the force of the speed. I tried to predict the moment of impact, but the smash came a couple of seconds later than I bargained for.

We were all thrown forwards, and we all checked the movement of our bodies, but the fireman flew on, and smacked into the fire-hole door, which he had (luckily for him or he'd have been clean through it) closed before the charge. He was down on the cab floor. I tried to give him a hand up, but he wouldn't have it. He sat bolt upright in the filthy cold dust and said, 'I've cracked my arm.'

I knew it was true, for he was dead white. The driver sat him on the sandbox that Bowman had lately occupied.

'Want me to take a look?' said the driver. He was not overly sympathetic.

The fireman shook his head. 'I can feel the bone – it's out. I don't want to see it.'

All the horror was under the sleeve, and that's where he wanted to leave it for the present. He just sat tight holding his right arm with his left.

'I can fire an engine,' I said to the driver.

He looked from me to Bowman, who said, 'And I can *write* about it, if that's any use.'

He gave a little grin, and tried to push his specs up his nose, only they weren't there. He'd had a couple of secret swigs from the driver's tea bottle, I'd noticed, and some of his high colour was now returned.

What the driver made of the pair of us, I couldn't have guessed, but I tried to put his mind at rest by taking up the shovel and opening the firehole door. The fire was thin at the middle, and the top left.

I turned and put the shovel into the coal, and took a long breath.

Then I was into it: the clockwork motion at twice the rate of the other fellow. The coal was flying off in a flat line straight to the points needed.

I heard the driver say something that might have been: 'All right then.'

At any rate, the whole man-machine started working around me. The driver looked ahead to the plough man; he then put on full reverse and took us backwards as I carried on shovelling.

I said, 'Shall we take a longer run this time, mate?' and he didn't answer but kept us rolling back fifty yards beyond the last distance.

As we came to rest prior to the charge, I was at the injector, operating the two valves to bring water into the boiler. I just wanted to be 'doing', but the driver said, 'Don't carry the water so high,' so I checked the flow. Being a little rusty, I had to think for a while about why he'd said that, but it came to me after a couple of seconds that each run at the snow made a rolling wave of water in the boiler. If the water slopped too high, it would carry over into the cylinders, the engine would prime and we'd be done for.

Beyond the driver's shoulder, the snow was increasing; the shadows were moving and the Highland ghosts were walking again. I looked at the fire, which was good and even, then back at the heather, where a black shape was flowing over the hillside. Could it be deer? The driver was leaning out, signalling to the bloke in the plough. The shadow on the hillside was not flowing as I had thought; it was moving in a rocking motion – on two legs only.

The driver was engaging forward gear.

'All set?' he said.

He was looking hard at the crocked fireman, who was now braced on the sandbox with his one good hand grasping the cab-side hard. It was a sight too late, but he'd learnt his lesson.

I stepped two paces from the fire to look out of the cab as the driver laid his hand on the regulator. Instead of looking forwards at the plough, I looked backwards. Small David was on the snow-dusted track, thirty yards behind. He walked with arm outstretched, as if that arm was a battering ram to clear a way through the snow-filled air. I pulled myself in and the first shot came as our acceleration began. Whether anyone besides myself noticed that first one over the roar of the engine noise . . . well, I do not believe they did. As we gathered speed, I moved again to the cabside.

'Keep still, would you?' said the driver.

Another shot came, followed directly by what sounded like a third. Or was it the first bullet striking the engine? When would we hit the snow? I pulled myself in. Had we made such an easy job of cutting through it that I had failed to even –

The smash came, and the great backward bounce – which just kept on. The wave of snow was made on both sides. We were enclosed in white walls, and I did not dare breathe as those walls held. We were slowing all the while, but still the snow was going up.

After ten seconds, the walls did begin to droop, though, and we were about at a stand as I looked out again through the low rolling snow and watched Small David running through the gloaming with arm still outstretched, just as though that gun of his was something we had dropped, and that he meant to return to us.

I pulled myself in and looked at Bowman. He was rocking forwards as the engine slowed.

'We're not in the clear yet,' I said.

But as I looked at Bowman he began to rock the other way.

'What?' I believe I said. Or maybe I just gave a gasp, for it seemed to me that our engine was now fairly floating – all thirty-odd tons of it.

'We're through?' I said to the driver.

He nodded, as much to himself as to me.

PART FOUR

Christmas

Chapter Thirty-one

That engine leaked steam like a bastard, not least because of the badly fitting smokebox door, as the driver told me under questioning. I asked him its class, and he said, 'E Class', 'D Class' or, for all I knew, '*declassed*'. I didn't like to ask again, for he seemed to find speech rather a strain. The good thing was that he didn't ask too many questions, or in fact any. I told him I was a detective on a case, but whether he *took* that, I don't know. I was certain, though, that he was not aware of having been fired on; nor was any man in that cab. They'd have mentioned it, after all, if they *had* noticed.

I felt sorry for them in a way, for I knew the danger I'd been in, and was able to weigh the value of freedom and life, and the best sort of life at that: the engine-driving life.

We made good running after the snow block and pulled into Helmsdale twenty minutes after. A train there was fairly itching to get to Inverness, having been kept back by the weather all day, and we were in luck again at the Highland capital, being just in time for the east-coast sleeper, which would take me directly to York and Bowman on to London, but we were not quite so pressed that I couldn't go to the telegraph office in the station, and wire the wife to say I'd be back next day. The telegram cost two and four – which was a bit of an eye-opener.

We happened to board the train in the restaurant car, and Bowman said we deserved some proper grub. I had a good sluice-down in the WC, but we were no doubt the filthiest pair that ever sat down to a railway dinner, and a Christmas railway dinner at that. Bowman couldn't read the menu, so I read it out to him – turkey and all the extras was practically forced on you.

The wine list came separately, and Bowman said, 'Jim, when I was lying in that damned barn, I said I'd never touch spirituous liquor again, didn't I?'

'Aye,' I said.

'Did you believe me?'

'You sounded as if you meant it,' I said.

'You *did* believe me, then?'

'Yes.'

'You were quite wrong to do that,' he said, and he passed me the wine list.

As I poured out the wine he'd asked for, he gave a grin, saying, 'Up to the top of the church windows!' His face was back to its usual colour, but perhaps, looking at his reflection in the window, he felt that it needed a little touching up here and there. He then clinked glasses with me when the wine was poured, which he had never done when all those gallons had gone down at Stone Farm and in Fleet Street, and which I think is a foreign habit that they've picked up in London. He continued in good spirits throughout the first two of the three courses we put away, his observations coming with a twinkle rather than the world-weary, sighing tone I'd been used to, whereas my own mood was now a dangerous light-headedness rather than happiness. I'd been jerked out of my tedious groove by the whole business, but jerked out of my *income* as well. Once I'd paid my half of the present supper bill, I would have next to no money – perhaps a quid or so, I dared not look to see.

And in about ten hours' time I would walk into the York police office and be given the boot, for I had belted Shillito and I had *not* settled the matter of the Travelling Club. I kept returning in imagination to the day I was stood down last from the Lancashire and Yorkshire Railway. There'd been a bit of money owed, and I'd been called into the wages cabin alone to receive it. That was the worst bit – to receive my wages alone, and at an odd time, whereas normally there would be such a press of cheerful, shouting blokes in that office.

Then again, though, it was as if another man was in all that bother. I could not quite believe it was me, for I had come out of my Scottish adventure with a whole skin, and if a fellow is spared he is spared for a reason, isn't he?

At first, the two of us had plunged into technicalities. Marriott, according to Bowman, had to be lying dead somewhere between the cottage and the railway line. He thought it doubtful that Small David would go to the bother of hiding the body; it would suit him for it to be found, if it really had been a suicide.

'But is he telling the truth about that?' I asked.

'Why would he lie?' Bowman replied.

'Because he himself might have killed him.'

'If he had done, I don't think he'd bother to lie about it,' said Bowman, with glass raised. 'Small David's a man of mixed character morally, in that, if you get to know him at all, he's quite honest about the murders he's done. Besides, Marriott was his source of income.'

'But he's *had* all of Marriott's bread. This might just have been the right time to do him.'

Bowman shook his head.

'I think the matter is concluded as far as Small David is concerned. He's done his job and had his wages.'

Bowman then told me a little more about Marriott's decline.

He'd never been any great shakes as a brief. He'd started in London chambers, but left after a row and moved to the North for a quiet life. His office in Middlesbrough he shared with Richie, but it was no place for a barrister. There wasn't even an Assize Court in the town. Instead, he would appear at the Quarter Sessions doing small, something-or-nothing pleadings. He struck everyone as a queer sort: a snob, and nervous as a cat – flashing into rage at nothing – but always beautifully turned out.

'And what *about* the boy?' I asked. 'What's become of Richie, do you reckon?'

Bowman shrugged.

'He might still win through to France. Small David won't stop him – quite the contrary. He likes the kid . . . Would *you* stop him making away after all he's been through?'

And it was that particular question that put the crimp in.

Bowman turned to gaze through the window, playing with his wine glass, and seeing nothing. It was a sad do that his eyes, given the chance of acting without the aid of glasses, were not able to rise to the challenge. He saw me eyeing him, and brushed his fingers along his funny nose. He sighed, for the first time in a while.

After an interval of silence, another question came to me: 'Do you know Small David's name?'

'Surname's Briggs,' said Bowman. 'I know that much.'

The other diners left the dining car; the train rattled on through silent, white-dusted stations, most crammed with empty baggage wagons, but that's how it always is on a night train: a feeling of excitement followed in short order by one of loneliness.

'Do you know what that place is called?' he said. 'The hill on which the deer house stands, I mean?'

'They don't run to place-names up there, do they?'

'Fairy Hillocks,' said Bowman.

'It is wrongly named.'

'But that's what you put on a letter. I wrote to them the day after meeting you, and I suppose the letter's still there somewhere, lying abandoned with all the other papers.'

It was a piece of evidence – that's what he was getting at.

He sighed again.

The waiter, who had sat down at one of the empty tables, was watching us. He had not cleared the table alongside us, and a knife jingled against a glass there. The waiter would not interfere; he was banking on the noise driving us round the bend, and off to our beds.

'I'm glad of my time there in a way,' said Bowman. 'It's put me to rights in a number of ways.'

If he wanted me to ask what *sorts* of ways, I would not do so, for I was trying to compose my own thoughts.

'I find I have a taste again for writing,' said Bowman, 'and I mean the proper stuff, or at least the longer stuff. I might go back to my novel, or try my hand at another.'

Silence except for the glass and the knife.

'It was an African adventure,' said Bowman. 'Rather in the Rider Haggard line.'

Another pause.

'It came like winking – I'm sure I'll be able to place it if I give

214

another push.'

'Have you been to Africa?' I said

'Not *literally*,' said Bowman, turning to the window once again. He rubbed his eyes, as if trying to start them working. 'One place I have been is Scotland, so perhaps I'll get up a Highland story.'

The waiter was approaching, having given up on the knife and the glass.

'An advantage of novel-writing,' said Bowman, 'is that it can be carried on anywhere – in any circumstances, I mean.'

'I must write up a report,' I began, 'and of course –'

The waiter was presenting the bill to Bowman, who squinted at it for a while.

'I'll stand you this,' he said, taking out his pocket book.

'I won't hear of it,' I said. 'How much?'

'The total is one pound nineteen shillings.'

I took out my pocket book with a feeling of fear. But before I put my hand into it, the waiter had been paid by Bowman and had left – which queered things still further between my companion and me.

'You were saying about your report?' said Bowman.

I sat back.

'Small David cannot be on this train, can he?'

Bowman frowned. I did not wait for his answer, but stood up, saying, 'I mean to go and take a look.'

'But you have no ticket, Jim. Let me buy you a sleeping berth.'

Evidently, Bowman had gone north with plenty of gold about him, which was only sensible in the circumstances.

'The warrant card will just have to serve,' I said. 'You turn in now.'

I stood up. Bowman did the same, and we shook hands.

'You must make out your report, Jim,' he said. 'I will answer for anything I've done wrong, which is a good deal, I know.'

I almost walked to York, considering that I was back and forth along the dark corridors of that train many times before arrival. Small David was not aboard, as far as I could tell with most of the compartment blinds drawn down. He could not have been – he'd have had to have ridden the slow plough with us in order to make the connection for Inverness at Helmsdale.

Chapter Thirty-two

I stepped down at York feeling light as a feather from want of sleep. I was one of only four to climb down there. It was six o'clock, and the station was coming to life in a series of crashes, and in the barking of the exhaust on the first passenger train of the day for Hull, which was pulling away from Platform Thirteen. I stood on Platform Four. A cold wind was sweeping along under the roof, and I could not contemplate removing my hands from my coat pocket.

I walked towards the door of the police office. It ought to be open by now. The Chief was often the first man in, filling the place with the sour smell of his cigar smoke as he read the night's telegrams and the first of the post. But it was locked, and a notice was pasted to the door glass: 'Monday 20 December. Closed. Police training day. Passengers seeking urgent assistance please find Stationmaster's Office by the booking hall.'

I had forgotten this was a training day.

In fact, training days were a species of holiday and generally ended in the bar of the Railway Institute. There were sometimes physical jerks directed by the Chief, sometimes lectures on dry subjects such as 'effecting arrest' or 'railway trespass'. The Chief was required to lay them on, but he didn't really hold with them, and wouldn't mind if you missed one, providing the cause was anything other than bone idleness.

I looked at the notice again. It annoyed me that anything as normal as a training day should be allowed to go on after all that I'd been through. Still, at least I couldn't be stood down on a training day.

I walked on. It was too early to go back to Thorpe-on-Ouse. I'd only wake the wife and Harry, and the boy needed his sleep. I picked up a *Yorkshire Post* at the bookstall and the fat man who ran it said, 'First one away today, mate.'

On the front page, I read 'Leap from an Omnibus' and 'Hull Soldier's Bad Behaviour'. Nothing had happened, but the paper had to come out all the same.

I walked out of the station, and saw that the snow had gone, leaving only the ancient city of York and a little rain. I went into town, and breakfasted at the Working Men's Café by the river at King's Staith. It was the cheapest breakfast going: fried egg, two rashers, tea or coffee and bread and butter all in for a bob. All of yesterday's Yorkshire papers were lying about on the tables, and it turned out that nothing had happened *yesterday* either, except that the snow had been expected to stop, which it obviously had done. It would apparently be returning, however.

I came out of the café and watched the river blokes take a load of coal off a barge until they began to shoot me queer looks, at which I went off into the middle of town.

Should I make a report on my investigation? Bowman wanted me to drop it. He felt he was owed this, having rescued me from the house at Fairy Hillocks. But I would at the least be required to give an account of where I'd been if I wanted to keep my job.

I pushed on. The shop blinds were rolling up, like the weary opening of a person's eyes on a day of cold. The narrow streets were full of the delivery drays, and the shouts of the early morning men. In St Helen's Square, a great consignment of Christmas trees rested against the front of the Mansion House.

I *would* be willing to put the thing on ice, but for Small David. There were more murders left in him, and that was a certainty. He had to be run in.

I looked up. I had found my way to Brown's, the toyshop that lay just off St Helen's Square. I walked through the door and the ceiling seemed to be sagging, but it was only the hundreds of paper chains stretched across. I turned and saw a great multi-coloured house. It had been built from Empire Bricks. All around it were boxes of same, and some of the smaller ones contained only half a dozen bricks, but I didn't care to look at the price ticket even on these. Beyond the books were dolls – and they were all lying down, so that their part of the shop looked like a mortuary. Then came the narrow spiral staircase that led up to more toys. This was the feature of Brown's: it was helter-skelter-like, almost a toy itself, and it was now all wrapped in green tinsel. I climbed it, feeling an ass at having to turn so many times in order to go up such a little way.

The second floor of Brown's seemed at first one great parade ground of miniature soldiers. A man moved along fast by the far wall – he looked almost guilty at being full-sized. I walked on and the soldiers gave way to trains. The clockwork engines were in the North Eastern style – well, they were painted green at any rate. Small, leaden railway officials stood among them. The engines had keys in their sides, and some were much smaller than the key that operated them, and looked ridiculous as a result. I put my hand on the smallest engine that was not dwarfed by its key, and looked at the price: seven and six. Many a York citizen kept house for a week on that. I took out my pocket book and fished out one ten-bob note. I knew it was the last, but I still had some silver in my pocket and that might make another ten bob.

I paid for the engine, and then walked to Britton's in Gillygate. I stood under the sign looking in the window for a while. The sign read: 'Britton: Coats, Skirts, Furs', and it worried me that the gloves in the window were only draped about to offset the articles mentioned on the sign, and were not really of any account in themselves. But only the gloves had prices in shillings rather than pounds. Besides, the wife had especially mentioned that she wanted a new pair. I went inside and asked the assistant about one particular pair, and they were ten bob exactly. I pulled all the loose change out of various pockets, and it turned out I had enough, although I coloured up in the process of bringing it to hand.

'I'm sure the lady will enjoy them, sir,' said the assistant, and I thought there was something a bit off in that 'sir'. A gentleman ought not to buy his wife a present out of loose change.

For some reason, when the gloves were all wrapped up and ready to be taken away, I asked the assistant, 'What are they made of, by the way?'

'Deerskin, sir.'

Well, I couldn't take them. It was seeing that herd in the Highlands that had done it; and then dreaming about them. I had to take a calfskin pair, which cost another bob again.

I walked back to the station, picked the Humber off the bicycle stand and rode to the edge of York, and then past the six wide fields to Thorpe-on-Ouse. As I walked along the garden path, I heard the wife typing in the parlour, and so left the gloves in their parcel in the saddlebag while pocketing the clockwork engine. I opened the front door and the wife's greeting rang out. She was happy. She'd got the job, I was certain of it. The two telegrams I'd sent were on the mantelpiece, together with some Christmas cards, and a letter in an envelope addressed to the wife – there was nothing from John Ellerton at the Sowerby Bridge shed.

We kissed, and the wife, looking at my sodden suit, said, 'It's rained just in time for Christmas' – adding, 'Mrs Gregory Gresham has written to confirm the appointment.'

'Very good,' I said. 'How's Harry?'

'Much better. He's gone back to school.'

It was all very good, but again I felt strongly my own unimportance. I produced the little engine from my pocket.

'He'll adore that,' said the wife. 'He'll think he's got the moon.'

He would have a few other things besides, but not much: a top, a ball, a bag of chocolates. We walked through to the kitchen now, where a pot of tea was on the go. A seed cake stood on the table in brown paper.

'That looks an expensive item,' I said.

'The Archbishop's man brought it,' said the wife.

The Archbishop of York had his palace at Thorpe-on-Ouse. At Christmas, one of his servants went around the village houses in a coach delivering cakes and sweetmeats cooked in the Palace kitchens. Given that we didn't have any money to speak of, this felt a little too much like receiving charity.

'You don't mind taking it?' I asked the wife.

'I like the Archbishop,' she said.

'Why? You wouldn't have charity from any other sort of gentry.'

'The Archbishop is different.'

'How come?'

'Because he's religious . . . well, sort of.'

She grinned at me. I liked that; she looked smaller when she grinned.

'Did you trace out any murderers in Scotland?'

'Several,' I said.

'But did you find who'd killed the men in the picture?'

'Yes.'

'Then you will have your promotion . . .'

'There are complications,' I said.

'Such as?'

'None of the guilty men has yet been taken into custody, for one.'

'Where are they then?'

I shrugged.

'They're all over the shop.'

She looked at me narrowly.

'But you made progress?'

'Yes. Do you want the detail of it?'

'No,' she said, walking over to the larder and pulling back the thin curtain that hung there.

'I've been quite housewifely over the past two days,' she said.

There were some new items in the larder: in pride of place were about a dozen plums and four tins of pineapple rings. The wife explained that the plums were all for Harry. A vegetarian diet was recommended for a weak chest. Everything that cost *money* was recommended for it

'As for the pineapple,' said the wife, 'I thought we'd have it on Christmas Eve, Christmas Day, Boxing Day and the day after Boxing Day. What do you think of that as a plan?'

'I would like them with custard,' I said.

She ignored that (for she couldn't make custard, and refused ever to learn), saying instead, 'I'm dead set on making jam roly-poly.'

I pictured her about it. She would start enthusiastic, and then turn silent. It was best to be out of doors when the wife cooked. She was looking at me.

'You're all in, our Jim. You'll have to go to bed.'

'I don't think I'll get off,' I said. 'I've too much on my mind.'

She was still smiling. She had no inkling that I might be out of a job by the end of tomorrow.

'I'll bring you up a bottle of beer if you like.'

'I'll tell you what – I haven't had a fuck for a little while,' I said.

'I should think not,' said the wife. 'You've been in *Scotland* for a little while.'

She stepped back and leant against the cold kitchen wall, saying, 'What were the women like up there?'

'I didn't really *see* any women.'

'That is a very good answer,' she said, grinning again.

I followed her upstairs. On the bed, I got the wife's dress up. She wasn't going to take it off because she had to take some letters across the road to the post office for the two o'clock collection . . . but it did come off eventually, and we were in the middle of a rather hot tangle, with the church clock striking two, when I asked:

'Now, are your boots upstairs or downstairs? The elastic-sided ones, I mean?'

'Why on earth do you ask?' said the wife, stopping what she was about.

'Well . . .'

'They're by the stove, I think. I was hoping you'd have a go at them with Melton's cream.'

'Oh.'

'I was going to wait until Christmas Eve,' I said, '. . . only I thought of Uncle Roy, who would sort of make Christmas come early. About a week before, he'd come over from Stafford with a couple of pounds' weight of sugar balls, you know, and it struck me that –'

'Sugar *what*?' said the wife.

'Sugar balls,' I said.

'But what have they got to do with boots?'

A sudden reversal occurred at that moment, so that she was looking down at me as she asked:

'What have they got to do with *anything*?'

I couldn't come out with it.

'Nothing,' I said. 'Nothing at all – let's just carry on.'

And we did; and afterwards, when she was getting dressed, the wife said, 'I'm going to see Lillian this afternoon. I'm going to ask if you can wear Peter's suit for the interview. He's about your size.'

'Not the suit he digs graves in?' I said.

The wife was backing towards me with her hair pulled up. As I fastened the hooks of her dress, she said, 'Peter Backhouse has three suits. One for digging graves, one for attending the important funerals and one for getting drunk in the Fortune of War. The point is that the mourning suit is of quite good broadcloth, and I think you should wear it on Friday.'

If she wanted me to wear it, I would wear it. It wouldn't matter what I thought or what Peter Backhouse thought. Lillian Backhouse would go along with the wife's scheme; she would do anything for Lydia and vice versa. They were both New Women, and that sort came with an uncommon amount of push. The wife was now 'doing up' the bedroom, and the sound of rain beyond the window was fainter, so that I couldn't tell whether it was falling from the sky, or just trickling away in the gutters.

Finding a comfortable position for sleep, I said, 'You can't really have jam roly-poly without custard, you know.'

'Custard needs lemons and we haven't got any.'

'Why not?'

'Because I didn't choose to buy any.'

'I don't see what you have against custard.'

'Have you never tasted a jam roly-poly so good that it didn't need to be drowned in pints of the flipping stuff?'

'No.'

'Well then, I feel very sorry for you, I really do.'

But she really did *not*.

'If the rain stops,' the wife said as she was quitting the bedroom, 'we'll go for a walk with Harry after school. We're to give him a turn in the fresh air whenever possible.'

Lydia woke me at four, by which time the rain *had* stopped.

Harry was not a bit exhausted by his first day at school in a long while, and once he'd had his cup of beef tea, a bit of bread and cheese and one of the plums (which was more than he'd eaten in weeks), he was keen to walk along the river a little way for a look at the swing bridge that brought the London expresses over Naburn locks and into York.

It was a beautiful blue evening, if cold. We walked along the river towards the little village of Naburn, which was a strange business. The way took you through dripping trees, across a couple of silent fields . . . and then you struck the huge iron bridge with signals riding above and flashing lights. As we stood alongside it, an unruly goods came over – mixed cargo, going on for ever. It was as if a whole factory had been dismantled and entrained.

'What do you reckon to that?' I asked Harry.

'It's eee-normous,' he said.

He was sitting on my shoulders and kicking my chest – which hurt. We were about to turn around and go home, when the high signals shifted.

'Eh up,' I said, 'another one's coming.'

It was a big engine that brought the carriages – the biggest of the lot. I could scarcely credit it, but it was a V Class Atlantic that was coming riding over the locks of the Ouse.

'Now you don't normally expect to see that on a London run,' I shouted up to Harry, as the thing came crashing over. 'It's called the Gateshead Infant!'

'Why, our dad?'

'It's called "Gateshead" because it was *shopped* out of Gateshead, and "Infant" . . . well, because it's *big*.'

'Are you *trying* to confuse the boy?' said the wife.

'What do you think, Harry?' I shouted up, when the last of the carriages and the brake van had finally gone over.

No answer.

'Better than an aeroplane any day, wouldn't you say?'

I craned around to see his face, and I could tell he was thinking it over. The question, like many another just then, was rather in the balance.

Chapter Thirty-three

The next morning I walked through to see the Chief, who waved at me to sit down, which might have been good or bad. His office was full of cigar smoke. The great shield his team had won in the shooting match was propped on the mantelpiece, which was barely wide enough for it.

'What do you think this place is?' said the Chief, with the cigar still in his mouth. 'A bloody boxing ring?'

But the Chief, having called me in for a rating, had already gone distant. He was shifting some papers – mostly telegrams – from one side of his desk to another; he read each one very quickly as he slid it across.

'I lost my temper, sir' I said. 'I daresay I ought to apologise.'

I would go no further than that. I would not be made to eat dog. That had been the whole point of striking out, and that was also the reason the Chief had *told* me to strike out. He had done it to bring me on.

Or was he about to give me the boot?

'Where *is* Detective Sergeant Shillito, sir?' I enquired, and for the first time it struck me that I might have landed the bloke in hospital, for I had not clapped eyes on him since my return.

The Chief looked up from one of the telegrams, saying in a dreamy sort of voice, 'Seems there's a bad lad on the loose.'

'Sir?' I said.

The Chief always talked in mysterious fragments, and I got hold of his thoughts in spite of, and not because of, the words he used. I knew of one bad lad on the loose, of course, and the whole of my difficulty rested in that person, namely Small David. The departure for France of Richie Marriott – the suicide (if it had really happened) of his father – I could give these events the go-by. But it was not possible to keep Small David under my hat. His crimes could not be dodged.

The Chief slid two more pieces of paper from one side of his desk to another, but he fixed on a third. He was now leaning low over his desk in a worrying sort of fashion. It seemed he was trying to turn his cigar into smoke at the fastest possible rate; to disappear into a fog of his own making.

Presently he looked up, saying:

'No, alarm's off.'

'What, sir?'

The Chief pushed his chair back, put his feet on his desk with a clatter that threatened to bring down the shooting shield and said, 'Circulars from the Northern Division. We were to keep an eye out for a mad Scot. Big bloke, not over-keen on coppers, believed to carry a revolver. Battered his own brother to within an inch of his life . . . He was seen first thing today at Middlesbrough station buying a ticket for York.'

'Is a name given?'

The Chief looked again at the paper in his hand.

'Briggs.'

He dropped his cigar stub to the floor, and lowered one boot from his desk on to the cigar.

'Seems he was dead set on coming to York – you've gone white, lad,' he said, eyeing me more closely.

A beat of silence.

'Any road,' the Chief went on, 'they've just sent word to say they've got him.'

'They've run him in?'

The Chief raised his boot back on to the desk.

'Now you've gone red,' he said. 'Aye – they've shot the bugger dead.'

The Chief scratched his head, setting his few strands of hairs wriggling. On his face was a complicated expression. He looked at me for a while from behind his boots – watched me as I thought on.

Small David. He'd returned from Scotland on Monday morning, had his set-to with the troublesome brother and then he'd tried to come after me. I took a breath, for I meant to start in on my account of events at Fairy Hillocks. But then I held the breath.

The Chief suddenly pulled a pasteboard envelope from a desk drawer, and swept all the papers on top of his desk into it.

'You've been away from the office for two working days,' he said, 'Friday and Monday. Do you have anything in your notebook to show for it?'

'Not in my notebook, no.'

'Why not?'

'Because I didn't set anything *down* in my notebook.'

'Why not? No pen to hand?'

'That's not why.'

'You had a pen to hand?'

'I carry two at all times.'

'Indelible?'

'One indelible; one – whatever is the opposite of indelible.'

'Can you give me one good reason why a young detective should carry any pencil other than an indelible one?'

'Trust, sir,' I said, '. . . that's what it all comes down to. If I was trusted more, then I could write in normal pencils, but I am not trusted.'

'"If I *were* trusted more" I believe is the correct English.'

'That proves my point exactly, sir.'

'To return to the notebook,' he said, lighting another cigar. 'You didn't make a note . . . because nothing happened?'

'Because too much happened.'

'Do you want to have been on leave?'

I couldn't make him out.

'It is not a good idea to frown at me in that way,' said the Chief. 'Do you find the question unclear?'

'You're saying I don't have to tell you what happened.'

'That's it.'

I thought it better to leave a moment of silence before giving my reply.

'I accept.'

My difficulties were falling away at a rate of knots, but the fact that I had been let off the need to explain what I'd been about in Scotland did not mean that I would be allowed to keep my position.

'Am I to be stood down?' I asked.

'Shillito means to speak to you about your future,' said the Chief, rising to his feet.

It was not the answer I had hoped for.

Chapter Thirty-four

I walked into the main office and Shillito was waiting there, holding a leathern notecase under his arm. There was a mark on his forehead that I'd made. He watched me come out of the Chief's door, and motioned me towards my own desk. Wright was looking on from his corner – the best ringside seat.

Shillito sat at his own desk, which was directly opposite mine, and he began to eye me. Was he going to ask for my notebook? As he continued to stare, Wright sharpened a pencil without looking at it. His eyes were on me. A great train was leaving from Platform Four, and the noise made my heartbeat begin to gallop.

Just then, the Chief came out of his own room and quit the office without a look back. It was all no good; I was for it.

Now Shillito was speaking.

'As a body of men we must stand together, would you not agree, Detective Stringer?'

'I would, sir' (I found I didn't object to calling him 'sir' as long as I fixed my eyes on that mark that I'd made.)

'We're up against it on all fronts,' he said.

I nodded. The train had gone, leaving only the steady, slow scrape of Wright's pencil-sharpening blade.

'We do not have the privileges of the ordinary public detectives,' Shillito ran on, 'and the travellers are frequently against us.'

I nodded again.

'They chaff us, will not give up their tickets when asked.'

I was tired of nodding.

'And do you know what the other classes of railwaymen call us?'

'The pantomime police.'

'Just so.'

(He hadn't reckoned on me knowing that.)

'We must stand together, then.'

'I have already agreed to that.'

I was pushing it with Shillito, but I seemed to have decided that it was all up for me in any case.

'Very well then, try this: *we must not deal each other blows.*'

Whatever reply I made to that, he wasn't listening, but was standing up, removing some papers from the notecase.

'You want to get your promotion – there it is.'

He dashed the papers down on my desk.

'Now I'm overdue at home,' he said, and he strode out of the office without another word.

There were half a dozen pages, torn from a magazine, a railway journal – not *The Railway Rover* or the *Railway Magazine* or anything I'd heard of, but some little journal out of the common. I caught them up, and looked across at Wright, who was still scraping away at the pencil.

'What the hell's going off?' I said.

'You did yourself a good turn when you clouted him,' said Wright.

He put down the pencil, sat back and folded his arms.

'It's Christmas,' he said. 'Do you want an orange?'

There was no sign of any orange, so this might have been a sort of bluff. I thanked him and said that if he was after doing me a good turn, he might record in the log book that I'd gone out on the search for Davitt, the fare evader. I then quit the office and walked under a sky that threatened more snow, to the Punch Bowl in Stonegate, which was known for its twopenny pints of ale. It was a secret-looking pub with many small, half-underground rooms that got smaller the further back you went from the street, so that it was like drinking in a coal mine. In the very furthest snug from the street, I began to read the bundle of papers that Shillito had given me. It was a very strange return for having hit him; in fact, the papers were strange all ends up.

Chapter Thirty-five

On Christmas Eve morning, Harry was up at half past five, setting
a marker, I supposed, for the next day. I came downstairs at six in
Peter Backhouse's funeral suit; the wife passed me a cup of cocoa
and said, 'It fits to a tee.'

The suit was in fact blue. I had mentioned this to Backhouse
over a pint in the Fortune of War, and he'd said, 'Don't say that.
It's meant to be mourning black. I'll lose confidence at the funerals
if I think it's blue.' But I wasn't over-concerned, since Peter
Backhouse didn't have any confidence to begin with.

After breakfast, I opened the front door, and was fairly blinded
by the whiteness. The sight of all the new-fallen snow made Harry
break out into a kind of hopscotch in the warmth of the kitchen.
On the doorstep, the wife passed me my topcoat, which she'd
given a good brushing. She then gave me a special kiss of the sort
normally reserved for late evening and handed me my bicycle clips.

'Buy a paper at the station bookstall, our Jim,' she said. 'One of
the cleverer sort, you know. Then go into the interview with it
under your arm.'

'To create the illusion of intelligence, you mean.'

'No, Jim, you *are* intelligent.'

I put on the bike clips.

'Please try to remember that, Jim,' said the wife.

I went down the side alley, where the Humber was covered by a
tarpaulin against the shocking weather. As I walked it along the
front path, the wife called, 'And if you get the promotion . . . I'll
think on about the boots.' Harry stood behind her, grinning fit to
bust, just as though he knew exactly what she meant.

231

The six wide fields were all piled with a smooth whiteness like well-made beds. I made the bicycle stand at York station after twenty minutes; I then stood there for a further three, blowing on my hands to make them work again. As I blew, I thought of Captain W. R. Fairclough, formerly of the 5th Lancers. Under this gentleman, whose acquaintance I would be making very shortly, the North Eastern Railway Police had grown from sixty-seven men of all ranks to three hundred and forty-two. He was all plans, and I'd been made privy to what was surely the strangest of them by Shillito; or at least, that seemed to be the case, but I could not quite dismiss the thought that it was all a great jape designed to pay me out for hitting him.

I had brought the papers along with me. They were in the side pocket of my topcoat as I approached the bookstall, where I bought both the *Manchester Guardian* and *The Times*. Brainpower in journalism did not come cheap, I decided as I handed over the coin, but having learnt that I would be keeping my job, and that there would be another payday after all, I'd been a little freer with the loose change I had remaining. I stuffed the papers into my pocket, and walked over to the police office, where Wright and Constable Baker were the only men about.

Wright turned towards me and gave me my wages: three pounds and seven for the past week, and a pound Christmas bonus. I was so relieved to be in funds that I almost tipped him – almost went back to the bookstall for another clever paper as well. Wright also handed me a telegram along with the wage packet. It came folded, so I didn't read it just then, but walked over the footbridge to take the train for Whitby, where I would, as usual, change for Middlesbrough. Wright had been civil enough, but he'd barely looked at me as he'd given over the wages and telegram. He'd lost interest in me now that I was no longer in bother with my superiors.

As I crossed the footbridge, the telegraph lad came bounding along.

'Morning, squire!' he shouted.

'What are you doing here?' I said. 'It's Christmas, en't it?'

'It is for some,' he said. 'You had a wire from London, you know. Come in just now.'

'I've got it, thanks,' I said.

The message had evidently come first into the main telegraph office rather than the police office – but that was often the way.

There were many distractions on the Whitby train, and they took my mind off the wire in my pocket. There were more kids about than usual and the adults were a sight livelier than on any normal day. It was Friday and it was Christmas Eve – as a combination it was nigh-on unbeatable.

All the corridors were blocked by giant trunks and going-away portmanteaus and brown paper parcels, and it took me a good ten minutes to find a seat. When I sat down I took the newspapers out of my pocket: 'To-Day's Speeches,' I read on the front page of *The Times*. I then put my hand in my pocket to get out the telegram, but it wasn't there. I hunted through all my pockets, under the wondering eyes of every person in the compartment, but it was nowhere to be found. I had somehow mislaid it.

It could only have been from Steve Bowman, for he was about the only man I knew in London. I didn't want him waking up the whole case of the Travelling Club now that I'd seen my way clear to dropping it, but it was not in his interests to do that. I then remembered that he still didn't *know* I'd dropped it. As far as he was concerned, he had a gaol term in prospect, and no doubt the telegram had been expressing anxiety on that score, and looking out for my answer.

I would try to reach him by telephone before the day's end. There was no sense leaving him stewing all over Christmas.

I couldn't quite get on with the clever newspapers, and so passed the rest of the journey looking at the white landscape beyond the window, and reading again over the papers given me by Shillito, which seemed no less weird now than they had at first sight in the Punch Bowl tavern.

Chapter Thirty-six

Stepping off the train, I walked past the Middlesbrough police office, hoping not to run into the two-faced Detective Sergeant Williams who'd dished me to Shillito; or attempted to. It seemed that Shillito, having been soundly belted, had come round to me and removed the bar he'd placed on my way to promotion. There was no great mystery involved. He was a double-fisted man himself, and I'd spoken to him in the language he understood.

The police office was separate from the police headquarters, which lay on Spring Street, the very place in which Paul Peters's camera had been lifted. It was not a *long* street, and so the camera must have been taken practically on the doorstep of railway police headquarters – a fact it might be better, all considered, not to mention to the head of the force. (I also made a mental note not to bring up the matter of the shooting of Small David, for I was sure it had not been a planned event, and that the force would count it an embarrassment.)

The Spring Street offices had only been taken temporarily for just as long as it took to do up the ones at Newcastle, and the desk that had been placed in the hallway of the building at the foot of a staircase had a lonely look of not belonging. The same went for the bloke sitting at it – he wore a police uniform with a topcoat over, and pointed up the staircase when I told him I had an appointment with Captain Fairclough.

'Third floor,' he said, and his voice echoed against the cold stone, which made me more nervous than I was already.

I climbed the stairs and a black door with the words 'Capt. Fairclough' painted on it in scruffy white letters stood before me. I knocked, a voice called out and there he was.

He was a handsome man; looked the part of a leader, with grey-black hair and a grey-black beard. He sat at a sizeable desk in a room otherwise more or less empty, and it held the wide-awake smells of coffee and paint. It was freezing too, for behind the wide desk was a wide window, with the sash propped open.

But it was all on account of the view, for Captain Fairclough's window looked clean across the Company rows to Ironopolis. Standing before the desk, I took it all in: the great red clouds coming out of the blast-furnace tops, like slowly blossoming flowers; the trains of all shapes and sizes rolling through the snow; the wagons being hauled and lowered; and the tiny, lonely-looking men by the rails, or on the gantries of the blast furnaces or crossing the wastes in between, where, for the present, the snow had killed the ash.

'Sit down, Detective Stringer,' said Captain Fairclough.

I did it – and too quickly. I still wore my topcoat, and the clever papers, folded in my side pocket were sticking into me. They could not be seen by Captain Fairclough, and so had proved a waste of money.

'Do you know Middlesbrough?' he asked by way of preliminary.

It was good that he'd asked, for it meant he'd not heard of my troublesome investigations into the Travelling Club. But then again: what was the correct answer?

'I am not very closely acquainted with it, sir,' I said.

Try not to talk like a copy book, I told myself.

'Now you came to us from footplate work –' said Captain Fairclough.

I nodded, thinking guiltily of the letter I'd written asking for a return to it.

'I have a good general knowledge of railway working, sir,' I said. 'I find it comes in handy to know the business of a marshalling yard or engine shed.'

That was a little better.

'You had the solving of a murder, I believe.'

He meant the business of my first weeks on the force. I began telling him all about it, but after five minutes he checked me and I coloured up at that.

'The tale does you great credit,' he said, but not over-enthusiastically, and I wondered whether he considered me boastful.

After a little more rather strained conversation, I noticed that Captain Fairclough was looking down at a few pieces of paper.

'I have good accounts of you from your superior officers,' he said. Now I'd expected it of the Chief, but it was quite a turn-up to hear that I'd got a recommendation from Shillito. I'd really fixed him with that blow.

Captain Fairclough now fell to thinking about something, and turned to give me the benefit of his profile as he did so. But I was looking beyond him. The snow was coming down again, and it didn't seem to make much difference to Ironopolis until you looked closely and saw that the men were now moving through it as though blind. I looked back towards Fairclough. I had not convinced him that he ought to promote me, that was a certainty, and if I didn't manage it soon then Lydia would not be able to take up her own position. There was nothing for it. I would have to trust to the new-found good intentions of Detective Sergeant Shillito.

'I think dogs might do a good deal in police work given a little more experience,' I said.

I had made my shot; there was no going back. Captain Fairclough turned sharply towards me.

'Dogs?'

'Yes.'

'Did you say "dogs"?'

I was sitting in tight boots now.

'A fine body of trained dogs, yes.'

He turned away from me and looked through his window, taking it all in right across to the Tees with one great intake of breath. Had Shillito been guying me? The pages he'd given over had been from a journal of the Great Western Railway, of which Fairclough had been governor before he'd come north. They had been an account of the use of dogs in police work. It was an idea that had not caught on very widely, as the writer of the article admitted. In fact it had caught on only in Belgium, at a spot called Ghent, which had a dock that needed a lot of guarding. A single sentence in the article was to the effect: 'It is believed that the chief officer of our railway force, Captain Fairclough, favours putting dogs to work in this way,' and I had trusted my whole future to those words.

'A canine police, now . . .' Fairclough said, turning back around slowly. 'What gave you the idea?'

I had what I thought a good lie ready for this.

'Just forever walking past signs reading "Beware of the dog", sir. And I thought – why not for police purposes?'

'What breed would you favour for the work?'

The ones in Belgium had been Airedales. An Airedale was the biggest sort of terrier, as I'd discovered in the reference division of York Library. But I ought not to look as though I'd got the whole thing from the article.

'A big enough breed to put fear into a villain,' I said. 'But the animal must be intelligent with it.'

'Would the dogs be on a leash?'

'Yes, and muzzled.'

That was how they had them in Belgium.

'I believe that other forces use them,' I said.

'Where?'

He had me now. I kept silence, hoping he'd put another question.

'Well then,' he said, '*where?* Are you aware of any area of operation?'

'Belgium, maybe?'

That might easily have queered the whole thing, for it surely proved that I'd cribbed the notion of dogs from the article, but perhaps Captain Fairclough had never *read* that particular article, even though he'd been mentioned in it, for he rose to his feet saying, 'I will not keep from you that I have been thinking on remarkably similar lines myself. For thief-taking, or simply as a deterrent, it strikes me that dogs must have a place in our work.'

And I knew from his 'our' that I had done it; or that Shillito had done it for me.

'Imagine some loafer in that goods yard of yours at York,

Detective Stringer – pockets bulging with pilfered whisky bottles and baccy. You approach him with a dog leashed; you ask him to come along quietly . . . Now I'd say he'd do it, but let's imagine he refuses your request. You threaten to unleash the beast. You warn him it is trained to attack every man not wearing a police uniform . . . He'd come along then, wouldn't you say?'

'He'd come along all right, sir . . . why, like a lamb I should think.'

Captain Fairclough laughed a little at that.

'Now,' he said, when he'd stopped, 'any other suggestions?'

'I think there ought to be a special class of men to do things like ticket inspections and lost luggage reports,' I said.

'I see.'

'I believe this is not a good use of the detective mind.'

'And who would do the work instead?'

'Men developed from the grades of clerks,' I said, thinking: let's give Wright some bloody work to do; get his nose out of other folks' affairs. What Captain Fairclough made of my idea I don't know, but he made a note of it. He then strode around his desk to shake my hand.

'I have enjoyed our talk very much, Detective Stringer,' he said. 'You need have no apprehension as to the outcome of it. A very happy Christmas to you.'

'A very happy Christmas to you too, sir.'

Chapter Thirty-seven

Well, I was on velvet. My job was safe, and I had secured my promotion, which in turn meant that Lydia could take up the job of her dreams. Our money troubles were at an end. And the case seemed to have resolved itself beautifully. It was like a mathematical problem that had looked very involved but that, after a long, head-racking while, was discovered to come out at zero. Marriott had killed himself or been killed by Small David, and there was some justice in either outcome. If it had not been suicide then it would have been made to look like it, for Small David seemed to be a great hand at that. There need be no questions asked.

The inquest into Peters would return a verdict of suicide. It was a shame that Peters should be set down for ever as having done away with himself – but then, how could that ever have been disproved except by confession of Small David, which had never been likely?

As for Lee and Falconer – Lee was deemed to have been murdered and he had been. The wrong man had swung for it; but not, by all accounts, an entirely *innocent* man. Falconer was put down as disappeared, and no injury was done to his name and reputation as a result. It was perhaps a more dignified fate than the one that he had met in reality. Small David had got his deserts just as surely as Marriott himself, and the men who'd deserved to come out of it with unstained characters had done so: Richie Marriott was on the Continent, where he would no doubt remain, and only he and I knew of Bowman's involvement. We in fact were the only three who knew the cause of the Travelling Club's disappearance, and it seemed to me fitting that only three *should* know, for there was no rightness or dignity in the explanation. A word from my schooldays came to me: the business had been a *shameful* one from start to finish.

But it was now played out.

I walked in a happy haze about the snowy streets of central Middlesbrough, where the shops were all either full to bursting or closing early – nothing in between. I had half an eye out for the Middlesbrough Brown's. I would buy Harry a lead man to go with his clockwork loco – a guard with arm raised, forever giving the 'right away' to the little engine. It struck me that I could also run to a scarf to go with Lydia's gloves. Of course, the situation called for a pint as well, but it would be a risk to slip into a pub so close to Captain Fairclough's office. In the end, I decided to put it all off to York: I would take an early train back.

I hurried up the steps at the back of the station that gave on to the 'up' platform. In the parcels office they were still stamping and labelling like mad. At the platform ends, salt was going down, and I had a moment of alarm about the weather. If there'd been drifting, I might be kept on the coast for Christmas, and that really would be a calamity.

I could not stop thinking of all the things I might do being once again in funds and, happening to give a glance in the direction of the telegraph office, I remembered Bowman. It was half past midday. I had another ten minutes until train time, so I darted in to send a wire, which took longer than I'd expected because of a queue full of people sending their love to all points of the compass, whereas if they'd really meant it, they'd have posted Christmas cards long since or gone to see the love objects in question.

I climbed aboard the Whitby train with seconds to spare – no time to look at the engine. I fretted that it might be pushing a snow plough of some kind. We rocked away and, as Ironopolis came into view, I saw that only a few furnaces remained in blast, and that all the strange little wagons had been tidied away into sidings. Our train was only a quarter full; the light was fading already, and I felt that most people had already gone to their Christmas places. I had a compartment to myself, and I looked at first to the seaward side, where the holiday town of Redcar soon came up, with the black sea crashing beyond the lonely 'Tea' flag. A few minutes later, the snow was coming down slantwise again on Marske. There was a sudden crashing to my right, and I turned and saw a full-sized snow plough being taken on the 'down' line between two ordinary engines, as though the Company was trying to smuggle the thing through to Middlesbrough. We were in and out of Saltburn in very short order. The platform lights blazed, and I watched half a dozen muffled-up people hurrying away to Christmas.

For a moment there was nothing but the swinging station sign.

We pulled away and were soon flying through Stone Farm, where I thought I saw Crystal standing stock still on the platform and being snowed upon. I made a move towards the window, meaning to drag it down and call out 'Happy Christmas!' to the miserable old fossil.

Next thing we were in the town of Loftus, gliding along the high street in the same direction as the snow. From the platform there came nothing but a few throat clearances out of sight. We pulled away into the country and a seabird flew alongside the window – and then suddenly it was taken higher, as if yanked up on a wire.

I turned the other way and the door of the compartment opened. Small David sat down over opposite me with his tweed coat spread wide, a smile on his face and a revolver in his hand.

But it could not be Small David. Small David was shot.

'Are you . . . Sanderson?'

'Och, ye've sniffed me oot.'

He had addressed the top of my head, with his own great head tilted back.

But he couldn't be Sanderson either – Gilbert Sanderson was hanged.

There was some bloody complication: a mass of dried blood under his flat sporting cap – the cap was welded to the head by the stuff, and yet he was grinning. It was Small David all right; he hadn't crowned his brother. He had been crowned *by* his brother.

'I can see ye're thinkin' hard.'

I was thinking how the police had taken him for Sanderson, and now *I* had confused him with his *brother*, with the same disastrous consequences. He gave a glance towards the window: the white fields rolled on under the blackening sky. There were farms and what looked like farms but with flames rising above, farms on fire – and these were the mines.

'Yer brain's too wee, de ye ken that?' said Small David.

My mistake had arisen because I had not been able to think of him as suffering at the hands of another man, but only as the *cause* of suffering. I looked down at his yellow socks – there was blood on them too, and sweat and filth, and all the horrible leakage of his great body.

'Smart eh!' he said, and I saw that he had no teeth, just like a great baby. Had they been lately knocked away by his own brother? I saw through the window a summerhouse in a garden of snow coming fast by the window – that was all wrong. I turned again to face Small David.

He said, 'Ye'll alight the train in a wee while.'

'Will I?'

'Aye, ye wull.'

'It was the brother that was shot by the police –'

'Aye, gone for ever.'

'He gave you a good battering.'

'Och, he could nae batter a fish.'

'Why didn't *you* shoot him, Small David?'

'I was savin' the bullets for yersel'.'

'Where's Marriott?'

'Hum? Stull deed.'

'The son, Richie?'

'He's awae tae France.'

'But you've taken all of his father's money.'

'A guid deal of it, aye.'

He looked away from me and he looked back.

'My *fair share*,' he said.

We were both being rocked as the train slowed. I looked to the left and down. At Flat Scar mine, the endless rope still turned,

242

sending the swinging buckets out towards the mine station, where a mineral train waited with a fuming engine at the head. The fly-wheel turned inside the wheelhouse, and the sea smashed against the little jetty beyond. It was Christmas for some, the telegram lad had said, but not for the blokes of Flat Scar, and not for me. Snow had been scraped away and piled up all around the mine, like so much white slag.

There came a fluttering from beyond the right-hand window, and I thought at first that another seabird was flying close by, but it was the rattling wind gauge that marked the start of the Kilton Viaduct. The train noise was different now, as we slowed and ran on to the viaduct, and it galvanised Small David, who rose to his feet, motioning with the revolver for me to do the same.

As I stood facing the man, I realised that I stood taller than him; but he held the gun. He drew open the door of the compartment and motioned me into the corridor, which was empty. I had the feeling that we were the only men aboard. Small David pushed the gun into me, indicating that I should walk along the corridor.

The corridor went on for ever, but we slowly closed on the car-riage door. As we did so, he spoke:

'I was no quite comfortable while ye were left alive.'

'How did you know I'd be in Middlesbrough?'

'Yon bottle man told me.'

'Spoken to him recently, have you?'

'I have nae.'

I knew then what the telegram had been: a warning from Bowman that he had at some early stage let slip the fact that I had an appointment at Middlesbrough.

We were now at the door.

'I wull be calling upon the bottle man presently, but ye have the honour of being the first tae dee.'

Small David opened the door, and the snowy gravel was flowing along beneath our boots. On the other side of it stood the low wall of the Kilton Viaduct, and beyond that lay the long drop to the beck and the mineral line.

'Oot,' he said.

I jumped, and he followed directly after.

We were alongside the carriage bogies, and the wheels them-selves were horrific and merciless when seen close to. The carriage walls towered above us, and they came on, and came on.

'Stir yersel',' said Small David. He meant me to walk to the mid-dle of the viaduct, and there he would make me leap.

I leapt early.

One hand on the viaduct wall and I was gone. From the middle of air, I saw the mine, the endless rope turning under the darken-ing sky. My bowler was falling in advance of me; it was disloyal, abandoning ship. Well, a bowler was a ridiculous article in any case. My limbs were just so many floating things, and by slow degrees it seemed that my boots were becoming higher than my head. I wondered whether I would make a full somersault before I smashed. I was no detective sergeant; it was not meant to be. I was an engine man who had missed his way, and that was all about it.

Chapter Thirty-eight

It ended neatly enough, for I landed in a perfect grave – a grave of snow. I lay in it, and thought about what had happened. The fall had not ended with the smash, but had continued for a little while after with a sort of dark, burning roar, and the notion that the word 'Chute!' was being shouted very loudly into my ears.

Above the top of my snow-grave I could see the side of the viaduct. I had leapt from the point at which it began, and fallen perhaps only thirty feet on to the top of the valley side. I began an upwards crawl out of the snow, and my hands seemed small and very red, and my back was ricked. It was easier to move to the left than to the right. But I came out all right, and stood up, a little bent over. A sea wind was coming up at me; it blew the snow through the legs of the viaduct. The sky had a look of dangerous dark blue against the whiteness all around, and I knew this was the coldest day I had seen, but I could not feel it. The snow was my friend now, even though I had fought it all my life.

I seemed to be very high as I stumbled forwards. I was on a high ridge of snow – it had been made when a track to my left had been cleared. The track ran down to the beck, and the zigzag mineral line. The mine itself lay far below, and an echoing rattle was coming up the valley from there. The mineral train was leaving the mine station, or attempting to do so. The ironstone wagons were all hitched. The train was jerking back and forth, as if it was trying to unfreeze itself.

I climbed the bank side for a little way, and was quickly underneath the viaduct at its lowest point. I moved underneath it. My back was all right as long as I held it in a certain position, but I had to move a little way crabwise. I climbed on to the eastern side of the viaduct top (whereas I had jumped from the western side). I crouched against the viaduct edge, and the wind gauge was there: one small, mad windmill. No, it was like a trapped bird, and it was frightening to be near it. The thing's arms turned at a furious rate, and the thing *itself* was spinning bodily. Small David stood fifty yards beyond me, and on the opposite side of the single track. In the gathering dark, he was peering over the western viaduct wall, looking down at the zigzag line where the iron train had stopped – looking for me. I began walking towards him. I did not care if he saw me. I did not know what would happen if he did, because I was not thinking. Instead, I walked, with the line beside me. No trains would come, I knew that – we were quite safe from interruption.

Small David was now moving along a little way – going away from me. But I kept up my steady, bent-over advance. There was now a steadier clanking coming from below the viaduct. The mineral train was moving.

I veered to my left and gave it a glance. It was coming up to the legs of the viaduct. Small David looked down at it too, but he did so from a stationary position in the middle of the viaduct. I looked to the right. It hurt to do it, but there was the Rectory Works. The fires leapt from the kiln tops, more beautiful than any Christmas decoration, and it was the strength of *purpose* that made them so.

In the middle of the sound of the sea, and the sea wind, and the clanking train, I stood to the rear of Small David. He was leaning over the viaduct wall. It was hardly decent, but I reached forwards and took hold of the tweed of his topcoat where it lay over his arse. I lifted it and I pitched him away into the wind. I had done with him.

I leant over and watched him go.

In the middle of air Small David looked like a frog I had once seen making a leap: too thick about the middle, arms and legs of no account, although these did move about a little as he flew. He hit a middle wagon of the iron train, and then – thank Christ – he stopped moving. I could not have stood the sight of him squirming

246

on the ironstone, but then again, what would have happened if that sight had indeed met my eyes? I looked along the viaduct wall to the wind gauge. It operated a signal that checked trains in any really strong blow, and it was still thrashing away for all it was worth, not aware that the disaster had in fact already occurred.

I turned about again and looked at the kilns of the Rectory Works. A strange red spirit crawled upwards from the top of each one. On the gantry that ran along the tops stood a single man. I remained for an hour on the Kilton Viaduct, and I watched every wagon from the train rise to the point where it was tilted by automatic process. Sometimes the gantry man was visible in his upper world, sometimes not. He came and went from a metal shack attached to one end of the gantry platform. Whatever he was about up there, he did not pay attention to what was being pitched into the kilns. Anything that came up with those wagons was for burning and no questions asked.

Presently, a train came along the viaduct. It would be at about five p.m. – I could not have said at the time. I stopped it with my hand. I believe that I made the driver aware of my warrant card, but it may be that he'd said, 'Let's have you in, mate,' before seeing it.

I was taken up on to the footplate, and I took up a position directly before the fire, causing the fireman, as I seem to remember, to curse all the way to the terminus. But I believe that I was magnetised by that fire, for the driver had to shift me bodily away from it at Whitby West Cliff, explaining that here they must pitch it away, having reached the end of their turn.

Chapter Thirty-nine

I made my way out of the station with my new, bent walk, but I felt that I was straightening up by degrees.

The town of Whitby was freshly covered in snow, which was ruffled by great gusts coming in from the sea. The black water was low in the harbour, and the ships and boats were all a little skew, as if drunk, which their owners very likely would have been at that moment. The pubs and hotels around were all ablaze with light as I walked first around the grand new buildings on the west side.

I was trying to walk off the effects of having killed a man.

A car was turning outside the front of the Metropole, and half the guests – in their finest clothes – had turned out to watch the manoeuvre. They looked like the most innocent people in the world.

I went across the harbour bridge to the east side, and walked along the road on which stood the offices of the *Whitby Morning Post*. They were closed now, and I squinted inside at the heap of back numbers on the long table. Old papers made a litter. You ought not to look back. But still I turned – or was it the wind racing in from the sea that *made* me turn? – towards the Bog Hall sidings, spread out beyond the station, where all the wagons and carriages were arranged in neat lines for their Christmas rest. One of them had been something special once, for the saloon built to the instructions of the Whitby-Middlesbrough Travelling Club was doubtless still in there. The wind rose again, stirring the boats and lifting the snow crystals from all the rooftops, and the high graveyard of St Mary's church. I didn't quite like to look towards the church, for I had hardly turned the other cheek back there on the viaduct.

I looked instead towards the town of Whitby in general. Amid the flying white particles, I saw a softer, rising whiteness from beyond the station roof. It was Christmas Eve, and the men at the controls of that steaming engine would be anxious to be away. I made towards them.

I boarded the last train of the evening for York with seconds to spare. Another man came into the compartment just as I had settled myself. He was a tall, pale man and wore a good, fur-trimmed topcoat. He leant over my outstretched legs and yanked down the leathern strap that controlled the window. He knew it was not quite correct behaviour on such a night, but he required the refreshment of the cold air. As he sat down, and as the train began drawing away out of the station, he eyed me, challenging me to speak out.

But I made no objection.